# The Tale of The Farrell:

# The Serpent in the Glass

## by D.M. Andrews

Third Edition

Published in 2012 by FeedARead.com Publishing – Arts Council funded .

A CIP catalogue record for this title is available from the British Library.

# DEDICATION

*To all those who believe, who dare to dream,
and who never let go...*

# ABOUT THE AUTHOR

D.M. Andrews has been writing fiction since his early teens. He enjoys reading historical, fantasy and children's novels. Find out more about him and his writing at www.writers-and-publishers.com

# ACKNOWLEDGMENTS

*To R.J. Locksley for her help with editing this third edition, to Alex Hausch for his fine cover artwork, and, most of all, to all my readers.*

## – CHAPTER ONE –

# *The Birthday Key*

A badly painted garden gnome with a look of surprise upon its face sat atop a bright red toadstool. In its hand it held a fishing rod, the hook of which hung unmoving in the windless Hertfordshire air several inches above a small pond's still surface. The gnome's eyes seemed fixed on the other side of the garden where a greenhouse sat in the shade of a crab apple tree. Every other pane of glass had been painted lime green so as to create a checkerboard effect.

Thomas stood on a large wooden box in the loft, his eye pressed against the hole in the roof as he stared down through a broken tile. He rolled a marble between his fingers. The day felt every bit as muggy as the day before, but he knew better than to wander into the garden without permission. Last time he'd done that he'd trodden on the dandelions, Mrs Westhrop had shrieked at having her 'prize flowers' crushed, and Thomas had been sent straight back into the house by a very angry Mr Westhrop.

Thomas's attention switched back suddenly to the greenhouse. Mr Westhrop had emerged and was looking up. Thomas pulled his eye away from the hole and ran a hand nervously through his short ash-blond hair. Had he been spotted? Thomas chanced a look through the hole again. Mr Westhrop was now making his way purposefully indoors. Thomas knew that walk and that look. A moment later a small copper bell tinkled. He'd been summoned.

Thomas barely had his shoes on before the monotone voice called up to him. He poked his freckled face over the edge of the hole in the loft. On the landing below, looking up at him, stood Mr Westhrop in his beige summer suit. He didn't wear dark suits. Perhaps he thought they would emphasise his rapidly greying hair, what was left of it anyway. He had a calculator in his hand. Mr Westhrop was an employee of Swivet, Stibbard & Waverly, a prestigious firm of accountants, and, as far as Thomas could tell, this meant he had to count things.

Mr Westhrop brushed something invisible from his suit. 'Did you polish the taps?'

'Yes, sir.'

Mr Westhrop slipped the calculator into his breast pocket. 'I hope you've done it well. You know how my wife likes to see her face in them. Those taps have lasted us twenty years and they're as good as the day we bought them. No sense in forking out for things a little elbow grease will preserve.'

Jonathan Westhrop described himself as 'extremely careful' when it came to money, though not a few of those who lived in Holten Layme used other words to describe this trait. Thomas wasn't sure what a 'miser' was, though he thought the word very similar to 'miserable', and that summed up Mr Westhrop very well. Thomas had once overheard a neighbour tell Mr Westhrop that it took far more muscles to frown than it did to smile. Mr Westhrop replied that he would henceforth save himself a lot of effort by doing neither.

Thomas often felt miserable too. He had none of the trappings of a normal boy his age. He didn't even have a watch, let alone a computer or mobile phone. He did have a clock, a very old clock that needed to be wound up every other night before he went to sleep. Mr Westhrop didn't hold with batteries; they needed replacing and that meant money – money, said Mr Westhrop, the family couldn't afford.

Anyone entering the Westhrop home on Birch Tree Close wouldn't have thought them poor. Behind the oak door with its beautiful brass knocker lay a welcome mat; though few ever were. Inside, expensive carpets covered the floors, and then of course there was Mr Westhrop's plush office complete with aquarium – full of tropical fish of all shapes, colours and sizes – that ran the entire length of one wall. And the whole house was well kept. Mrs Westhrop liked to keep a clean house. A very clean house. An obsessively clean house.

All of this stood in stark contrast to Thomas's 'bedroom', if that word was appropriate, for it contained no bed – unless one counted the large dog basket in which he slept. Indeed, it wasn't really a room at all, because Thomas lived in the loft. A naked bulb hung from the rafters, though it did little to dispel the darkness. Mr Westhrop wouldn't allow anything higher than a twenty-five-watt bulb, it saved electricity, he said.

'My wife would like you to scrub the patio again and to pay particular attention to removing the lichen and moss, and then I'd like you to clean the windows of the greenhouse – inside and out. Mind you don't knock the tomatoes! We should save a pretty penny this year if my yield projections are correct.' He tapped the pocket containing the calculator. 'But first make tea, as Jemima will be in from the garden shortly.'

'Yes, Mr Westhrop.'

Thomas never addressed his adopted parents as 'Mum' or 'Dad'. It'd never felt right. Besides, the only time Mr Westhrop ever spoke to Thomas was when he was giving him chores or financial advice, though the latter seemed pointless to Thomas as he received no pocket money. Mrs Westhrop, on the other hand, spoke to herself more than to anyone else, and seemed particularly fond of addressing the spider plant in the kitchen.

'Good. I'll assign you some more chores when you're done. I expect tea in ten minutes.'

\* \* \*

Before Thomas had even finished tying his shoelaces, he heard the front door slam, followed by shoes thudding up the stairs, into a room below, then back out onto the landing. Jessica Westhrop was home. A few seconds later a pleasantly countenanced girl beamed at him, braces and all, from the top of the ladder that led into the loft.

'Happy birthday, Thomas!' Her chestnut hair was its usual mess, not surprising for a girl who preferred to run rather than walk.

Thomas flashed a smile back at her. 'Thanks, Jess.'

Jessica climbed into the loft and sat on a box, dropping her backpack. The wooden floor, the source of many a splinter, supported little furniture: the basket, complete with pillow and sheets, served as Thomas's bed; a wardrobe provided a home for a school uniform and a few other clothes; and several boxes, dotting the floor like seats for guests who never came, contained a few of Thomas's personal items. Mrs Westhrop didn't enter the loft even to clean. Mr Westhrop seldom came up here either. There wasn't much to come up for, unless one was looking for a cobweb.

Jessica's face turned serious. 'So I'm not a year older than you anymore?'

Thomas smiled. 'That's right!' Jessica's birthday fell a couple of weeks before his, and she always teased him about being a year younger for that fortnight.

She grinned. 'So what did you get from her this year?'

Aunt Dorothy was the only person who regularly bought him presents, except for Jessica of course.

'A woollen hat.' Thomas looked around the sultry loft. Jessica's aunt had a knack of buying out-of-season gifts. He pulled the bright yellow hat from a box. 'I guess it'll help keep me warm in the winter up here.'

'Anything from my mum?'

'No, not this year.'

'Sorry,' said Jessica.

'That's OK. You know how she is.'

Mrs Westhrop didn't always remember birthdays. Two years ago she'd bought Jessica her present four months early, and then forgotten it altogether the following year. Thomas had fared worse still, having received but one present in the last three years: a baggy pair of corduroy trousers that remained too large for him to this day. Unlike his wife, Mr Westhrop had quite a good memory, especially for figures. This made no difference, however, because Mr Westhrop didn't hold with what he termed 'frivolous expenditures', such as cards, Easter eggs, or presents of any kind.

'Well, I got you something!' Jessica announced gleefully, as she reached down for the bag she'd thrown on the floor.

They always gave each other something at Christmas and birthdays; it was their way of making sure they had at least two gifts to open every year. Usually they made things for each other, as Thomas had no money, and Jessica rarely so. Jessica, unlike Thomas, did receive pocket money, but sometimes weeks would pass before Mrs Westhrop remembered to pay her.

Jessica pulled a card from her bag and passed it to Thomas. 'I made it before I went out.'

It was homemade. Jessica had drawn a cartoon of a schoolboy at his desk, with a teacher bringing him a chocolate cake with eleven candles. Mr Westhrop didn't allow parties, but Jessica's drawing helped Thomas imagine what it would've been like.

Jessica handed a velvet pouch to Thomas. 'Now you can play properly!'

Inside he found an assortment of marbles – some metallic, others like precious gems, and yet others like clear crystal glass.

'They're beautiful, Jess!' Thomas loved marbles, but he'd only ever had the few he'd found in the street. He sniffed the bag. 'I can smell peaches.'

Jessica bit her lip. 'The bag split, so I put them in the one Mum gave me. I think it had perfume in it. Still, maybe scented marbles will be all the rage this year?'

Thomas smiled and then they both laughed.

The Westhrops hadn't wanted to adopt Thomas. Mr Westhrop had made that quite clear to him on several occasions. They didn't even want to have another child after Jessica. Mrs Westhrop had utterly refused to put her 'poor nerves' through the ordeal of a second child, and Mr Westhrop had positively sweated with anxiety at the cost. But the then three-year-old Jessica was such a bundle of energy that she affected Mrs Westhrop's 'poor nerves', Mr Westhrop's wallet, the household's general appearance and, on one occasion, the location of several of Mr Westhrop's tropical fish. Even the pet dog, Jags, took to hiding from Jessica after she'd tried to see if he would fit through the cat flap.

The Westhrops had decided that the only solution was to find her a playmate. When Jessica spotted Thomas at the orphanage, she'd taken to him straight away and wouldn't let go of his hand. They tried to separate them, but Jessica cried so loudly that Mrs Westhrop became very flustered and Mr

Westhrop agreed to adopt Thomas on the spot. And so Thomas, a boy whose mother had died and whose father had abandoned him, came into the Westhrop home.

Thomas proved to be a wonderful playmate for Jessica. But this didn't stop Mr Westhrop from taking an immediate dislike to the new addition to his home. The first thing that annoyed Mr Westhrop was that the boy's father had left instructions that Thomas's surname not be changed. Secondly, the boy daydreamed during the day, and had nightmares during the night. But these were small matters compared to Thomas's eyes.

About two years after his adoption the Westhrops noticed that Thomas's eyes were growing greener. 'Eyes like a couple o' burning emeralds' was how Mrs Taft from number twelve described them. Mrs Westhrop even began to suspect that Thomas was possessed. She had never spoken to Thomas since. 'Tell Thomas to clean his teeth!' she would say to Jessica, or 'Tell Thomas to finish his dinner!' or 'Will you tell Thomas to cover his mouth when he yawns!'.

Sunglasses had been provided for Thomas, with the instruction that they be worn whenever he left the house. It wasn't permitted for Thomas to wear sunglasses at school, so the Westhrops had been compelled to take the extraordinarily expensive step of providing Thomas with contact lenses that made his eyes look a more 'acceptable' blue. Although he had excellent eyesight, Thomas had been forced to wear them ever since – only removing them when he went to bed.

It wasn't long after Thomas's ninth birthday that Jags had died. Thomas not only inherited the dog's basket, but also many of the pet's duties such as bringing Mr Westhrop his paper and finding his slippers. Over the last two years those duties had only multiplied. He felt more like a servant than a son.

* * *

The patio would have been quite normal if it were not for the dandelions that sprouted in the place of several missing slabs. The uprooted slabs had been removed to the far end of the garden where they now stuck out of the soil in what Mrs Westhrop called a 'decorative rockery'. A trellis sat at the top of the rockery, casting its mocking shadow over the climbing plants that would never reach it.

Cleaning the patio was taking longer than Thomas had anticipated, although he had been distracted. Soon after he'd started, Thomas noticed Mr and Mrs Westhrop in the living room. They seemed to be discussing something in great earnest. Thomas got the impression that Mr Westhrop was trying to convince Mrs Westhrop of something, or at least calm her nerves.

Jessica had, true to her word, come to help, but she proved even more interested in her parents' conversation than Thomas. She was still only on her third slab after half an hour.

'Are you sure you can't pick out any words?' Jessica had her ear against the patio window again.

'It's double-glazed, and they've shut the windows,' Thomas said as he scrubbed away at a stubborn patch of lichen. 'My hearing isn't that good.'

A scraper clattered to the ground. He looked up to see Jessica smiling through clenched teeth at the door to the patio. The net curtains had been drawn back and Mr Westhrop stood looking at them both. Thomas swallowed hard. He would probably be told off for not going fast enough, and then told off some more because Jessica was helping.

Mr Westhrop opened the patio door, and the children awaited their fate. 'Thomas, you forgot to remind me it was your birthday today.'

Thomas looked across at Jessica, and she looked back, as confused as him.

Mr Westhrop looked down at the patio as if he wanted to say something about it, but then he shook his head and looked up at them. 'Go and get cleaned up. You want to be presentable for your party later on.'

Jessica raised her eyebrows. 'Party?'

'Yes, it's lucky your mother reminded me,' Mr Westhrop added. Thomas and Jessica looked at each other in compounded disbelief.

'It starts at six o'clock sharp. So both of you upstairs and wash your hands. And don't forget to put on your best clothes!'

'What's going on?' Thomas asked Jessica once they were up the stairs and out of earshot.

'I don't know, but there's no way Mum reminded him about your birthday. Still, a party, Thomas! A party!' Jessica disappeared into the bathroom with a smile.

* * *

The 'friends' Mr Westhrop had mentioned turned out to be Jessica's school friends. Jessica had the gift of making friends. Thomas had managed to get through his entire junior school without any.

From their conversation, the girls seemed to be under the impression that Jessica was having a late birthday party. Thomas felt glad they'd not had time to buy presents, or he might have ended up with a doll or a hairbrush. Mr Westhrop hung around the front door for some reason. Mrs Westhrop, judging by the noise of plates and glasses, was busy in the kitchen, either that or she'd put the crockery in the washing machine again.

The guests ate their salad without a word to Thomas, preferring to talk to Jessica about shoes and clothes. Thomas salted a piece of celery and bit off the end with a crunch just as the lights went out.

One of the girls asked Jessica if her parents had paid the electricity bill, but before she could answer, Mrs Westhrop's off-key falsetto filled the room.

'Happy Birthday to You! Happy Birthday to You! Happy...'

Thomas cringed. The girls joined in, but even Jessica's enthusiastic addition to the chorus wasn't enough to drown out Mrs Westhrop's contribution. When the song got to Thomas's name, the girls had to correct themselves when they realised it wasn't Jessica's birthday after all. Thomas reddened. He disliked the song. It made everyone stare at him.

Eleven candles stuck haphazardly into a chocolate cake floated toward the table. It was just like the one Jessica had drawn on his card, except smaller. Mrs Westhrop told Jessica to tell Thomas to blow the candles out and make a wish, though he doubted it would come true; after all, what were the chances of everyone forgetting the *Happy Birthday to You* song before his next birthday?

The doorbell rang just as the lights came back on. At first Thomas thought it must be another one of Jessica's friends, but before he could get so much as a peek at the visitor, Mr Westhrop had whisked the newcomer into his office, no doubt to show them his tropical fish – a fate to which many a visitor had been subjected. The office door opened just as Thomas finished his slice of cake. It was their first birthday cake since Jessica had turned eight.

Mr Westhrop appeared at the doorway. Behind him stood a tall man, perhaps in his mid-thirties, wearing the sharpest suit that Thomas had ever seen. The man's brown hair had a hint of ginger at the temples.

'Thomas,' Mr Westhrop began in an uncharacteristically pleasant tone, 'this is Mr Bartholomew.' He turned to the well-dressed man. 'As you can see, Thomas is just finishing his birthday party with his friends.'

'Ah, popular with the girls I see!' Mr Bartholomew joked in a Scottish accent.

Thomas flushed.

'Have you had enough of that big chocolate cake, Thomas?' Mr Westhrop asked, his lips lengthening in an attempt at a smile.

Thomas thought about saying no, and telling him it was far from big, but Mr Westhrop carried right on.

'Well, Thomas, would you join Mr Bartholomew and myself in my office?'

'Yes, Mr Westhrop,' Thomas said, as he stood up and wiped his mouth. At least he'd be away from the girls. Some of them were now giving him menacing looks.

'Good. Say goodbye to your friends,' he said, as he turned back to Mr Bartholomew. 'My wife will see to them. She's very good with children.' The two men walked back into the office.

Thomas looked at Jessica and she shrugged. What would anyone want with him? Was he in trouble? 'A party with no music?' one girl said to another just as Thomas slipped out, leaving Jessica and Mrs Westhrop to say goodbye and see them on their way.

Mr Westhrop already sat at his desk when Thomas walked into the office, and Mr Bartholomew opposite. A briefcase stood on the floor beside the latter's well-shod feet.

Once the door was shut, Mr Westhrop continued, the forced smile still upon his face. 'Mr Bartholomew's a solicitor, Thomas. He works for Bartholomew & Runfast.'

Thomas nodded awkwardly. What did this have to do with him?

'Bartholomew & Runfast dealt with your placement in the orphanage under the direction of your father, Mr Farrell,' Mr Westhrop explained.

Thomas suddenly felt very strange. Did this Mr Bartholomew know something about his father? Yet despite the mounting questions, and an increasing heart rate, he stood there silent.

A look of distress came over Mr Westhrop's face, as if he'd suddenly remembered something very important. 'I'm sorry, Mr Bartholomew, I forgot to ask if you'd like a drink or something to eat?'

'Thank you, I wouldn't say no to a cold drink.' The Scottish solicitor smiled as Mr Westhrop got up and left the room. Mr Bartholomew turned to study the aquarium. 'You've a nice home here, Thomas.'

This was Thomas's chance. 'Did you know my father, sir?'

Mr Bartholomew looked a little taken aback. 'Mr Runfast dealt with Mr Farrell. I'm afraid your father never returned after leaving you with us. We don't even have his first name or address. He must have been well off though. He paid in gold, you know.'

'Gold?' Thomas wondered if Mr Westhrop knew that.

Mr Bartholomew nodded. 'Yes, and very generously too, according to Mr Runfast's record of the transaction.'

Thomas took a step closer. 'Maybe Mr Runfast could tell me more? What he looked like. That sort of thing?'

Mr Bartholomew gave Thomas a thoughtful look as he stood up. 'Mr Runfast unfortunately died a couple of years ago – run over by a bus, a tragic and most ironic death.'

Thomas nodded. 'And my mother? I know she died, but –'

Mr Bartholomew put a hand on Thomas's shoulder. 'Sorry, lad. She passed away before you were brought to us. That's all we know. Perhaps some answers may lie in my briefcase.'

Just then Mr Westhrop came back with drinks. He eyed Thomas suspiciously. Mr Bartholomew thanked him, sipped his orange juice, and resumed his seat. There were ice cubes in his glass. The Westhrops had pulled out all the stops. Thomas wondered why. But more than that he wondered what Mr Bartholomew had in his briefcase.

Mr Westhrop took his position behind the desk again. 'My wife will be but a moment. Perhaps you might like to see my Egyptian Mouthbreeder –'

'Ah, Mrs Westhrop,' Mr Bartholomew said, standing up as she entered the room. Mr Westhrop frowned hard, abandoning his own advice to never do so.

Mrs Westhrop smiled, shook hands with Mr Bartholomew, and sat down next to a rather large Yucca plant. Mr Westhrop turned back to the solicitor. 'Yes, anyway, perhaps you should proceed, Mr Bartholomew?'

'Yes, yes, of course,' the solicitor said.

The front door closed and Jessica's footsteps came to a stop outside the office door. Thomas looked around. No one else seemed to have heard the eavesdropper.

'Well,' Mr Bartholomew began in his rich Scottish voice, 'this is something that all three of you will be interested in, I'm sure.'

Four, Thomas thought, as he glanced at the door.

'Thomas, on the day your father brought you to us he left a certain item in our care.' Mr Bartholomew pulled his red leather briefcase up onto his lap. It opened with a couple of clicks and the solicitor pulled out a white envelope. 'He left instructions that this should be placed into your hands on your eleventh birthday.'

Thomas tried to read what it said on the envelope, but before he had a chance the solicitor whipped out a piece of paper.

'I'll need this signed by Thomas and by one guardian. It's just to say I've delivered the item.' Mr Bartholomew placed the paper on the desk.

Mr Westhrop read it carefully, signed it, and then pushed it toward Thomas. 'Well, your turn.' Mr Westhrop held out his gold Swivet, Stibbard & Waverly pen.

Thomas signed it as best he could. He hadn't perfected his signature yet. Each time he wrote it out it looked different. Thomas handed the piece of paper back to Mr Bartholomew, and would have given him the pen too if it had not been deftly intercepted by Mr Westhrop.

Mr Bartholomew placed the envelope into Thomas's hand. Thomas lifted it up and saw that Mr and Mrs Westhrop were eyeing it every bit as keenly as him, especially Mr Westhrop. Upon it in black flowing ink were written the words:

*Master Thomas Farrell*

Was this his father's handwriting? Thomas looked upon it in awe.

'Well, Thomas,' Mr Westhrop said. 'Mr Bartholomew doesn't have all day. Open it!'

Thomas opened the envelope cautiously and tipped the contents into his hand. There in his palm lay a card and a gold key. Thomas checked the envelope to make sure he hadn't missed anything. It was empty. Thomas turned the card over in his palm. Upon it an address had been written:

*Bay Barch Bank, Selkirk, TD7*

'Ah, yes, I know that bank. Selkirk's where we have our office. Looks like you've a key to one of its deposit boxes,' Mr Bartholomew said. 'Your father must have left something there for you before he' – the solicitor paused – 'before he went away. Perhaps some more of that gold, eh?' He winked at Thomas.

'Bank? Gold?' Mr Westhrop said, his eyebrows raised. 'Deposit box, you say?'

'Yes, it's the oldest bank in town. Driven past it plenty of times.' Mr Bartholomew stood, briefcase in hand, and straightened his already-straight tie. 'Well, I must be off. It's a long journey. Thank you for the drink.'

'Mr Bartholomew?' Mr Westhrop asked. 'I wonder if, before you go, you might give me directions to this bank?'

'Certainly, Mr Westhrop. I'd be delighted. Do you have some paper?'

'Of course,' Mr Westhrop said, grabbing a pad of paper from a shelf by his aquarium and almost knocking the fish food into the water.

\* \* \*

Thomas held the envelope tightly as he stood in the doorway and watched the solicitor drive away. Mr Westhrop stood next to him, the map Mr Bartholomew had drawn clutched equally as tightly in his own hand. Somehow Thomas regretted the goodbye, as if a link between him and his father had just been severed. He gripped the envelope a little tighter. There was just the key now. It was his gift from his father, his birthday key. Once that box was opened perhaps he'd know who his parents were and why his father had placed him in an orphanage. Perhaps he'd know, for the first time in his life, who he really was; and that filled him with a strange mix of excitement and anxiety, like a hundred Christmas Eves at once, but with no certainty that, come morning, there would be any presents under the tree.

'Well, we shall go to this bank just as soon as possible,' Mr Westhrop said as he closed the door, but Thomas had the impression that Mr Westhrop didn't even know he was standing next to him.

## – CHAPTER TWO –

## *An Heirloom and an Invitation*

Outside, the overcast sky drizzled all over Mr Westhrop's pallid-green Morris Minor. It was one of those showers Mother Nature teased people with, perhaps in the hope of catching as many as possible by surprise when the real cloudburst struck.

Thomas sat in the car with Jessica, while Mrs Westhrop made a final check to ensure all the windows were closed, doors locked, electrical equipment unplugged, and the oven turned off. Mr Westhrop sat in the Morris Minor tapping his fingers on the steering wheel. She sometimes took twenty minutes to give the house a good check, and once Mrs Westhrop had forgotten they were all waiting for her and Mr Westhrop had returned to the house to find her making banana bread. That was unlikely to happen this time; Mr Westhrop had repeatedly told his wife about the importance of this journey.

Mr Westhrop had attended to the planning of the trip with an eagerness that had surprised Thomas. Soon after Mr Bartholomew's departure, Mr Westhrop had asked for the key Thomas had received. Just in case Thomas 'misplaced' it, he'd said. Thomas had reluctantly agreed and hadn't so much as seen the key since. He still had the envelope though. It now lay in his treasure box along with the slip of paper summing up all he knew about himself and his adoption. He'd spent many hours that week staring at the writing on that envelope. His father's writing. To know that, to see it, to possess it, made Thomas feel he at last had something, however small, that linked him with his parents.

The past week at school seemed to have dragged on for at least a fortnight. Thomas's class was buzzing with talk about which secondary school each pupil would be going to in September. Jessica had told Thomas on Wednesday that Mr Westhrop had wanted to get them both into St Prudence-in-the-Fields, but Thomas didn't have much interest in the matter after Saturday's events, though he did briefly wonder how the school received its name.

Thomas had spent most of his lesson time daydreaming, even more than he normally did. He'd dreamed of going to the bank and opening a box filled with photographs of his parents. He'd dreamed of finding a chart displaying his family history clear back to the Norman Conquest. He'd dreamed of finding a note telling him that his father was still alive, living in a small cottage on the outskirts of Holten Layme, and that he was invited over for tea. Today he would find out.

Jessica sat quietly in the backseat, but she didn't fool Thomas. He could tell that she was bubbling with excitement. Neither of them had been to Scotland before. Why Mr Westhrop had arranged the trip with just a week's notice, Thomas didn't know, but he was glad they were going so soon. Well, if Mrs Westhrop ever finished checking the house, that was.

As if summoned by Thomas's thought, Mrs Westhrop appeared from behind the burgeoning mass of wisteria that clambered up the side of the house. Mr Westhrop sighed with relief as his wife got into the car. Jonathan adjusted the rear-view mirror and started up the engine. After Mrs Westhrop had asked Jessica if she had her seat belt on, and asked Jessica to ask Thomas the same thing, they were pulling out of the drive of number six, Birch Tree Close and Thomas's heart was beginning to race with the thought of what might await them at the end of their journey.

* * *

Thomas opened his eyes and rubbed an aching nose that had spent the last hour squashed against the arm of the door. He must have nodded off. His belly rumbled. They'd stopped off twice at the motorway services, but Mr Westhrop had only allowed them a small amount to eat each time because of what he said were 'exorbitant prices'.

The rain clouds had gone and the sun now rode high above. They were in the slow lane, which meant Mrs Westhrop must've been driving. She wasn't a very good driver by her own admission, but Mr Westhrop needed a rest, and stopping was out of the question. Time was money, after all. Mrs Westhrop drove very close behind other vehicles, a unique situation in that it was the only time her nerves were fine whilst Mr Westhrop's were not; which was why the latter chose to close his eyes but never quite drift off.

To Thomas and Jessica's delight the slow lane was left behind as Mr Westhrop – who remarkably opened his eyes just at the right point – instructed his wife to turn off the motorway and onto an A road.

'Thomas?'

Thomas sat up. 'Yes, Mr Westhrop?'

'That sign up ahead, what does it say?'

Thomas looked up to a blue sign with white lettering. 'Welcome to Scotland.'

'Good, good. Then we should be in Selkirk soon.'

Jessica looked up from a brochure she'd grabbed from the house. The Westhrops maintained a large collection of tourist-information literature, mainly because it was all free and provided the next-best thing to going on holiday – which, of course, would've actually cost money. 'Oh, it looks the same as England.'

Thomas looked around, half expecting to see a haggis shop or a bagpiper, but all that met his eyes were hills, grass and a few scattered trees.

'We're in the Cheviot Hills right now. They lie on the border of England and Scotland, you know,' Jessica continued.

'I do now,' Thomas replied, yawning before breaking into a smile that Jessica returned. The hills were pretty though. He liked hills. Holten Layme could've done with more of them.

'So what will you do if your dad has left you lots of money?' Jessica suddenly asked.

Thomas frowned. He looked at Mr and Mrs Westhrop. The music was playing too loudly for them to hear. 'Well, I think if there's any money your dad wouldn't let me spend it, at least not until I'm older.'

'But if there was, and you could spend it?' Jessica persisted.

Thomas thought hard. 'I would buy myself a giant bag of marbles filled with every size and variety I could imagine. And I'd buy you some shoes and a giant bar of chocolate. I might even buy a new garden gnome for Mrs Westhrop!'

'Oh, Thomas, that's so sweet!' Jessica said. 'But I think it would be fairer on the gnome if you let someone else buy it.' Jessica made this last comment quite seriously, before she reached into her bag and plucked out a new brochure entitled *Discovering the Scottish Borders*.

Thomas thought there might be money. It was a bank after all. But money wouldn't answer his questions. It wouldn't tell him who he was or who his parents were. Had his father just abandoned him after his mum had died? Did he have no grandparents or extended family anywhere? Was he alone in the world?

* * *

They drove into Selkirk not much later. It was a little more built up than Thomas had imagined. After finding a free car park, Mr Westhrop led the way quickly to Bay Barch Bank, guided by Mr Bartholomew's map. Getting somewhere fast was an important life skill to Mr Westhrop. Needless to say, he'd become an excellent map reader, unlike Thomas. Thomas had managed to get lost on the way home from school no less than three times in his first two weeks of junior school.

'Well, here we are,' Mr Westhrop said with some pride at having found it so quickly.

There on the corner stood an old-looking building with the words *Bay Barch Bank* engraved over the door. They walked up the steps to the heavy, but thankfully open, metal-embossed doors. They were greeted by a very clean room with a polished marble floor and a smart wooden counter that ran the entire length of the room. Behind the glass of the counter many computer screens flickered. Most of the positions had big notices saying 'Closed'.

Mr Westhrop led them over to a part of the counter behind which a young man sat. He seemed to be trying to find something in a drawer. Mr Westhrop coughed.

'Uh, hello. How can I help you?' The clerk shoved the drawer closed.

'My name's Mr Westhrop. I'd like to make a withdrawal from a deposit box. It's in the name of Thomas Farrell, I believe. Here's the key.' Mr Westhrop pulled Thomas's key from his light grey waistcoat and placed it on the counter.

The clerk eyed the key as if it were some strange creature he'd never seen before. He didn't touch it. 'Excuse me, I'll get someone who can show you to the box.' He disappeared through a door.

Less than a minute later an older man, dressed somewhat like Mr Bartholomew, appeared on their side of the counter. 'Hello, Mr Westhrop?' He greeted them with a surprisingly warm smile. 'You've a safety deposit box key, I believe? May I see it?'

'Yes, of course.' Mr Westhrop handed him the key from the counter.

The man examined the key. 'Ah, yes. One of the old boxes. If you'll follow me, please?' He took them through a corridor that ended at a large desk behind which stood a secure-looking door.

'Excuse me one moment,' he said as he pressed a few keys on a computer on the desk. He looked up. 'Thomas Farrell?'

'That's me,' Thomas said.

The clerk dropped his eyes to Thomas with one eyebrow raised. 'Oh, I see. Do you have some identification, young man?'

Thomas looked back at Mr Westhrop.

'Here you are.' Mr Westhrop pulled a letter and certificate from his jacket pocket. Thomas caught the words *Adoption Papers* at the top of the letter. He'd seen them before, when he was six, if he remembered correctly. Mr Westhrop had got them out to provide evidence to Thomas that he wasn't their son. It had been something Mr Westhrop had done with great care – care in the sense that he wanted there to be no misunderstanding on the facts of the matter.

The clerk scanned the documents and gave them back to Mr Westhrop. 'Well, let's proceed.'

The door opened and Thomas and the Westhrops were ushered through to a room lined with small metal panels, each with its own keyhole.

'Here it is,' the clerk said, 'safety deposit box two hundred and six.' He inserted the key into the box and turned it. It clicked and the clerk pulled open the door.

Thomas was just tall enough to see inside. It lay empty except for a brown envelope and a small cloth-wrapped bundle. Thomas reached in and pulled them out. The cloth was tattered and the object inside round and hard. The envelope bore similar words as the one that had held the key. It read:

*To Master Thomas Farrell*

But it was, to Thomas's surprise, not written in the same hand. He could tell. He had studied the other envelope's words, followed their curves and lines with his eyes every night since Mr Bartholomew's visit, until sleep had taken him.

Mr Westhrop, looking somewhat disappointed, thanked the clerk, as did Mrs Westhrop. Jessica didn't thank anyone because she was too busy staring at the bundle in Thomas's hand.

Once back in the car, Mr Westhrop looked at him. 'Well, let's not be all day about it.'

Thomas would've liked to open them in private, but he was lucky Mr Westhrop allowed him to open them at all. He hesitated to unwrap the bundle, though he didn't know why. Dismissing his unfounded fears, he removed the layers of old cloth from the object within – and promptly dropped it.

'Careful, it might be valuable!' Mr Westhrop barked.

A glass sphere, a little larger in size than a golf ball, now rested on the backseat of the car between Jessica and Thomas. But it was what it contained that had made Thomas drop it, for suspended in its centre hung a snake.

Mr Westhrop held out his hand. 'Give it here.'

Thomas picked it up gingerly and handed it over.

'Hmph,' Mr Westhrop grunted, 'nothing more than some family heirloom, I'd guess. Probably worthless.' Mrs Westhrop eyed it with a look of disgust as her husband dropped it back into Thomas's hand. 'Open the envelope, then.'

Thomas opened the envelope. Inside he found two sheets of paper.

Mr Westhrop tapped his fingers on the steering wheel. 'Well, what does it say?'

The front sheet consisted of a short letter, but it wasn't from his father. He read it out:

*Dear Thomas,*

*I have been instructed by the representative of your late father's estate to provide an education for you at Darkledun Manor, School for Gifted Children. I am glad to inform you that this has been paid, and a place is open to you as of your eleventh birthday. A sum has also been arranged to compensate any legal guardian(s).*

*I enclose all necessary details regarding Darkledun Manor, which you should show your legal guardian(s) without delay.*

*Yours Most Sincerely,*

*M. Trevelyan, Head.*
*Darkledun Manor*

Before he could look at the details to which this Mr M. Trevelyan referred, Mr J. Westhrop had grabbed them along with the letter.

Jessica sat forward, eyes bright. 'What's it mean?'

'It means,' Mr Westhrop began with that familiar look of glee, 'that your good mother and I will finally have some compensation for our challenges over the last few years. Which is, of course, quite right and proper.'

But Thomas, lost in thought, didn't hear Mr Westhrop.

When younger, Thomas thought his father might visit one day, but when the visits never came Thomas began to accept that his father was dead. The confirmation of it comforted him, in a way; if his father had still been alive, Thomas wouldn't have understood why he'd never come to see him. The invitation to the school gave him hope. The writer of the letter, or this representative, must've known his father. At last he might be able to find out who his father really was.

Jessica turned to Thomas. 'The name sounds a bit sinister.'

'What? Trevelyan? It doesn't sound sinister to me.'

'No, the school! Darkledun Manor.'

'Well, that's good fortune,' Mr Westhrop said, as he finished studying the sheet attached to the letter. 'Everyone wait here, I'll be back in ten minutes.'

Mr Westhrop took fifteen minutes, not ten. He returned quite pleased with himself. 'I've just been on the phone to this Mr Trevelyan and have arranged for us to stop by on the way home.'

As the car pulled off, Jessica started rummaging through her bag, but Thomas paid little attention to her. This was all rather sudden. He was going to meet Mr Trevelyan. The thought that this man might be able to tell Thomas more about his father sent his heart racing, though whether with excitement or fear, he couldn't tell.

'Dad?' Jessica asked just as Mr Westhrop turned onto the main road.

'Yes, Jessica?' he said.

'I didn't know there were special schools for gifted children.'

Thomas looked at his adoptive sister. He hadn't picked up on that. Why had he been invited to a school for gifted children? There was nothing special about him.

'Obviously this' – Mr Westhrop waved the invitation to Darkledun Manor in his hand – 'was extended without any personal knowledge of Thomas. I think they'll still take him. After all, it's already paid for.'

Jessica ignored the remark. 'If Thomas goes to this school, how will he get home each day? I think it might be very late when he gets in. And you know how he gets lost so easily. Maybe we can meet him somewhere?'

Mr Westhrop looked at his daughter in the rear-view mirror with impatience. 'Jessica, Darkledun Manor students don't come home every day. It's a boarding school.'

Thomas hadn't heard of one of those before. Did they make boards there or was the school itself made of boards?

Seeing the confusion written on the two small faces in his rear-view mirror, Mr Westhrop went on. 'A boarding school is where students sleep overnight. They don't come home at the end of each day or even at the weekend.'

'You mean if Thomas goes to Darkledun Manor we won't see him again until he's an adult?'

'Thomas will come home in the holidays, Jessica.' He didn't seem particularly pleased about the idea from the way he spoke. 'Now, no more questions. I have to concentrate on the directions.'

Jessica tried to fold up the map she'd been looking at, but wasn't having much success. She seemed agitated. Thomas paid little heed to Jessica though; he was, after all, going to see a man who might know something about his father.

# – CHAPTER THREE –

## *The Headmaster of Darkledun Manor*

It wasn't far to Darkledun Manor. After leaving the main road from Selkirk they headed west along a much quieter road that came to follow the course of a river. A few minutes later they crossed a bridge. It was at this point that Thomas saw a sign that read *Carterhaugh Forest*. He looked at Jessica, but her head was turned the other way. She didn't seem very interested anymore. In fact she'd said very little since leaving Selkirk. Perhaps the trip had tired her out.

After crossing the bridge, Mr Westhrop pulled the car over and consulted the map. About a mile later he turned off down a lane marked with a wooden sign upon which *Darkledun Manor – 2 miles* had been painted in black. The trees became denser, so much so that Thomas was unable to see anything but a wall of green.

Eventually the lane ended at a pair of large iron gates. The one on the left bore the word *Darkledun* at its top, wrought in iron and painted white, and the gate on the right sported the word *Manor*. Mr Westhrop drove through the open gates and parked. Thomas and the Westhrops piled out of the car, Jessica (unusually) last.

They stood at the bottom of a hill upon which sat a manor house with a tower at one end. A cobbled path led up the incline to the front door. They approached the school somewhat warily, especially Mrs Westhrop who appeared concerned she might trip on the cobbles. Thomas walked behind the Westhrops, staring up. Jessica trailed behind, sparing only the odd glance at the school. The door had a bell, a brass one from which hung a chain of dark metal.

Mr Westhrop tugged on the chain. The bell rang, and the chime echoed through Darkledun Manor's empty grounds. A moment later the door opened and they were greeted by a lady not much taller than Jessica. Thomas guessed her to be in her middle years. Her long, dark brown dress clung tight to her waist, a perfect complement to the short, dark brown hair that left her neck and ears exposed.

'Good morning. I am Miss McGritch, the Housekeeper of Darkledun Manor. You must be the Westhrops?' she said in a voice as austere as Thomas had ever heard, but with only a hint of a Scottish accent. The short lady looked at each of them. Her eyes rested last and longest upon Thomas.

'Yes, that's right,' Mr Westhrop replied.

Miss McGritch smiled slightly and beckoned them in. 'If you will follow me, I will take you to the Headmaster.'

Mrs Westhrop's high-heeled shoes clattered noisily on the stone floor of the sunlit entrance hall as they followed Miss McGritch. The Housekeeper walked so prim and proper and straight-backed that Thomas thought she must have practised with a book on her head.

Stairs led up to another level, but instead they went left and the Housekeeper led them down a couple of featureless corridors, and past a number of doors all marked with a number and letter such as 3A and 5B, until at the end of the last corridor they arrived outside a door upon which were affixed the words *Headmaster's Office*.

Miss McGritch knocked and an enthusiastic, but not-at-all Scottish, voice answered. 'Yes? Who is it?'

'The Westhrops, Headmaster.'

'Well, 'blige me, they were quick! Do show them in!'

The Housekeeper opened the door. Thomas walked into a room not much bigger than the Westhrops' living room. A large desk sat beneath two tall windows that looked out onto a small copse. In front of the desk stood a man of average height and build, though a little portly around the waist, with grey hair that hung long enough to cover his ears but was entirely absent from his crown and forehead. He wore a grey tweed suit and a shocking yellow tie with black spots, which didn't go at all with the purple shirt beneath. The man's round face and blue eyes were full of vigour despite him being, as far as Thomas could guess, about twenty years older than Mr Westhrop. He held a monocle to his eye as if examining them all in minute detail. After a few moments, the balding man dropped the monocle and it swung down to his tie. Thomas could now see it was attached to a thin silver chain that hung around his neck.

'Hello, it's jolly nice to meet you all! I'm the Headmaster, Mr Trevelyan.' He shook them all enthusiastically by the hand, starting with Mr Westhrop and ending with Jessica; this seemed to lift the latter's spirits briefly. They sat down on some rather comfortable orange chairs dotted around his desk. Mr Trevelyan opened a cabinet and pulled out a tray of glasses which he placed on his desk. He then took a jug of juice from the same cabinet as well as a plate of fairy cakes. He gave the latter to Mr Westhrop who, not having a sweet tooth, passed them on to his wife. Mr Trevelyan, meanwhile, filled the cups with juice.

'This must be a little strange for you,' Mr Trevelyan said after seating himself behind his desk.

Mr Westhrop forced a smile. The Headmaster's accent was hard to place, but Thomas thought it must have been from somewhere in England rather than Scotland.

Mr Trevelyan took a sip of juice. 'I'm sure you have many questions, as will Thomas most of all, of course.' When no one responded the Headmaster carried right on. 'I can have Miss McGritch show you around. It's all quite modern – electricity, lights, that sort of thing.'

Thomas looked up from the yellow-topped fairy cake he'd just bitten into. He couldn't imagine a building without electricity, even though his own bedroom-loft barely possessed it.

Mr Westhrop frowned. 'No, no. I'm sure it's quite all right.' He pulled his small calculator from his inside breast pocket. 'Your letter mentioned some financial matters?'

If he was shocked at Mr Westhrop's frankness, Mr Trevelyan didn't show it. Thomas stole a glance at Miss McGritch who stood behind them. Her face was hard to read, but Thomas thought he caught a glimmer of disapproval.

'Yes, of course. Miss McGritch, perhaps you'll take the children on a quick tour? If that's all right?' Mr Trevelyan looked to Thomas and Jessica, and then back at Mr and Mrs Westhrop.

Mr Westhrop gave an indifferent nod and Miss McGritch led Thomas and Jessica out of the room. Thomas took a look behind him before he left the office. Mr Westhrop was fiddling with a piece of paper and his gold Swivet, Stibbard & Waverly pen. The Headmaster, or so it seemed, flashed a boyish grin at Thomas before Miss McGritch closed the door.

*  *  *

A sports field spread out behind the Manor, its edges dipping down the hill into a bank of trees and blackberry bushes. A forest surrounded the whole hill, and the only discernible features on the horizon were the peaks of three hills far to the east.

Thomas looked back and saw the tower he'd first seen from the car park. 'What's in the tower, Miss McGritch?'

Miss McGritch's face became even more serious. 'The tower is out of bounds.'

Miss McGritch led them back inside. She showed them one classroom, with small wooden desks and plastic chairs surrounded by walls painted the same cream as the corridors, before leading them out of the block and up the wide flight of stairs they'd seen on the way in.

'To the left is the girls' dormitories, to the right, the boys' rooms,' she said, as they reached the landing. She allowed them a quick peek into one of the rooms: a bed, wardrobe, chest-of-drawers, chair and small table all fit into a space not much larger than the Westhrops' loft. To Thomas it was like a palace. He couldn't remember what it was like to sleep in a proper bed.

Miss McGritch's office sat on the landing between the girls' and boys' dormitories. As they passed it, Miss McGritch shifted her gaze to a glass-panelled room filled with bookshelves on the other side of the landing. 'You will wait in the library over there while I check to see if Mr Trevelyan and your parents are ready to have you return. Perhaps you will take the time to educate yourselves a little?'

Jessica wasted no time in exploring the library. The bookcases, chairs, tables and stands had been spread out across the landing overlooking the hall below. There was a row of shelves dedicated to science, a row on technology, another on history, languages, and quite a few other subjects too. Jessica had found a shelf holding some big and old-looking books.

Thomas remained by the stands. He ran his finger across a nearby shelf, but he wasn't really looking at the books. Eventually he sat down. It was only then that he realised that Jessica stood looking out across the hall to the window high above the door to the Manor. She hugged a book to her chest.

Thomas leant back in his chair. 'Did you find a good book?'

Jessica didn't turn around. 'It's beautiful.'

'What's it called?' Thomas couldn't see the book's title from where he sat.

'I think Scotland's a beautiful place, don't you, Thomas?'

Jessica still faced the window. Thomas realised she wasn't talking about the book.

'Yeah, I guess,' Thomas said.

'It's a nice school, too. I think you should accept the Headmaster's invitation.' Jessica sounded as if her thoughts were miles away. Perhaps she was homesick?

Thomas could see no reason not to accept. The school was a link to his father. Mr Westhrop would probably decide for him anyway. 'I guess I will.'

Jessica turned to face him. 'You don't seem to care very much either way!' She dropped the book heavily on a table.

Just at that moment Miss McGritch appeared in the hall below. The Housekeeper paused, gave Jessica a disapproving look, and called them down.

Thomas followed Miss McGritch, but didn't speak to Jessica, who looked as if she'd bite his head off if he tried. Perhaps she was jealous. She'd said it was beautiful. St Prudence-in-the-Fields was a nice enough school no doubt, but probably not as picturesque as Darkledun Manor. That must be it, Thomas thought. He'd been thinking so much about what Mr Trevelyan might know of his father that he'd given no thought to the implications of him going to school here. He had to make a decision that would affect his life for at least the next five years. Had Mr Westhrop thought about that? Yet Thomas felt strangely comfortable with the idea of living here for most of the year, excited even. Though he wasn't sure what the Headmaster would do once he found out that he had no special gifts. Or perhaps Mr Westhrop had already told Mr Trevelyan about Thomas's lack of talent. By the time they got back to the Headmaster's Office Thomas had made up his mind on the matter.

Miss McGritch took up her place by the door, like a guard, whilst Jessica and Thomas returned to their seats under the delighted gaze of the Headmaster. Mr Westhrop looked pleased with himself, though it was hard to gauge Mrs Westhrop's mood as she picked at a pink-topped fairy cake.

'Ah, welcome back the both of you!' Mr Trevelyan said. 'I trust you have enjoyed the tour? Sorry it was so brief.'

Thomas nodded and smiled, though Jessica said nothing.

Mr Trevelyan leaned forward and raised his eyebrows. 'Well, Thomas, your guardians have agreed to your enrolment here. That only leaves me to ask you whether you wish to attend?'

Mr Westhrop's eyes widened. Clearly he hadn't been expecting the question. Thomas looked at Jessica who sat staring out of the window. 'Yes, very much.'

Jessica didn't show any reaction, though Thomas thought Mr Westhrop gave a very faint sigh of relief.

'But I wondered if – if it would be possible for –' Thomas stammered, much to Mr Westhrop's irritation. 'I mean, would it be possible for Jessica to go to school here as well?'

Jessica looked up, her eyes wide. But she wasn't the only one.

'My Jessica, come here?' Mrs Westhrop almost whimpered. She looked at her husband for support.

'We couldn't afford to pay for Jessica. You see' – Mr Westhrop turned to the Headmaster – 'the school we've picked out, St Prudence-in-the-Fields, is very reasonable in its costs.'

'Please, sir,' Thomas began, 'I don't know how much my father left, but if there's enough I'd like to pay for Jessica too.'

Mr Westhrop looked as if he were about to disapprove, but then stopped himself. Thomas recognised those eyes. Mr Westhrop was doing some mental calculations at a speed way beyond Thomas's ability.

'Yes, Thomas, your father left enough,' Mr Trevelyan said. 'You cannot spend the money though. You see, it was put in trust until you come of age.'

Thomas felt disappointed, and his face didn't hide it.

'However,' Mr Trevelyan continued, 'I am sure the representative of your late father's estate would release funds for such a magnanimous gesture.' Mr Trevelyan smiled warmly and Thomas reddened quite deeply.

'That's if it's all right with Mr and Mrs Westhrop?' the Headmaster asked, casting his blue-eyed gaze their way.

Mrs Westhrop looked undecided, but Mr Westhrop didn't. 'It certainly is all right. Yes, it is very acceptable.'

Mr Trevelyan looked at Jessica. 'And that's OK with you?'

By this time Jessica's eyes were all but popping out of her head. 'Oh yes! Yes! Thank you!'

Thomas smiled awkwardly. He was glad she'd agreed.

'Well, that's settled then!' Mr Trevelyan announced. 'The school year begins on the first Tuesday of September and we expect all students here the day before. I will send a letter nearer the time regarding the travel arrangements and so forth. You won't need to buy anything. The uniform and books are all covered by us. Miss McGritch here will take Thomas's and Jessica's measurements before you leave. Now, do you have any questions?'

Thomas wanted to ask about his father, but it felt awkward with Mr and Mrs Westhrop present. Jessica, however, had lots of questions, and she asked the first one before Thomas would've had a chance to ask his own anyway.

'Mr Trevelyan?' Jessica said, a look of some concern on her face.

'Yes, Miss Westhrop?' Mr Trevelyan responded as Miss McGritch wrapped a yellow tape measure around Jessica's waist.

'Are there any shops near the school?'

Mr Trevelyan contained a grin and rubbed his plump chin. 'Well, let's see. I'd recommend you make use of one of those new-fangled bicycles we keep here. Most students use them. No bus, you see. There are a few small shops around in the villages, and there's the town of course – bit of a ride, but that'd be your best bet.'

Bicycles? New-fangled? Thomas was sure bikes had been around long enough not to be called new-fangled anymore, though he'd never owned or even been on one.

'Thank you,' Jessica replied. Thomas felt certain she was taking notes. Perhaps she was working out how much shopping she could carry on a bike.

Miss McGritch finished with Jessica and moved on to Thomas, who endured it silently. Jessica continued to ask questions all the way down the corridor after Miss McGritch had recorded Thomas's measurements. Questions such as how many books were in the library, what sort of dishes were on the school menu, and whether or not there'd be any hockey. Eventually they reached the door, and Mr Trevelyan wished them all farewell.

Thomas paused and, when the Westhrops were a little way ahead, turned back to the Headmaster, who waited patiently. 'I thought maybe you knew my parents?'

The Headmaster looked at Thomas with gentle eyes. 'Sorry, Thomas, I can't say I knew Fearghal and Eleanor.'

'Fearghal and Eleanor? Those were their names?' Thomas asked.

'Well, bless my soul, you didn't know? No, you wouldn't have, I suppose.'

Fearghal and Eleanor Farrell. It almost felt like too much information. All these years not knowing, and then to find out by way of a brief comment. Thomas decided he wouldn't tell anyone about this. It would be his secret.

Thomas took a deep breath. 'Do you know how my father died?'

The Headmaster paused, as if thinking what to say. Thomas thought he saw Miss McGritch cast a wary sidelong glance at the Headmaster before he answered. 'He died in battle,

Thomas, soon after he left you. That's all I can tell you, I'm afraid.'

'What about other relatives?' Thomas asked.

'I don't know about your mother's side, but your father was an only child and his parents no longer walk this world,' Mr Trevelyan explained.

'I see,' said Thomas. 'Thank you. I had to ask.'

'I understand. Maybe we will talk some more when you return.'

He wanted to ask more of course, but now wasn't the time. Mr Westhrop had almost reached the car.

'Yes,' Thomas agreed with a smile before he turned and hurried down the cobbled path to catch up with the others. At the bottom, back again beside Mr Westhrop's green Morris Minor, Thomas turned and gave a final wave to Mr Trevelyan and Miss McGritch. The Headmaster of Darkledun Manor waved back, but the Housekeeper only looked on, unmoving and straight.

# – CHAPTER FOUR –

## *Of Dreams and Serpents*

'I found it!' Jessica appeared at the top of the ladder holding a map. Only the crown of her chestnut head was visible above it. Before Thomas could ask what she was talking about, she'd knelt down and spread the map flat across the dog basket's covers, despite the fact that Thomas still lay in the bed.

Found what? Thomas stared up at the glowing bulb he'd switched on at the sound of Jessica's feet on the ladder. And what was the time? Thomas looked at the old wind-up clock on the box beside the dog basket. It was a little before eight o'clock in the morning. It had taken Thomas a while to get to sleep, but the tiredness still hadn't left him. Jessica, however, had made a full recovery, and had no doubt been up at least an hour already.

Thomas looked at the map through sleepy eyes. He would've preferred breakfast. 'What have you found?'

'This!' Jessica pointed to a pale patch of green on the map.

Thomas wiped the sleep from his eyes. Just above Jessica's finger lay a splash of light green with the words *Carterhaugh Forest* written across it.

'Don't you notice anything strange about the map?'

'Erm – no.'

Jessica sighed. She did that when Thomas couldn't keep up with her. She pointed at the concentric lines drawn upon the map. 'I reckon that must be the hill the Manor's on, but there's no Manor there on the map.'

'Maybe it's an old map,' Thomas suggested.

'I checked the date. It was printed two years ago.'

Thomas shrugged. 'Well, maybe they don't put everything on the maps, or it got missed or something.'

Jessica looked unconvinced. She saw a mystery in everything. It was probably those adventure novels she read.

'I've been reading a bit about that forest too.'

'You have?' Thomas asked, yawning.

She sat down on the floor. 'According to legend, it was a haunt of fairies!'

'A haunt of fairies?' That was another tourist-brochure quotation if ever he'd heard one.

Jessica crossed her legs. 'Yep, and not all of them very pleasant.'

'Well,' he began, accepting that he wouldn't be getting back to sleep, 'I didn't see any fairies.'

'But there must've been some there.'

Thomas frowned. 'How'd you know that?'

'Well, who made the fairy cakes?' Jessica grinned as Thomas groaned.

Jessica had certainly cheered up after their visit to Darkledun Manor. In the car on the way home, Thomas had got a full review of all the places to visit, where all the main shopping centres were, and a host of other information Jessica had gleaned from the brochures. He was glad of Jessica's change of spirit. He didn't like it when she got upset; though he wouldn't admit it, he relied upon her to fill an otherwise friendless world. And yet something else had entered his world now. A purpose. He was at last doing something with his life that his father would have wanted – receiving an education paid for by Mr Fearghal Farrell. And knowing that was the best thing in the world.

Thomas shifted and his hand brushed against a round, hard object under the covers. Pulling the blanket back, he found his father's glass orb. He'd been examining it last night and must have nodded off and dropped it into the covers.

Picking it up, he held it close to his face. The 'snake', he'd decided, was probably a lizard of some kind. He couldn't tell if it was real or not. He'd never seen any lizards except in a zoo. And then it'd just been their tails poking out from beneath branches and leaves in glass tanks. Thomas had spent most of the time, at Mr Westhrop's insistence, in the building housing the tropical fish, so there'd been little time to see anything else.

The creature in the orb had two horns upon a head that ended in an odd-shaped snout. Four legs, each with a clawed foot, stuck out from the sinuous body, and its tail wrapped back on itself as if the lizard, or whatever it was, had been captured in mid-turn. It certainly looked very lifelike. A horrible thought occurred to Thomas. Perhaps it had been cast alive into the hot glass when the orb was made? Thomas shuddered. He had no love of snakes or lizards, but he wouldn't wish such a terrible fate upon one. The creature, though a subtle green in colour, had a metallic sheen to it as if thinly coated in silver. The silvery sheen changed its hue as Thomas moved the orb around.

Jessica furrowed her brow and stared at the glass orb. 'Do you think it's real?'

'I don't know, Jess. I don't even know what this thing is.' Thomas shrugged. 'Perhaps it's a paperweight or something.'

'They have to have a flat bottom, Thomas, otherwise they just roll off the paper.'

Thomas wasn't thinking. He was still tired.

'Most likely an heirloom, like Dad said,' she added.

Thomas nodded. He'd heard the word of course, but wasn't entirely sure of its meaning.

'I looked it up in Father's big dictionary in his office. An heirloom is a rare or unique item a family passes down to their children, or at least something that stays in the family a long time.'

'Like your mother's frilled slippers?' Mrs Westhrop had had them as long as Thomas could remember.

'Something like that, I think. Though I'm not sure I want her to pass *them* down to me.'

Thomas leant closer to the orb. 'It looks so – well, like it's still alive, watching.'

Jessica pointed to the creature's back. 'Look at those.'

Thomas peered closer. Two small folds of skin were wrapped close against its back. He hadn't taken much notice of them before. 'Maybe it was shedding its skin when it was killed – well, I mean if it's real.'

Jessica's eyes widened. 'They look like wings, Thomas. Snakes and lizards don't have wings!'

'Wings? Are you sure?' He looked again at the thin folds. They did look like wings, now that Jessica mentioned it.

* * *

June was soon gone, the stormy showers passed, and a hot July in full swing. Only a couple more weeks of school remained, a fact that put a spring into the step of most students at the end of school that day as they made their way down the tree-lined avenue leading from the school gates. Not so with Jessica Westhrop. She always had a spring in her step, whether the end or beginning of term. Thomas walked alongside her unaware of his sister's or anyone else's steps, and certainly with no spring in his own.

He was tired. He'd spent his lunch hour in the library with Jessica looking through books. Jessica had been searching the library for a week to see if she could find a picture of the creature in Thomas's glass. She'd had no success and so employed Thomas's aid. Thomas thought he must've seen a picture of every type of lizard and snake on the face of the planet. But not one of them looked like the creature in his father's orb.

'I meant to tell you about something I found in the library today. I forgot about it when we got into those books on reptiles,' Jessica announced, as they left the tree-lined avenue.

Thomas looked up from the cracks in the pavement he was trying to avoid. 'You did?'

'Yes, I was helping Bernice Flanagan with her project for Mrs Prowse.'

'And?'

'Well, I've got something you can add to your essay.'

Mrs Prowse had asked everyone to write a page about their family tree. Thomas had finished the essay two nights ago; at least he'd written what he could. It was a pity that Mr Trevelyan hadn't known his parents. Maybe he knew where his parents were buried. He wasn't going to give up.

'I handed it in.'

'Oh, well, you won't want to know what I found out then.' Jessica gave Thomas a mischievous look.

'Jess?' Thomas said, following. She did like to tease him.

'It was about the Farrell surname. It's Irish too, like Bernice's.'

Thomas didn't feel Irish, though he didn't feel English either. He felt as if he belonged elsewhere, some place far away and yet very close. It was a feeling that had always been with him, as far as he could remember.

'It comes from the name Fearghal,' Jessica added.

It was Thomas who stopped this time. Jessica went on quite a way before she realised Thomas was no longer beside her.

'Thomas?' she shouted back. 'Are you OK?'

'Yes, yes,' Thomas replied, beginning to walk again.

Jessica eyed him with concern, but then her face returned to its normal exuberance. 'It means "valorous man". One of your ancestors must've been called Fearghal!'

Thomas nodded as casually as he could. Jessica had no idea just how close that ancestor was. How strange that his father's surname should have the same meaning as his first name. Jessica of course had no idea. He'd told no one.

\* \* \*

It was getting dark outside when Thomas heard Jessica's familiar footsteps racing up the ladder. The next thing he knew, a book landed on his chest as he lay there in bed.

'Mum and Dad are watching that silly programme again, so I thought we'd make good use of the time.' Jessica sat down beside Thomas's dog-basket with a book in her hand.

Thomas didn't know what 'silly programme' she was referring to, but he sat up and stared at the book. 'What's this?'

'A book.'

'Yes, I know – I mean –'

'It'll complete our research. That book and this' – she held up *Snakes and Other Reptiles of the Amazon Basin* – 'were the last ones in the wildlife section. I booked them out of the library after you left to eat.'

Thomas looked down at the title on the black cover: *Beasts of Legend*. He rubbed his eyes and looked at the receptacle that held his filtered contact lenses. Jessica was the only person who ever saw his bright green eyes these days, eyes that had become far brighter than Jessica's as the years had passed.

Thomas flicked the book open and found the first page with a picture: a unicorn standing in a forest by a pool of water. He yawned and looked up at Jessica. She was lost in her book. The nearest thing they'd found to the creature in the glass so far had been a lizard with a web of skin around its limbs, but it was still a poor likeness.

'I think this was on the wrong shelf, Jess.' He turned another page, half expecting to see a mermaid or something similar, but instead saw something he wasn't expecting at all. 'Look at this!'

A black-and-white drawing of a creature very similar to the one in the glass stared up at them. Thomas looked at the title: *The Great World Serpent*.

Jessica read out the words beneath the image. 'In myth, a serpent was another name for a dragon or wyrm, usually of the longer, more sinuous variety.'

Thomas grabbed his father's orb and compared it with the image. They were a good match, even down to the small wings upon the back.

Jessica closed her book with a snap. 'Well, it looks like we found it! It's a serpent!'

\* \* \*

Thomas held the Serpent in the Glass – for that was what he'd decided to call it – for some time after Jessica had crept off to bed, taking her books with her.

He wondered if his father had also stared into the depths of the Glass. It was a thought that made Thomas feel suddenly sad. He would never see his father.

Thomas couldn't remember what his father looked like, of course. He was only a couple of years old when he'd been taken to the solicitors. But there was the dream.

Exactly when he'd first had the dream, he couldn't remember, but he'd been very young. Since then the dream had come many times, sometimes only weeks apart. His father was in the dream with him. He didn't know where they were, but he did know it was a safe place. There was a gentle glow – like a great fire in a fireplace, except all about him. Thomas lay in his father's arms, but unable to see his face. But Thomas didn't long feel this comfort, because he would then have the sensation of being carried away to some distant place, as if some darkness were pursuing him and his father. Then the fear came. His father was gone. He was alone. And he would always wake.

Perhaps these lingering dreams of his father explained Thomas's feelings toward him. He'd no such recollection of his mother. Not even in dreams. Thomas suddenly saw the reflection of his own face in the Glass again, his green eyes flashing back at him like a couple of emerald stars. Forcing himself up, he pulled on the piece of string that turned off the bulb. He got back into bed and pulled the covers up close, but he didn't surrender the Glass to the darkness of the loft. He kept it clutched in one hand as if it would stop him losing his father again.

* * *

It was night. Thomas stuck his head out from beneath the covers. A pale light filled the loft. It came from the hole in the roof lining – a silver glow that fell upon the wooden boards and cast strange yet pleasant shadows in the corners and above the beams. He climbed out of the converted dog basket and made his way over to the hole. Being careful to make no noise, he stepped up onto the box and put his eye to the hole.

Outside, the back garden was bathed in moonlight brighter than Thomas ever remembered seeing. But something felt different. He looked around. Suddenly Thomas caught a movement on the lawn near the greenhouse. He strained to focus on the shadowed area beneath the crab apple tree. Then he saw it. There, in the shadow, nestled a huge dark mass about the size of a small car. Thomas couldn't tell what it was, though it certainly wasn't a car. It moved again and its surface glittered as if it were made of metal.

Then, without warning, the mass unravelled outwards into the light of the moon and Thomas realised what it was. It looked at first like a huge snake, but then Thomas saw a leg, and then three other legs, each with a huge claw on the end; above them a pair of long, black leathery wings sat upon a scaly back. It was a giant serpent, just like the one he'd seen in the book from school, just like the one in the Glass – and it was in the Westhrops' back garden!

As if in response to Thomas's horror the serpent lifted its large head and flicked out its tongue, tasting his fear. It lifted its body up on its hind legs as far as it would go so that the snouted head rose up level with Thomas. The moon struck the creature's face as it turned toward him, and Thomas stood frozen to the spot, not daring to move. Its eyes were just like those of the serpent in the Glass; jet-black vertical slits in pools of brilliant green – and they were looking directly through the hole at Thomas…

Thomas awoke with a start. His hand throbbed. He tried to clench it and discovered he couldn't: he still held the Glass. He pulled his hand out from under the covers, half expecting the globe to be on fire. It wasn't. In fact, it felt cool. He looked about. No moonlight spilled into the room. It was utterly dark. Thomas reached for the light and let out a sigh of relief when its glow filled the loft, dim though it was. Had it been a dream? It seemed so real. But it must have been a dream. Nevertheless, he couldn't help but take a peek through the hole in the roof lining before he went back to sleep. It was too dark to see anything outside of course. It always was.

Putting the Glass down, Thomas switched off the light and got back under the covers. But he couldn't sleep for some time. The image of the serpent kept on coming back into his head, clear and vivid. Eventually, after what seemed like hours, Thomas drifted back to sleep. There were no more dreams that night.

– CHAPTER FIVE –

## *Stanwell Clear*

Jonathan Westhrop had bought his wife a new coat, quite an expensive one by the look of it. She liked it a lot. Thomas could tell. Although the early September weather was still quite warm, Mrs Westhrop had brought the coat with her. Jessica and Thomas were under strict instructions not to touch it. Every now and again Mrs Westhrop glanced at the coat and smiled.

Mr Westhrop whistled a slightly off-key classical piece of music as he drove. 'Well, this'll be your last trip in this old car. I'm having a new one delivered next weekend.'

A new car? Mr Westhrop had owned the green Morris Minor since before Thomas could remember. Mr Westhrop had been buying a few things of late. Last week he'd purchased a new, even larger, aquarium along with several brightly coloured exotic fish to fill it. This spending spree, however, hadn't touched Thomas or Jessica. Nothing was bought for, and no money was given to, them.

Thomas wasn't at all sure that the Westhrops should be so happy on the day they were saying goodbye to their only daughter until Christmas. But he had no right to judge; after all, he felt happy too. He could taste freedom for the first time in his life. No, he wouldn't miss number six, Birch Tree Close.

Less than an hour later the four of them stood in the ticket office of Stevenage Railway Station. Jessica and Thomas cast their eyes eagerly about as people came and went. Arrangements had been made for someone from Darkledun Manor to meet them here at ten o'clock. They didn't have to wait long. About ten minutes after their arrival Thomas saw a thin man in a long, black, unbuttoned coat weaving his way through the crowded room toward them. In his gloved hand he held a large pocket watch attached to his black waistcoat by a long silver chain. On seeing them he stuffed the watch into a pocket, smiled and held out his hand.

'Mr Westhrop?' He had an accent Thomas couldn't place, but it sounded like he came from somewhere where they did a lot of farming.

'Yes. Mr Clear, I assume?' Mr Westhrop shook the other's hand.

The lanky man gave a short bow. 'That do be me, sir. Stanwell Clear at your services!'

Stanwell wasn't quite what Thomas had been expecting, and from the look on their faces the Westhrops felt the same. Thomas had imagined someone like Mr Bartholomew, educated and in a neat suit. Instead, Stanwell Clear's manner was one of little education and his black suit looked as if it'd been upon its owner for some weeks. It was obvious from Mrs Westhrop's expression that she disapproved, though she still smiled as pleasantly as she could. Jessica had no such affectation. Her eyes were as near to bulging as they could get.

Stanwell Clear's thin face was nevertheless kind, if somewhat grizzled. It didn't look as if he shaved any more often than he ironed. Wisps of grey and black hair shot out from under the black fedora he wore. He stuck his hand in a pocket of his jacket, and then in another, and another, until he found what he was looking for: a somewhat battered cream-coloured envelope, which he handed to Mr Westhrop.

Mr Westhrop opened the envelope and, after glancing briefly at the letter inside, nodded.

'Darkledun Manor be a fine school, sir. I'm sure your children are very grateful that you've decided to put 'em in it, so to speak.'

'Yes, yes,' Mr Westhrop said. 'How sharper than a serpent's tooth it is to have a thankless child, eh?'

Thomas swallowed hard, remembering his nightmare and the great fangs in the serpent's mouth.

'It's just a saying,' Mr Westhrop explained, as Mr Clear stared blankly at him.

Stanwell tilted his head. 'Oh, I see, yes, a sayin'. I must remember that one, yes.'

Mr Westhrop handed the letter back to Mr Clear. 'Well, I suppose we should go. We don't want Thomas – or Jessica – to be late.'

Mr Clear stuffed the letter back into one of his many pockets. 'No, we don't, sir, we's a ways to go and time and trams wait for no man.'

'Er – yes,' said Mr Westhrop, looking at Mr Clear with some concern. 'So,' he said, turning to Thomas and Jessica, 'we'll see you two at Christmas. Remember to behave yourselves!'

'Yes, goodbye, dear,' Mrs Westhrop said to Jessica, giving her a big hug, and quite unexpectedly becoming tearful. By the look on Jessica's face she was as surprised as Thomas.

'Tell Thomas "goodbye" too,' Mrs Westhrop whimpered.

Jessica smiled and looked at Thomas.

Mr Westhrop looked around uncomfortably. 'Now dear, pull yourself together, we may be losing Jessica for a while, but we'll be gaining a paying lodger. And don't forget that new gazebo we're going to buy tomorrow. Think how that will look in your wonderful garden.'

Mrs Westhrop brightened. 'Yes, I'd forgotten about that.'

'We're having a lodger?' Jessica asked.

'Oh yes, didn't I tell you?' Mr Westhrop said. 'He'll be staying in your room – well, you won't have need of it for a while. It's only short-term, but it'll help with the finances.'

Jessica looked shocked.

Mr Clear pulled out his watch again and looked at it with some concern. 'Yes, well, we do be best goin' now or we'll miss that tram.'

'Goodbye, Mrs Westhrop,' Thomas said. 'Mr Westhrop.'

Jessica's parents smiled with some effort as Thomas and Jessica turned and followed after Stanwell Clear, who'd kindly grabbed their suitcases, leaving them just a bag each to carry. As they walked away Thomas picked up the final snatches of the Westhrops' conversation – something about which colour gazebo would best suit the garden.

Stanwell Clear led the children to a platform where a large blue-green train awaited them. He didn't speak until he'd put their suitcases on the luggage shelves above the seats. 'You'll be enjoyin' the ol' Manor, that you will. We should be in Edinburgh in less than five hours, and at Darkledun Manor by tea-time I reckon. If there's no leaves, that is. They can stop trams, or so I've 'eard.'

The compartment was large enough to seat perhaps eight to ten people, but they were the only ones in it, so they had plenty of room to stretch out their legs.

Mr Clear sat down and swung one leg over the other. 'Now, don't you be mindin' if you need to catch up on some snoozin'.'

It wasn't long before they found Mr Clear didn't mind either; for he was very soon fast asleep and his hat – pressed against the back of his seat – in danger of lifting itself entirely from his head.

The train didn't stop for quite some time, though it passed through many stations. Jessica had been quick to voice her concerns about a lodger. 'He'd better not touch my things,' she'd said. Thomas thought it unlikely – Jessica's things were mainly old dolls, teddy bears and a shelf of adventure stories. She never played with the toys anymore, but she liked to keep them on a chair in the corner of her room. Perhaps she thought the new lodger might sit on them. As the journey continued, however, the conversation turned to the year ahead at Darkledun Manor. Jessica seemed to be as excited as Thomas, and for some reason that made Thomas feel very happy.

Eventually they pulled into a station and the train jolted to a halt, which caused Mr Clear to suddenly wake up and readjust his hat, which had miraculously remained balanced between the back of his seat and the back of his head for the entire journey.

'Ah, here be the First Stop!' Mr Clear announced, as he stood up and narrowly missed hitting his head on the luggage shelf above. 'You stay here. The tram do be stoppin' for only a few shakes of a sheep's tail, and I'll be back in two.'

Thomas and Jessica looked at each other and then back to Mr Clear as he disappeared out of the door.

'A strange character,' Jessica said after the door slammed. She'd adopted the phrase from her father who always said it after he'd been speaking with Mr Philpot who occupied the house two doors away from the Westhrops'. The man lived alone, but kept three pigs, eleven chickens and a goat in his back garden.

Thomas didn't respond to Jessica's comment. He was trying to see where they were, but a rather fat lady had unfortunately positioned herself right in front of the sign. The train began to make strange noises, as if it were some ancient engine ticking over with cogs, wheels and cranks. Then it hissed and gave Thomas a start. Where had Stanwell Clear gone? What if he didn't get back before the train left? Jessica didn't seem to be worried. She'd found an old broadsheet newspaper that someone had left on the seats, and was rooting through its pages.

Thomas glanced out of the window. 'Maybe we should go look for him, sounds like the tram's – I mean the train's – leaving?'

'Trains always sound like they're leaving, you get yourself all ready to move off and then they go as silent as the grave again.'

The train went quiet and Jessica gave Thomas one of her knowing looks. Thomas ignored her and looked out of the window again. The fat lady still blocked the sign. She wore a hat that looked as if it had a net over it. A couple of pale yellow flowers stuck out from one side. Had they been real Thomas would have thought them in great need of watering.

Mr Clear's face appeared at the window of the compartment door. Behind him followed a boy a little shorter than Thomas, but who looked to be the same age. He wore a large cream-coloured jumper and dark brown trousers that matched the colour of his hair. A wide grin spread across his large mouth on seeing Thomas and Jessica. He had a massive suitcase, which he dragged with tired arms.

'This be Marvin Plundergeese, no – Blunderguess, Blenderghost?'

The boy screwed up his nose. 'Penderghast.'

'Yes, yes that be it,' Mr Clear said, waving a hand at the boy behind him. ''E'll be startin' at the ol' Manor this year too.'

'But please, call me Penders, everyone else does.'

'Don't you like Marvin?' Jessica asked.

The boy shot her a hurt look.

Mr Clear closed the door and resumed his seat. Penders sat down next to him, looking awkwardly between Thomas and Jessica as the train began to shudder and whine slowly out of the station.

The boy sighed. 'It sorta sounds like a hamster.'

Jessica looked out of the window. 'The train?'

'No, Marvin.'

'Oh, I see,' Jessica said, although Thomas doubted she saw at all. 'My name's Jessica, Jessica Westhrop, and this is my brother, Thomas Farrell. He's adopted, that's why he's got a different surname.'

Ideally this was something Thomas liked to explain, but years of experience had taught him that Jessica was as unstoppable as a steamroller with no brakes in very icy conditions.

Penders nodded, still looking a little confused, though not daring to interrupt.

'We're from Hertfordshire, from Holten Layme. It's a nice enough village, I guess, but there's not many shops –'

'And,' Thomas broke in, 'where do you come from, Penders?'

'Oh.' Penders turned to Thomas and seemed to become more at ease. 'I live just north of here, in east Lincolnshire, but we only moved a couple of years ago. I was born in London.'

Jessica's ears pricked up. 'I hear they've got big shopping centres in London, and big shops that sell everything you could imagine.'

Thomas knew where this was leading. The conversation was heading back toward shopping. 'Are you excited about the new school?'

'Oh, yeah,' Penders replied. 'I can't wait to see what it looks like!'

'You didn't visit with your parents first?' Thomas asked.

Penders shook his head. 'Nope, my dad said a boarding school would be good for me, and that was that.'

Thomas nodded.

'D'you know who your real parents are?' Penders asked Thomas tentatively.

Thomas recovered from the unexpected question. 'They're both dead. I never knew them.'

'I'm sorry. That's harsh. I lost my mum when I was four. I guess I don't remember her much. Dad's remarried now, but his new wife doesn't like me much. It's been difficult for Dad, looking after me an' all. I guess that's why I'm going to a boarding school. It'd give him more time to get on with his research too.'

'Research? Is he a scientist?' Jessica asked.

'No.' Penders turned to Jessica. 'He's in sales. He does market research.'

Thomas wondered what researching markets involved. Counting how many fruit-and-veg stalls there were in a given town? Thomas suddenly realised that the subject was getting dangerously near to shopping again.

Thomas grabbed for the first question that entered his head. 'So, what's your gift?'

'Gift?' Penders asked.

'Yes, Darkledun Manor's a school for gifted children,' explained Jessica enthusiastically.

'It is? Well, the only gift I've got is for getting into trouble.' Penders grinned. 'What about you two?'

Jessica stared back blankly and shook her head, perhaps all too aware that her attendance at the Manor hadn't been by invitation.

Thomas shrugged. 'Do you think they made a mistake?'

'I guess we'll find out.' Penders grinned again, then leant back on his seat. Mr Clear was looking at them all with what Thomas thought a twinkle in his grey eyes.

'Where are you from, Mr Clear?' Thomas asked. The other two children looked at Thomas and then at Mr Clear.

'I be from the ol' Manor, Master Farrell,' he said in such a way as to make Thomas think it a stupid question.

Jessica frowned. 'Your accent doesn't sound Scottish.'

'No, I didn't say I grew up in Scotland.' Mr Clear didn't see fit to add where he had grown up – despite a considerable and intentional pause by Jessica.

'And what do you teach, Mr Clear?' Jessica asked.

'Teach?' the black-clad, wiry man replied.

Jessica nodded. 'Yes, at the Manor?'

A broad smile appeared on Mr Clear's stubbled face. 'Oh, I not be teachin'. No, no. I do be the Undertaker.'

'The Undertaker?' Penders said, swallowing hard. 'Does the school need one?'

'Oh, yes,' Mr Clear said emphatically. 'There do be a very great need, especially with so many young'ns about making a mess – and that 'as to be dealt with. And there's no 'alf measures taken at the ol' Manor, y'know. We go all the way.'

Penders' mouth hung open. Jessica looked more confused than afraid.

'Especially those crisp packets,' Mr Clear went on. 'They stuff 'em everywhere, y'know – but as I always says, you can't pull an ol' woolly jumper over Stanwell's 'ead without him findin' an 'ole.'

'Erm, Mr Clear, did you mean that you're the Caretaker?' Jessica asked.

Mr Clear shook his head. 'Yes, yes! Darn it! I do be always gettin' those words mixed up!'

Penders gave a sigh of relief, one Thomas echoed less audibly. It wasn't long before Mr Clear was off in the land of nod again, or at least that was what the three of them supposed as his fedora had fallen over his eyes.

Thomas watched Penders as he stuck a stick of gum in his mouth. 'Do you play marbles?'

Penders' eyes lit up. 'No, but I've always wanted to. Never had any marbles though.'

Thomas smiled. Pulling out the bag of marbles from his pocket, he eagerly opened it so that Penders could see his collection.

Penders' eyes widened. 'Craters! That's the biggest marble I've ever seen! Is that thing inside real?'

In his excitement Thomas had forgotten that he'd put his father's orb in the bag. He liked to keep both the marbles and the Glass on him, so it seemed only natural to keep them in the same place.

'I don't think so, it's a serpent – a sort of dragon,' Thomas explained.

'Where'd you get it?'

'It was my father's,' Thomas said.

Penders raised his eyebrows. 'Your dad played marbles?'

'Oh, it's not a marble. I'm not sure what it is exactly, but I'm pretty sure it's not a marble.'

Penders frowned at the Glass. 'It looks a bit creepy if you ask me.'

After Thomas showed Penders his favourite marbles they ate their packed lunches. The train came to a stop in Newcastle as Thomas bit into an apple. He idly wondered if there was an Oldcastle too.

Penders' words about the Glass seeming creepy floated around in his head. There was some truth to it. Why would anyone make such a thing? Perhaps it was just an ornament. The movement of the train lulled him so that his thoughts shifted more and more into the world of dreams. His hand drifted to his pocket and as his eyes closed his fingers slipped into the bag of marbles and gently wrapped around the Glass.

* * *

Thomas opened his eyes. The others all seemed to be asleep. The trees and meadows outside were still. The train had stopped, and they weren't even at a station.

He stood and asked Mr Clear what was happening, but he didn't wake up. He tried to rouse Penders and Jessica, even prodding them. Neither of them stirred. Something was wrong. Maybe he should find someone who could help?

He opened the door. He could see no one. Carefully he moved up the train toward the front. Eventually he found the driver's carriage but there was no one there. He turned and looked around the cabin and as he did so a shadow cast itself over the floor. Something huge and tall was behind him. He turned around slowly and saw it. The giant serpent swayed gently outside the train, its eyes boring into him through the glass. Its scales glinted silver-grey in the hazy sunlight.

It moved its massive head right up to the glass and Thomas saw its enormous fangs. He needed to run. Run! Thomas fled back through the cabin, but tripped as he went though the door, and as he fell he could hear glass breaking...

# – CHAPTER SIX –

## *Darkledun Manor*

Thomas hit the floor of the compartment as the train lurched to a stop. Jessica and Penders looked at him in surprise. Mr Clear seemed to still be asleep.

Jessica shook her head. 'If you fall asleep on a train, then don't be surprised if you can't stay on your seat when it comes to a stop!'

It must've been a dream. Yet it had seemed so real, like before at the Westhrops' when he'd dreamt of the giant serpent in the garden. The vividness of the dream still stood fresh in his memory. But, more than that, the fear of the serpent and its luminous green eyes still filled his beating heart.

Stanwell Clear moved his hat from his eyes. 'Almost three o'clock. You've been sleepin' for an hour or more I do reckon, which is a good thing as you'll be more to your senses for this evenin'. Journeys do be so tirin'.' He yawned on the final word as if to emphasise the point. 'Now, get your things, and follow ol' Stanwell!' He helped Jessica with her case, but the two boys had to struggle with their own. Once off the platform, they left the station and walked over to a large car park. There sat the ugliest thing Thomas had possibly ever seen on four wheels.

'Ah, there she be,' Stanwell said.

'What is it?' Thomas asked.

'That's the Darkledun bus. I do call her Bessie.' Stanwell beamed as he led them forward.

The Darkledun bus had custard-coloured paintwork and looked to be a relic from the 1970s. He'd seen pictures of Mr and Mrs Westhrop from that era. He hadn't asked to see them again. The small single-decker bus sported bubble-like fenders, rounded windows, and a large bonnet that reminded Thomas of a giant snout. Children about his own age filled the bus. Some of them looked a little embarrassed.

Mr Clear clambered awkwardly up a narrow ladder attached to the side of Bessie, dragging Jessica's suitcase with him. 'You children do go on in. Leave your luggage on the ground and ol' Stanwell'll put it up for you.'

On the roof of the bus a collection of suitcases and bags were slotted into metal stands and tied down with straps. It looked far from safe, and it made the bus look even stranger; as if it were a large store's luggage department gone mobile. All it needed was a till and a sales assistant. After climbing up into the bus, Thomas, Penders and Jessica found themselves confronted by ten pairs of eyes. Thomas looked about nervously, wishing the children would stop staring. Fortunately, Jessica and Penders didn't seem to share his self-conscious nature, so he hid behind them as they found a seat.

A woman with a clipboard stood up from a place behind the driver's seat. She wore a long, brown dress, and briefly reminded Thomas of Miss McGritch. But this woman looked a little younger and taller, though she fixed them with a face every bit as dour as the Housekeeper's.

The woman lifted her pen. 'Names!'

The three of them, afraid to disobey, gave their names all at once. However, she extracted the names from the simultaneous response and, after making three ticks on her clipboard, told them to quickly find seats.

Only one seat remained entirely unoccupied. Thomas headed straight for it. He dropped into the seat and pulled his bag onto his lap just as Penders sat down next to him. Jessica sat across the aisle, next to a very prim-looking girl with spectacles.

'My name's Jessica Westhrop,' Jessica said to the girl next to her.

They were seated halfway down the bus, so Thomas could see a number of faces. There were seven girls, including Jessica, and six boys, including Penders and himself. He wondered what their gifts might be. Maybe some were great musicians, others talented singers or mathematical geniuses.

The stern-looking lady now stood in the aisle, studying the clipboard with an occasional glance at the occupants of the bus.

'Who's she?' Thomas asked Penders in a lowered voice, but it wasn't so low that the girl next to Jessica couldn't hear, for it was she who answered his question.

'That's Miss Havelock, the Deputy Head. She met me and my parents at the station.'

Jessica, seeing the look on Thomas's face, introduced her new-found friend. 'This is Merideah Darwood.'

'Merideah *Constance* Darwood,' the girl corrected Jessica. 'Jessica has told me all about you,' she added, as she looked back at Thomas.

Thomas cringed, wondering what Jessica had told her. Once Jessica had told two of her best friends that Thomas couldn't find his marbles. He was nine at the time and it was perfectly true, but Jessica's exact words were that he'd 'lost his marbles' and so her friends went around telling everyone that Jessica's brother had gone crazy.

Merideah and Jessica were going to be friends. Thomas could tell. Something about the two girls was the same, though they certainly were opposite in appearance. Merideah's dark brown hair, cut just above the shoulders, hung perfectly straight and very neat. A black band held it back off her ears, and her round, black-rimmed glasses gave her the look of a librarian.

Merideah caught Penders' grinning face and she raised an eyebrow in response, but before either could speak Mr Clear started up the engine. The bus rattled no end to begin with, but then the noise died down to a level that allowed communication without the need for shouting.

'Gum?' Penders shoved a stick of chewing gum in Merideah's direction. She screwed up her nose and declined the offer.

Thomas bounced in his seat as the bus went over a speed hump a little too fast. He was glad there'd be no chance of dreaming on this leg of the journey. Not with Stanwell's driving.

\* \* \*

Bessie juddered to a halt inches from the Manor's rockery.

Stanwell removed his hat and wiped his brow. 'Well, another fine run, if I do be saying so myself! And no accidents to boot!'

The Caretaker jumped from his seat and made for the door as Miss Havelock began to usher the students off. Soon they'd all disembarked from Bessie and stood waiting in the car park.

As the Caretaker undid the straps holding the luggage to the roof of the bus, Thomas stared at the Manor. This would be his home now. His eyes followed the ivy as it climbed up the walls of Darkledun and, as his gaze reached the roof, his attention shifted to the tower. Holes ran around the tower, just below the pointed roof. Perhaps they were crude windows of some sort. Why did the school even have a tower? He dropped his gaze back to the rockery that fronted the Manor. Real rocks surrounded and dotted the feature. It was a far cry from the broken patio slabs that decorated Mrs Westhrop's rockery. Thomas smiled. He was glad to be back.

When the last suitcase hit the ground, Miss Havelock led them briskly up the cobbled path to the Manor door where the Housekeeper, Miss McGritch, stood waiting in the same brown dress Thomas had seen her in when he'd first visited. She nodded slightly at Miss Havelock and then opened the door wide. The children were herded through the entrance hall until they all stood at the bottom of the Manor's wide staircase.

Here Miss Havelock stepped up onto the stairs, turned to face the students and requested quiet. The Deputy Head gave Jessica a glare, and Jessica, who'd been talking to Merideah, fell silent with a guilty look on her face.

'Miss McGritch, the Housekeeper here at the Manor, will take the girls to their dormitories; Mr Clear, the boys. Please follow them and they will inform you of your room where you may deposit your luggage. You will all attend the assembly hall at seven o'clock promptly.'

Miss McGritch and Stanwell Clear led the children to the top of the stairs where they separated – Miss McGritch leading the girls to the left, and Stanwell leading the boys to the right. After they'd walked through a common room filled with low tables, red sofas, and comfy chairs of the same colour, they found themselves in a corridor lined with many numbered doors. Thomas remembered that these were the dormitories.

Mr Clear pulled a creased piece of paper from one of his numerous pockets. 'Ah, now let me see. There do be more of you every year, just like my perch – when the 'erons don't get 'em!' Others were put in their designated rooms as they went along, with Thomas being assigned to the last-but-one room on the left.

With a catch-you-later nod from Penders, Thomas moved his luggage into the room, took the key from Mr Clear with a grateful smile, and closed the door behind him. The room was much as the one he'd seen on Miss McGritch's tour, except that on the bed someone had left a sealed 'Welcome Pack' with a copy of something called *The Darkledun Manor Rulebook*. A note read *Please Open Immediately*.

He picked up the pack and looked around. His very own room, he thought. He felt quite overwhelmed by the new-found freedom. He dropped down onto the bed, and the welcome pack slipped from his hand. Mr Clear had been right: journeys were tiring. Thomas's bed felt far more comfortable than the dog basket in the Westhrops' loft. In fact it was very comfortable indeed.

It seemed to Thomas that no sooner had he drifted off into welcome slumber than a most unwelcome voice called him out of it again.

'Thomas, it's Penders.'

Thomas sat up wearily. Penders stood in the doorway. He wore a blazer and black trousers. He had an anxious look on his face.

Thomas yawned. 'What time is it?'

'About ten to seven, so you'd better hurry up and get changed!' Penders replied.

Thomas sat up and put his feet on the splinterless, carpeted floor and looked at Penders' new apparel. 'We have to wear our uniform?'

'Yeah, didn't you read the welcome pack?'

'I – erm – no,' Thomas mumbled as he looked down at the still-sealed pack on the bed beside him. 'I guess I was more tired than I thought.'

Less than five minutes later, Thomas finished tying his laces and stood up to pull the tie and blazer from the wardrobe. The shield-shaped Darkledun Badge upon the blazer's breast pocket had been divided horizontally into thirds; the top third bore the image of a green serpent. First he'd received the Serpent in the Glass from his father, then there was the dream about the giant serpent, and now the badge with the same creature on it. Could it be coincidence?

At the very bottom of the badge a narrow banner displayed the school motto *Aonfhuil is Aonchnámh*. Thomas had no idea what it meant. Maybe it was Scottish. It wasn't English for certain, and yet it seemed strangely familiar.

'Sorry?' Penders said.

Thomas hadn't realised he'd read the words out aloud. 'Oh, the words on the badge.'

Penders looked at his own badge. 'Is that the way it's said?'

'Oh, I don't know.'

Thomas looked from Penders back to the badge. How would he know how to pronounce the words? Maybe, if it was Scottish, he'd heard the language before? Maybe his father had been Scottish? It made sense. Why else would the representative of his father's estate have chosen a school in Scotland for his education?

\* \* \*

Thomas and Penders hurried into the assembly hall, stopping just in time to avoid falling over a group of boys sitting on the floor. All the first-year students sat on the polished wooden floor.

'Mr Penderghast and Mr Farrell, you are both late. Please sit down immediately.'

Thomas reddened even more as he looked up and saw Miss Havelock standing in front of a number of other teachers sitting on chairs. He scolded himself for being late. Being late meant that everyone looked at you when you walked in. As he desperately looked for a place to sit he spotted Jessica waving her hand. Thomas moved quickly over. Why did girls have to be so embarrassing? He felt a little more comfortable once he'd sat down, even if it was between Jessica and Merideah.

A hush fell among the pupils as Miss Havelock started talking about some very uninteresting matters, such as what to do in the event of a fire. Thomas took the time to look around the room. On the far side of the hall, a table stood laden with dishes, cutlery, serviettes and finger food. Penders kept eyeing the food, but Thomas turned back to the teachers.

The Headmaster, Mr Trevelyan, sat in the middle, a large orange tie poking out of the top of a mustard-coloured waistcoat draped with a tweed jacket. The Housekeeper, Miss McGritch, and a tall, muscular man, whom Thomas hadn't seen before, flanked the Headmaster. The man's apparel couldn't have been further removed from Mr Trevelyan's – a suit of dark grey, with a thin black tie around his broad neck, and the smallest sliver of the whites of a shirt at his cuffs. He might have been described as handsome were it not for the fixed look of dissatisfaction that marred the strong features of his face. Stanwell Clear was there too, but standing off to one side, by the fire exit. He still wore his long, dark coat, but his hat and gloves were gone. He had a smile on his face and seemed to be quite enjoying the meeting.

Several other adults were also present, but Thomas began to feel they were staring at him, so he fixed his attention on the trees he could see through the fire-exit doors, and pretended to be hiding there. It was a technique he employed whenever he couldn't deal with the eyes of others upon him. It had something to do with the pursuing darkness in his recurring dream. Somehow, if no one paid attention to him, it would keep him safe from the terror that sought his life.

Mr Trevelyan stood up and smiled. His trousers were pale orange and the monocle still hung from his neck by its silver chain. Thomas felt immediately more comfortable.

'Welcome to Darkledun Manor, School for Gifted Children!' Mr Trevelyan announced heartily. 'I trust you've all had a chance to settle into your new rooms by now?'

Penders shot Thomas a knowing look which Thomas did his best to ignore.

'My name is Mr Trevelyan. I am the Headmaster, and hope to be so for a long time. Miss Havelock here is Deputy Head.' Miss Havelock smiled briefly – very briefly – on hearing her name.

Mr Trevelyan introduced the teachers seated at the table, but Thomas paid little attention until Mr Trevelyan got to the stern-looking man dressed in dark grey.

'And this is Mr Gallowglas, our Physical Education instructor.'

Mr Gallowglas inclined his head toward the children. Thomas thought the man's grey eyes fixed onto him, but then he turned to say something to a bearded teacher sitting to his right. As Mr Gallowglas turned, Thomas saw that his jet-black hair had been tied back in a ponytail.

The Headmaster put his hands behind his back. 'I'd like to remind you to become familiar with the school rules in your welcome packs. I would particularly point out that no students are allowed near the tower.' Mr Trevelyan seemed to relax a little before continuing. 'Now, finally, I'd like to point your attention to our motto: *Aonfhuil is Aonchnámh.*'

Thomas caught his breath. Mr Trevelyan had pronounced it exactly the same way as him. He could feel Penders cast a glance his way, but he didn't take his own eyes off the Headmaster.

'It means "One Blood and One Bone". Here at Darkledun we are not many, but we are a family. We hope you will treat your fellow pupils – your brothers and sisters, if you will – well. And, if you have any problems, please view us, your teachers, as you would your own parents. Today our family has grown by more than any previous year, but don't worry' – he looked toward the tables at the other side of the room with a twinkle in his eye – 'we've still got enough food to fill all your bellies! Now, go find your seats at the table.'

The first-year students didn't wait for a second offer. They were up and seated within moments, but Thomas felt eyes on the back of his head as he approached the table. He looked back, but no one seemed to be paying him any heed. The

Deputy Head had her back to him. Mr Gallowglas was nowhere to be seen. The Headmaster was having a few words with Mr Clear, who seemed to be nodding a lot.

Thomas took the only remaining seat at the table, next to Penders. When he sat down he saw a little white card on the table with his name on it. The seats had been reserved.

'Sweet, eh?' Penders eyed the large plate before him, no doubt excited about how much food it would hold.

Thomas and Penders, being seated in the middle of the table, had to wait before the food worked its way down to them. 'My favourite!' Penders said excitedly, scooping a couple of spoons' worth of beef stew and dumplings out and passing it, somewhat reluctantly, to Thomas.

Thomas quite liked beef stew and dumplings himself, but he'd never had this much before.

After he finished, Thomas pushed his empty bowl aside and looked around. Some were still eating, some had finished and were talking amongst themselves, and some were trying to do both. Thomas suddenly had a feeling come over him, the kind of feeling he supposed people might have when they met unknown cousins, aunts or uncles at a big family event like a wedding or a funeral. Strangers and yet somehow connected.

He shook his head and the feeling went as suddenly as it had come. 'Scottish air probably.'

'Sorry?' said Penders, eyeing the pot of jam as if wondering if anyone might mind if he ate it neat.

'Nothing,' replied Thomas.

\* \* \*

Despite his unscheduled forty winks before dinner, Thomas fell exhausted into his soft bed not long after the meal. He awoke, quite suddenly, a little later and stared at the door in the gloom of the night. Had he just heard it close? He got out of bed, moved to the door, and pulled it open. He couldn't see anyone down the unlit corridor. It was too dark. But he could hear footsteps fading, the footsteps of someone, thought Thomas, with a slight limp.

# – CHAPTER SEVEN –

## *Dreams and Memories*

Thomas looked up at the bright blue sky, vaguely aware that a tall figure carried him away from a large building, from comfort, from home. The scene changed to one of sunlight and trees followed by a blinding light that left him and the man standing before a giant fireplace filled with glowing coals. Here they paused, but it didn't last long. A sense of fear descended upon Thomas. There came another blinding light, and Thomas felt a cold breeze as blurred images of a dark forest passed before his eyes. Then came the darkness and the silence.

Thomas awoke and looked at the wind-up clock he'd brought from the Westhrops. It was seven o'clock. It had been several months since he'd last had the dream. Strange, he thought, that it should resurface again on his first night at the Manor. Maybe the school's connection with his father had triggered it? He couldn't be sure if the dream was a true memory, but he felt sure the image was that of his father. Today, Thomas determined, he would ask the Headmaster about Fearghal. Mr Trevelyan had told him his father had died in battle, but Thomas hadn't had the opportunity to ask where he died. Maybe Mr Trevelyan could tell him how to contact the representative of his father's estate. Yes, he'd find the Headmaster at the first opportunity.

\* \* \*

The rest of the students had evidently turned up last night. Breakfast had been a sea of chatting strangers catching up on matters Thomas knew nothing about. He was glad when Penders finally pushed his empty bowl aside and they left the growing crowd to their toast, cereal, orange juice and chat.

'We've got maths as our very first lesson of the year,' Penders said gloomily, as they walked toward their form room. 'Whose bright idea was that?'

'How unlucky.' Thomas pulled his timetable out.

Penders nodded. 'Yeah, though I'm not sure which is worse – maths or Miss Havelock.'

'She doesn't teach maths,' Thomas said, looking at the teacher's name on the timetable: a Mr Guber.

'No, she's our form tutor.'

Penders was right: Miss Havelock's name had been scribbled next to the form box. Thomas sighed as they turned down a corridor. Why couldn't Mr Trevelyan be their form tutor?

The cream-coloured corridors had no windows, being lit by fluorescent lights. At the end of the first corridor Thomas and Penders found the form room.

They walked in together and saw Jessica and Merideah sitting in the front row. Thomas said good morning before sitting at the desk behind Jessica. Penders sat next to him and lifted the lid of the pine desk to see if there was anything inside. A white clock hung on the wall. A chair and small cupboard sat behind the teacher's desk, and a rolling blackboard covered most of the wall.

The door opened and in walked a tall, handsome boy, his dark uniform a stark contrast to his curly, blond hair. He smiled, nodded and sauntered into the seat next to Penders.

When Miss Havelock walked in everyone stood up. Thomas and Penders quickly did the same. That must have been something else in the *Rulebook*. Miss Havelock, Thomas thought, glanced briefly at him before she spoke.

'Good morning!'

'Good morning, Miss Havelock,' the class intoned as one.

Miss Havelock opened a thin, green book. 'I'm glad to see you're all on time. Now, please sit –'

Penders sat down and she glared at him. He stood up again, looking a little pinker.

'Please sit down once you've answered your name.' Miss Havelock took out a pen. 'Melantha Avebury?'

'Yes, Miss!' said the blonde girl to Jessica's left. She sat down.

'Merideah Darwood?'

'Yes, Miss!' Merideah responded. She took her seat to patiently await the end of the roll call.

Miss Havelock rattled through the rest of the register. Thomas couldn't remember all the names, nor did he try. When Miss Havelock called out 'Treice Montague' Thomas expected a girl to respond, but the tall boy with the curly, blond hair answered. Most of these names seemed very peculiar to Thomas. Perhaps a lot of people outside of Holten Layme had strange names.

'Well, now you all know each others' names' – Miss Havelock put the registration book down on the desk – 'welcome to the form. I expect you all to set an example for the school as first-year pupils. Do I make myself clear?'

'Yes, Miss Havelock,' the class intoned.

'Good. Now, we have registration promptly at half past eight every weekday morning and every weekday afternoon at a quarter past one. Today I'd like each of you to stand up and tell us a little about yourself. Half a minute each should suffice.' Miss Havelock glanced down at the register. 'Melantha Avebury first.'

Thomas didn't pay much attention to Melantha's remarks or those of the other children. He was to busy worrying about standing in front of the class. Then Merideah sat down and it was his turn.

Thomas stood up and took his position at the front. He could feel his face reddening. He swallowed hard and hoped no one noticed his shaking legs. 'My name's Thomas Farrell.'

He could feel his heart pounding. *Run, run!* a voice inside his head shouted. 'I was brought up in Holten Layme in Hertfordshire by the Westhrop family. I never met my real parents. Jessica' – he looked over at her, and the rest of the class did likewise – 'is my sister, well, as good as.' Jessica smiled and lapped up the attention. Thomas was all too glad to share it. 'And I like playing marbles,' Thomas finished and sat down quickly.

He controlled his breathing and calmed himself down. He touched the Glass in his pocket. It reassured him in some way he couldn't explain, maybe because it was his father's.

The rest of the children had their turn, but Thomas felt too flustered to listen.

'I'm glad that's over!' Thomas admitted as he walked out of the room with Penders after registration.

Penders nodded wearily. 'Yeah, me too. It was so boring.'

'You should show more interest,' Merideah said as she and Jessica caught up with them.

Penders smiled awkwardly. 'Oh, not your presentation of course, I mean the general, erm – the general Miss Havelock experience.'

Jessica gave Penders one of her are-you-going-to-change-your-tune-or-will-I-have-to-do-it-for-you looks. She was good at those and, as Thomas well knew, she had a plentiful supply of them. In front of them Treice Montague had Melantha Avebury and two other girls vying for his attention. All three were doing a lot of smiling for some reason.

'Well, maybe I should give her another chance.' Penders laughed nervously as the two girls glared at him.

Jessica nodded. 'That's a good idea.'

'Yes,' Merideah agreed, 'and this afternoon we've got Miss Havelock for Cultural Studies, so you'll get that other chance quite soon.'

Penders frowned and pulled out his timetable. Thomas did the same. The girls were right.

* * *

Using the map on the back of their timetables they found their way easily to room 5B, the venue for Mr Guber's mathematics class. Other than learning that the girls were far better than the boys at mental arithmetic – Mr Guber had wasted no time in informing everyone that calculators were banned from his lessons – the class passed without incident until the bell rang. At that point Thomas's pen decided to leak all over his hand. Perhaps, like Thomas, the biro had finally had enough of long division.

Telling Penders he'd catch up, Thomas ran to the washroom to clean his hands – he didn't want to miss break. Inside the washroom he turned on the hot-water tap, squirted out some pink soap, and tried to remove the ink from his hand. The stain had formed itself into the shape of the African continent.

Just as he tried to rub off Egypt, the door opened and Treice Montague backed in. He closed the door and pressed his forehead against it for a moment before he heard the tap running and realised someone else was in the room. He turned around quickly and seemed surprised to see Thomas.

Treice's casual look had gone and had been replaced with what Thomas could only describe as fear.

'What's wrong?' Thomas asked.

'Girls!' he said.

Thomas turned off the tap. 'Girls?'

'Yes, everywhere! Smiling, whispering, giggling girls! I was even asked if I could help with their maths homework.' Treice put his hand to his brow. Treice's crisp white shirt sleeves were fastened by silver cufflinks.

'I guess popularity has its drawbacks,' Thomas offered. He had very little experience with Treice's problem. Though he did understand why he'd want to avoid girls; after all, they might try to take you shopping.

Treice shook his head. 'I don't want to be popular. I wish they'd leave me alone!'

Thomas gave up trying to remove the stain. 'Well, you can always come and talk to Penders or me, I guess, if you need an excuse to get away that is.'

Treice took his hand away from his head. 'Really? That'd be a big help! I don't know anyone here yet.'

Thomas wondered if Treice played marbles. 'No problem.'

Treice offered his hand. 'Treice Montague, at your service.'

'Oh, Thomas Farrell, at yours.' Thomas shook the other's hand and then apologised as he saw the look of surprise on Treice's face. He hadn't dried his hands. 'Excuse me for asking, but isn't Trace –'

'A girl's name?' Treice interrupted.

'Well, I was going to say it was a little unusual,' Thomas explained.

Treice smiled. 'Sorry, most ask if it's a girl's name. It's spelt T-R-E-I-C-E. I've no idea why my parents called me that. I'm from Derbyshire. You said you were from Herefordshire, right?'

Thomas pulled a paper towel out of the dispenser and dried his hands. 'Hertfordshire.'

'Right. Listen, do you think we could sort of keep what I've told you a secret? You know, about the girls?'

Thomas dropped the paper towel in the bin. 'Of course. Now, let's see if we can find Penders. He doesn't like being called Marvin.'

Treice nodded as Thomas opened the door. 'Is the coast clear?'

Thomas stuck his head out and looked both ways. 'Yes! Let's go.'

Break consisted of all the students, apart from the Sixth Form, being ousted into the playground behind the Manor. Here the tuck shop opened its windowed shutter to the hungry students. Penders appeared from the crowd around the tuck shop. He had a half-eaten bar of chocolate in one hand and two bags of crisps in the other.

'Oh, hi, Thomas!' Penders looked from Thomas to Treice.

Thomas smiled. 'Penders, this is Treice.'

'Hi,' Penders said. 'I hope you don't mind me asking, but isn't Trace a girl's name?'

* * *

After he'd eaten, there was little time for Thomas to visit the Headmaster's office and ask him about his father. So, reluctantly, Thomas had traipsed back to his next lesson, history, and spent an hour learning about the Pictish peoples of ancient Scotland. At lunch he made his way to the Headmaster's office, but the room was empty.

It wasn't until after dinner, on his third attempt, that Thomas found the Headmaster's office occupied, though not by the Headmaster but by Miss McGritch.

'Yes?' she asked, seeing Thomas in the open doorway.

Thomas cringed under her austere gaze. 'Erm – I wanted to speak to the Headmaster.'

'He's very busy. Perhaps I can help?'

'No, I really need to see him.'

Miss McGritch's voice grew more stern. 'Mr Trevelyan doesn't have time to see pupils whenever they please. You'll need to make an appointment and –'

'It's all right, Miss McGritch,' the Headmaster interrupted. Thomas turned to see the Headmaster holding a steaming bowl of chocolate pudding. 'I'm sure I can spare a few minutes over dessert.'

The Housekeeper nodded as Mr Trevelyan showed Thomas into the office. 'Yes, Headmaster, of course.'

Miss McGritch left, glancing back disapprovingly at Thomas before she closed the door.

'You must excuse Miss McGritch.' Mr Trevelyan sat down at his desk and had Thomas pull up a chair. 'She's very good at what she does, but a tad over-protective at times.'

Thomas nodded.

'I do like chocolate pudding with custard, don't you?' Mr Trevelyan eyed the pudding excitedly. 'I was lucky to get some. There seem to be rather fewer puddings left over since the new school year started.'

Thomas had only just had some himself. Penders had had two helpings.

'Now,' Mr Trevelyan began, 'you've come to ask more about your father?'

Thomas's eyes widened. 'How did you know?'

'Well, it's only natural you'd want to know as much as possible, Thomas. Alas, there isn't much more I can tell you, but sometimes questions must be asked even when we don't have the answers.'

Thomas nodded. 'You said my father died in battle soon after he put me up for adoption? Do you know where he died? What war it was?'

The Headmaster sighed. 'Thomas, the representative of your father's estate has sealed all information about your father.'

Thomas didn't understand. 'But why? He's my father.'

The Headmaster spread his hands out on the desk. 'I think the representative feels it would be wise to wait until you're a little older.'

Thomas looked about the room, frustration filling his mind. 'Can I see this representative?'

Mr Trevelyan frowned. 'I'm afraid that person has requested complete anonymity. I must respect that. Although I didn't know your father, I knew *of* him. He was a good person from every account, Thomas. I think he would've supported the representative's decision.'

Thomas slumped in his seat. Would he ever find out more about his father? 'Can I at least visit his grave?'

Mr Trevelyan nodded. 'I hope to take you to it one day, but it isn't easy to get to.' The Headmaster stood and Thomas did likewise. 'Deep down inside us all is a yearning to know who we are and whence we've come, Thomas. We can seek for many things in life, but without that knowledge all seems empty.' Mr Trevelyan picked up his spoon and scooped some of the pudding into his mouth. 'Ah, just right. You see, Thomas, some things are better when we wait for the right moment, or else we might burn our tongue, so to speak.' He put a hand on Thomas's shoulder. 'Truth has a way of bubbling to the surface sooner or later, Thomas. Just be patient, and you'll find your answers.'

# – CHAPTER EIGHT –

# *The Tower with No Door*

Penders stood in the playing field behind the Manor. He eyed a cloud in the otherwise clear summer sky that had positioned itself right between the sun and the hill atop which Darkledun Manor stood. 'I hope we don't have to do anything too hard. I'm still digesting my food.'

Thomas stood next to him. Like Penders, he wore a long-sleeved T-shirt, a pair of shorts, and socks that came up almost to his knee. Thomas hoped the same as Penders, though thankfully he hadn't eaten anywhere near as much as his friend during break.

A deep, harsh voice sounded behind them. 'It is doing hard things, Mr Penderghast, that strengthens the sinews and the will.'

Thomas and Penders looked around to see Mr Gallowglas standing there, his black tracksuit a complete contrast to their own white P.E. kits. Thomas hadn't heard him approach. The teacher cast a stony gaze over them before he moved toward the centre of the field, ordering the boys to follow. Thomas noticed that Mr Gallowglas walked with a slight limp.

Penders let out a sigh of relief. 'Now there's a friendly man.'

Thomas nodded. Had it been Mr Gallowglas he'd heard walking away from his room on his first night at the Manor? Perhaps the teachers checked the students before they switched the corridor lights off?

Jessica crossed the field, talking to Merideah and two other girls. They all wore white socks, white tops, white trainers and knee-length pleated skirts of the same colour. Mr Gallowglas barked an order for silence. Next to the teacher stood a short woman looking very uncomfortable in a tight, navy tracksuit. It was several moments before Thomas realised the woman was the Housekeeper, Miss McGritch. She carried a net bag full of small red balls over her shoulder.

'As I'm sure you'll have seen from your timetable,' Mr Gallowglas began, his steady grey eyes sweeping between the boys and girls, 'Physical Education, unlike most lessons, lasts two hours. This denotes its great importance. Remember that.'

Penders gave Thomas a pained look.

'You will all be expected,' Mr Gallowglas continued, 'to have a clean kit at the beginning of each lesson – no exceptions. Is that clear?'

Everyone nodded, afraid to do otherwise.

Mr Gallowglas folded his arms. 'Good. Now let's get some exercise!'

Everyone had to complete three laps of the field as a warm-up exercise. Mr Gallowglas led the way and, despite his limp, managed to finish a half field ahead of Treice, the fastest student. After that, the children were lined up and put through various exercises, all of which Thomas thoroughly disliked and Penders utterly despised.

'Sinews and will!' Thomas said to Penders as they were half way through their squats. Penders screwed up his sweating face in disgust. Treice seemed to be having some difficulty with the exercise due to his height and the length of his legs. Thomas had another worry. He hadn't wanted to leave the Glass in the changing rooms as there were (despite the name) no locks on the lockers, so he'd stuffed it into the pocket in his shorts. Now it was rubbing against his thigh. Luckily, before the pain became unbearable, Mr Gallowglas bellowed the next set of instructions.

'Right, I want you in pairs, boys with boys and girls with girls.'

The children were quick to act, eager to pair up with someone they knew a little. The Housekeeper handed out a red ball to each pair and directed them to spread out across the field. Thomas and Penders made their way to the edge of the field.

'Listen!' Mr Gallowglas barked. Thomas wondered if the teacher had ever served in the army. His voice carried across the whole field. He instructed them to throw the ball to each other and to learn how to aim and catch effectively. Mr Gallowglas gave them two rules: not to stand less than ten yards apart, and not to lose the ball. It seemed simple enough.

Thomas threw the ball to Penders, who managed to catch it first time. Penders, pleased with himself, threw it back harder than he intended and the ball flew straight over Thomas's head and sailed toward the Manor. Thomas turned to see the red projectile hurtling toward the roof of the Manor, but it disappeared into the trees before it reached the building.

Thomas and Penders looked at each other.

Penders' expression was one of shock. 'Now what?'

Thomas shrugged. 'Best go find it, I guess.'

Penders glanced from the trees back to the field. 'Gallowglas isn't gonna like it if he finds out we've gone wandering off.'

Thomas looked back over his shoulder. Mr Gallowglas and Miss McGritch were on the far side of the field and not looking in their direction. 'Well, we're going to get told off for losing the ball anyway, so we might as well try and find it. Besides, they won't see us once we're in those trees.'

Thomas and Penders were soon out of sight and tramping through the trees to the west of the Manor.

'I don't know how we're gonna find it,' Penders muttered.

'I think it was somewhere near here. Let's split up.'

Penders, somewhat reluctantly, started rummaging around in some bushes. Thomas scanned the ground, moving away from Penders.

'Ouch!' Thomas said as he landed on his side. He glared at the gnarly old root that had tripped him.

'You all right?' Penders asked, looking up from a clump of tall nettles he'd been searching with a fallen branch.

'Yes, just landed on the Glass,' Thomas replied as he fiddled around in his pocket for the item. He pulled it out. 'Well, it's not broken, but my hip feels like it is!'

'What you carrying it about for?'

'I guess I just didn't like the idea of leaving it where someone might find it.' Thomas got up and rubbed his side. That was going to develop into a nasty bruise. As he went to put the Glass back in his pocket he thought he saw a glimmer of light within.

He held it up. It looked quite normal. Maybe he'd imagined it, or it had caught the sunlight. Shrugging, he went to put the Glass back in his pocket, but as he did so it glimmered again. He moved the Glass about and found the glowing increased as he held it out toward the path. He took a few steps back from the path and the glow faded, then a few steps down the path and the light came into the orb again.

'Penders! Look at this!' Thomas called.

Penders abandoned his stick to the bushes and came running over. He saw the Glass immediately. 'I never knew it could do that.'

'Nor did I,' said Thomas. 'The glow's getting stronger the further I go this way.' Thomas stepped cautiously so as to avoid tripping over the roots again. Penders followed, curiosity written all over his face.

The trees ended and they found themselves facing the wall of the tower. Thomas moved right up to the wall and the Glass glowed brightly. Thomas thought it must be as bright as a candle now.

'Craters!' Penders said. 'Wonder what it means?'

'Maybe there's something in the tower that's making it glow?' Thomas suggested.

'Maybe,' Penders replied.

'It won't take long to check. You go that way, and I'll go this way. First one to find the door, shout.' Thomas moved off to the left.

The tower soon came to an end as it merged with the side of the Manor. There was no door this way. Thomas walked back and met Penders coming the other way.

'Did you find anything?' Thomas asked.

'Yeah,' Penders replied, holding up a small red ball. 'Roach threw it further than we thought. I hope he never throws stones at me or I'll be full of holes!'

Thomas smiled. 'Any sign of a door?'

Penders shook his head. 'Not so much as a window, I'm afraid. I thought you must've found it.'

'No.' Thomas looked up at the tower. 'Strange that, a tower with no door.'

They rushed back to the field, Thomas stuffing the Glass into his pocket just before they emerged from the trees. Thomas felt a flood of relief as he saw no sign that anyone had missed them.

\* \* \*

As everyone walked back to the changing rooms, Thomas looked down at his dirt-stained clothes. Thomas wondered why on earth the colour white had been chosen for a P.E. kit. It was probably Gallowglas's doing.

'I don't think I'm gonna like Physical Education – indoors or outdoors. Gallowglas is a bit too demanding for my liking,' Penders moaned, as he traipsed beside Thomas.

Thomas's legs ached and he had a stitch. Gallowglas had made them do sprints before the end of the lesson. 'Well, at least we get four days to recover.'

Penders snorted, massaging his lower back. 'I think I need a month!'

'You'll get used to it sooner than you think, Mr Penderghast. Constant and consistent training is the key.' They turned to see Mr Gallowglas behind them. Somehow he'd managed to walk up behind them again without Thomas hearing.

'Training for what?' Thomas asked timidly.

Mr Gallowglas looked at Thomas through narrowed eyes. 'For life, Mr Farrell. And to stay alive.'

Mr Gallowglas moved past them, but then turned back. 'Oh, and if the ball's lost again, you'll ask for permission before leaving the field or you'll receive a detention. And my detentions, I assure you, aren't confined to desks, chairs and stuffy classrooms!'

And with that, Mr Gallowglas really did leave.

\* \* \*

Despite a very nice lunch of shepherd's pie followed by rhubarb and custard, Thomas still had a bitter taste in his mouth. Even Penders seemed to have lost his appetite a little, though not until after his second helping. Thomas couldn't stop thinking about Mr Gallowglas's words. How did he know they'd left the field? Did he see them?

'I wonder what Mr Gallowglas's detentions are really like?' Penders pushed his empty dessert bowl aside and leant on the table. 'A thousand press ups? Fifty laps of the field? Something like that I guess.'

'I don't intend to find out,' Thomas replied as Jessica and Merideah approached. Most of the other students had left the tables by now. Lunch was almost over.

'You two look like you've swallowed something sour,' Merideah said.

Penders looked up through tired eyes. 'No, we just had a run in with a very sour person.'

Merideah raised her eyebrows. 'And who was that?'

Thomas shifted. He didn't like being – or nearly being – in trouble, let alone telling anyone about it. 'Mr Gallowglas threatened us with detention for wandering off the field.'

Merideah gave them both a quizzical look. 'And why did you do that?'

'I threw the ball into the trees.' Penders slumped down into his arms, still tired from the two-hour lesson.

'You should be more careful.' Jessica nodded.

Penders opened an eye. 'I think Mr Gallowglas has the eyes of a hawk, and the ears of – of an animal that has very good hearing!'

'A bat?' Merideah suggested.

'Sorry?' Penders said.

'A bat has good hearing,' Merideah explained.

'Oh, right,' replied Penders, somewhat fazed. 'And he never smiles either!'

Jessica smiled wryly. 'I overheard some of the older students calling him "Grim Gallowglas".'

'I reckon that's about right,' Penders stated, with a light in his eye. 'It's a very good name, in fact.'

'Still, we found the ball, right over by the tower,' Thomas explained.

Merideah straightened her Alice band. 'The Headmaster said the tower's out of bounds.'

Penders lifted his head. 'Well, out of bounds or not, it sure made Thomas's Glass glow.'

'What Glass?' said Merideah. Penders looked blankly at Merideah before turning to Thomas with an awkward guess-I-said-something-I-shouldn't-have look upon his face.

The hall had nearly emptied of students now, so Thomas pulled the Glass from the bag of marbles in his blazer pocket.

Merideah looked concerned. 'You carry a lizard in a glass ball around in your pocket?'

'It was my father's. I never knew him, and it's all I have of his. I guess I like to keep it close. I'm not really sure what it is,' Thomas explained.

Merideah frowned as she looked at the object. 'May I?' She reached out and Thomas, somewhat reluctantly, dropped the Glass into her hand. She put her eye to the orb and then gave it a small shake. 'Hmm. I wonder how this lizard is suspended?'

'It's a serpent,' Thomas corrected her, but Merideah didn't seem to hear. 'I suppose it's just set in the glass.'

Merideah shook her head. 'Too light. It'd be heavier if it was solid glass.'

He hadn't thought of its weight before.

Merideah passed the Glass back to Thomas. 'And it glowed?'

'Yes, when we went near the tower.'

Merideah tapped her chin. 'Has it ever glowed before?'

Thomas shook his head.

'Perhaps the Glass has some strange qualities,' Jessica began. 'One of my friends showed me this necklace once. It belonged to her mother and had a stone set in it that changed colour when a beam of sunlight hit it.'

Penders looked at Jessica. 'There was no beam of sunlight. We were under the trees.'

'I'm sure there must be some scientific explanation. There's a lot of strange things in the world. My father showed me a stone that he said had some form of radiation in it. Maybe the tower has some source of radioactivity that reacts with whatever the Glass is made of? Maybe that's why it's off limits?' Merideah mused.

'I'm afraid,' began Penders, 'we'll never know, because the tower isn't just out of bounds' – he glanced sideways at Merideah – 'it also has no door.'

# – CHAPTER NINE –

## *A Serpent's Tooth*

'In science we're concerned only with facts,' Mr Goodfellow began, his ginger-brown moustache moving up and down as he spoke. 'Science, and the scientific method, doesn't deal in myth, in legend, in folklore or superstition. In short, our purpose in science is to discover the truth!'

Thomas continued to watch the lanky science teacher as he waved his finger, but soon he was staring unseeing at the charts and tables on the wall. One of them listed in pictorial form discoveries made about the solar system. Thomas wanted to discover the truth too. The Manor held a secret, and Thomas knew that it was connected with the tower. He couldn't explain how he knew; he couldn't make an appeal to Mr Goodfellow's 'scientific method', but he knew it was true nonetheless.

'Mr Farrell?' came a voice for what Thomas suddenly realised was the second time.

'Er – yes, Mr Goodfellow?' Thomas said. Everyone was looking at him. He reddened.

Mr Goodfellow looked at him with one eyebrow raised. 'I was asking the class if they could name the various branches of science. Now, young Miss Keavy here has offered "nature" as an answer, and Mr Quaint has suggested "chemistry". Can you think of another? I've mentioned them all this morning.'

Thomas cringed and silently rebuked himself for allowing his mind to wander. He thought hard. In his opening statement Mr Goodfellow had spoken about finding truth, that much Thomas remembered. Thomas had read a book about a man who'd found truth by making use of special powers he'd gained from an accident in a science lab. It was one of Jessica's books, a science-fiction book.

'Well, erm – has science-fiction got anything to do with science?' Thomas asked tentatively.

'Not a thing, Mr Farrell. It's fantasy, not fact. It's about things that don't exist, like myth, legend, folklore and superstition!'

Thomas felt his face flush red. If only everyone would stop looking at him. As if in answer to his wish, Georgiana Keavy suddenly screamed. Thomas turned to see her stand up and point. Within seconds several girls had jumped up on their chairs, also screaming. Thomas and Penders couldn't see what they were looking at, but several others stood up or pushed their chairs away from the vicinity, all except Demelza Luard who stood up and moved to where Georgiana had pointed.

'There you are!' She bent down and then stood up with a rat in her hands. It's coat looked the same colour as Demelza's hair. 'Where have you been?'

'Miss Luard!' Two red cheeks now flanked Mr Goodfellow's moustache. 'This rat belongs to you?'

She nodded. 'Yes, sir. His name's Tregeagle.'

'Don't you know that you're not allowed to keep pets in your room?'

'Oh, I don't keep him in my room. He sort of wanders around the building where he wants,' Demelza explained, her face a picture of innocence. Several of the girls made gurgling noises.

Mr Goodfellow folded his arms. 'And do you think it appropriate to allow a rat to roam around the school, Miss Luard?'

'Well,' Demelza began, looking a little confused, 'there are plenty of other rats doing the same thing. I don't think one more would make much difference. Tregeagle has made so many more new friends –'

At this several of the girls started looking about nervously, except Jessica, who was trying to keep from laughing out loud. Merideah sat there as if everyone – except her of course – was being thoroughly silly. Some girls were now clutching each other as they cast furtive looks around the floor from their vantage point atop their chairs.

Demelza held the rat to her face and looked him in the eyes. 'Tregeagle says he doesn't mind. He thinks it's quite a nice building actually.'

Mr Goodfellow held up a finger. 'Now, now, Miss Luard. There's no need to pretend you can talk to rats.'

Demelza walked back to her seat. 'It's not talking really, more a sharing of thoughts.'

'Don't lie, young lady.'

'It's not a lie!' Demelza surprised Thomas with the passion of her words.

Mr Goodfellow looked somewhat taken aback by the response from the small, normally quiet girl. 'Well, do something with that rat, or it goes out the window.'

From her bag Demelza pulled a shoebox with holes in the lid. She opened it and gently placed Tregeagle inside before replacing the lid and putting it back in her bag.

\* \* \*

Thomas awoke suddenly and found himself lying on his bed. How long had he slept? Five minutes? Fifteen minutes? An hour? He'd only meant to lie down for a minute. Jessica had challenged him to a game of marbles after the excitement of the unexpected visitor in the science lesson. Thomas had only popped back to his room to drop off his schoolbag. He looked at the old brass clock on his table. It was half five but not ticking, which was strange because he'd only wound it up last night. Thomas gave the key a few turns. It remained silent. He shook it, but it still made no sound. 'Great!' Thomas muttered. The clock had never failed him from the day Mr Westhrop had found it in a charity shop on Thomas's fifth birthday.

Thomas stood and made sure his marbles were still in his blazer pocket. He didn't want to be any later than he already was, so he made straight for his door.

Penders, to Thomas's surprise, stood outside his room.

'Penders? Am I late?'

Penders didn't reply. Penders seemed frozen in mid-step as if he were about to open the door. Thomas waved a hand in front of Penders' eyes and even tried prodding him. There was no reaction.

'Erm – Penders? Are you OK?'

Whatever could be wrong with him? He knew people had seizures, but they usually collapsed. Thomas began to grow concerned. He needed to find a teacher. They would know what to do.

'Hang on, Penders. I'm going to get help!' And he ran down the corridor to the boys' common room.

A few students dotted the chairs, all of them in the same state as Penders. Thomas stared around in disbelief. Had everyone been struck down with the same illness? Perhaps there'd been something in the food? Maybe there was something in the cauliflower. He hadn't eaten that.

He flew down the stairs, reaching the assembly hall at a run. Here he stopped and looked around in amazement. Some students sat unmoving at their tables staring blankly into bowls of half-eaten lemon meringue. Others stood with open mouths, frozen in the middle of conversations. Three girls huddled together, staring at something across the room. Thomas followed their line of sight and saw Treice sitting alone at a table, his chair cocked back and his foot resting coolly on the knee of his other leg.

'What's wrong with everyone?' Thomas asked himself just before he spotted Jessica and Merideah unmoving in the doorway. They both wore quite composed faces, but by their posture they looked as if they were on the warpath.

Then something caught his eye behind Jessica and Merideah. Something moved in the trees near the very spot he and Penders had entered to find the lost ball. Thomas walked out onto the field. The air was still, unnaturally still. Furthermore, he could hear nothing. No rustling trees, no birdsong, no grasshoppers.

Then something glistened again, this time in the trees nearer the boys' changing room. Thomas made his way hurriedly over. Maybe it was Stanwell. Perhaps he hadn't eaten any cauliflower.

Thomas entered into the trees, but Stanwell was nowhere to be seen. Suddenly a large head emerged from a bush. Thomas immediately recognised the luminous green eyes with the vertical black slits. It was the serpent. It was here in the school grounds! Here at Darkledun!

Thomas bolted through the trees toward Stanwell's shed. The serpent's body and legs scraped against the ground as it followed. Bracken rustled and flattened as the weight of the monster passed over it. Thomas's heart now beat so hard that he could feel the thumping in his head.

The tower blocked his path. He turned, but the serpent had already reached him. It reared its ugly snouted head up as if to strike. Venomous eyes burned into him as he backed up against the side of the tower. This was it. He was going to die. The serpent opened its mouth and revealed its deadly fangs…

'Thomas!'

He broke from his sleep, opened his eyes, and found Jessica shaking him by the shoulder. It had been a dream; only a dream.

'Are you OK?'

'Yes, of course, Jess. What are you –' Thomas stopped as he realised Penders and Merideah were standing at the foot of his bed looking at him as if he'd nearly died. Perhaps he almost had. The serpent had seemed so real. But it was just a dream.

'Oh, sorry. Gallowglas's lesson the other day must've taken more out of me than I thought. I hope you're not too mad –'

'Thomas,' Jessica interrupted, 'the Glass, it…' She seemed unable to find the right word as she stared at his hand.

Thomas remembered now. He'd taken the Glass out of his marble bag so he could get to the marbles. 'It what?'

'It was glowing,' Penders said. 'I mean really glowing. Went out when you woke up.'

'It did?' Thomas said uneasily, as he stared down at the orb. It seemed quite innocent there in his hand.

'Yes,' Jessica confirmed.

'Like at the tower?'

'Brighter, a lot brighter!' Penders corrected.

Jessica frowned and sat down on the bed, but she didn't take her eyes off the Glass.

She wasn't the only one thinking. Thomas had suddenly realised something. Something very significant. 'I had a dream,' he said. 'I've had it before, well, sort of the same one.'

Penders and Jessica gave him blank looks. He hadn't told anyone about the dreams. 'Each time I had this dream I was touching the Glass – at home, on the train and just now.'

'What was the dream about?' Penders asked.

'It's weird,' Thomas explained, feeling a little embarrassed. 'but so real. Everyone is – I don't know – kind of frozen. As if time has stopped.' He decided not to tell them about the giant serpent. He wasn't quite sure why. Maybe it was something he and he alone had to deal with. Sharing the experience would somehow make the battle not entirely his. 'I saw Penders outside my door in my dream, and you and Merideah were coming in through the fire exit into the assembly hall looking, well, rather angry. Of course, I guess that was just a dream because you are all here.'

'Thomas,' Jessica said after a slight pause, 'Penders came to your room alone and then went to find a teacher, but ran into us as we were coming up the stairs to go back to our rooms. We were a little – er – upset. We were waiting out back for you, and when you didn't turn up, well, we came through the assembly hall just like you said.'

Merideah leant on the bottom of Thomas's bed and gave him a stare, the sort a nurse might give a troublesome patient. 'Still, it's not beyond the realm of possibility that he merely dreamt what was likely. If he was late for the game, he might well have thought that Penders would come knocking on his door, and that we would be angry at his poor timekeeping, though we ought to be used to it by now.'

Thomas swallowed hard. 'Well, yes, you're probably right. I mean Treice was in my dream sitting on his own eating some meringue – and how likely's that?'

'Very likely. Meringue was the only dessert on the menu at dinner,' Penders said.

'No, Penders,' Merideah began. 'I think Thomas meant the likelihood of Treice being on his own and not surrounded by silly girls.'

Penders puckered his brow. 'Oh, right.'

'But Treice was there,' Jessica said.

Merideah raised an eyebrow. 'And how do you know?'

'Well, I, er – noticed him out of the corner of my eye. And,' she continued, ignoring Merideah's eyes, 'he was eating meringue on his own.'

'Leaning back on his chair?' Thomas asked.

'Yes,' Jessica confirmed.

'You've a very good corner of your eye,' Penders teased, which made Jessica redden.

Thomas sat back down on his bed. Maybe something strange was afoot after all. How could he have seen what was going on downstairs when he was upstairs asleep on his bed?

'Perhaps one of us should try holding the Glass when we sleep?' Penders suggested in an attempt to fill the silence that always came when something weird dawned upon a group of people for the first time.

'I think that would be a good idea,' Merideah agreed. 'It would need to be supervised. No sense taking any risks. And we should be scientific about it. There should always be an objective observer. Jessica and I can take turns and Thomas can supervise Penders when he has his go.'

Penders smiled nervously as he eyed the Glass still in Thomas's hand. 'I said *one* of us should try.'

Jessica grinned. 'Oh, you didn't want to have all the fun and be the only one to try, did you?'

'No, of course not. In fact I didn't want any "fun" at all. I'm very selfless that way, Jess,' Penders said.

Jessica nodded. 'I'm sure you are, Marvin.'

Penders looked hurt. 'It's Penders!'

'It's Jessica!'

Thomas smiled. She only allowed him to call her Jess. Not even her best friends got that privilege.

'OK!' said Penders.

'Excellent.' Merideah readjusted her black Alice band. 'I'm glad we're all willing to give it a try.'

'No, hang on,' said Penders, 'I meant about the name, not the –'

'I suggest we leave before someone reports us for being in the boys' dormitories,' Merideah said to Jessica before Penders could finish.

'Good idea.' Jessica stood and followed Merideah out of the room. Thomas was sure they were both wearing smiles as they left. Penders, however, most certainly wasn't.

## – CHAPTER TEN –

# *Grim Gallowglas*

October in the borders of Scotland felt colder than Thomas had anticipated. Already the leaves on the trees around Darkledun Manor had turned a rather pleasant autumnal yellow. The wind, however, was anything but pleasant.

Thomas had finished his breakfast and now stood staring out at the field. He was glad there was no P.E. today, it looked even more windy than yesterday. The last few weeks had passed by quite quickly, and Thomas had now settled into a routine. P.E. and Outdoor Skills, also taken by Mr Gallowglas, were his worst lessons. Still, Thomas had learned how to build a fire, construct a basic forest shelter, identify edible fungi and, more importantly, avoid the poisonous ones. But in every lesson his thoughts kept on coming back to the tower. A stone's throw away, yet it might as well have been in another country. Mr Gallowglas seemed to be keeping an extra eye on the tower at break, lunch and during outdoor lessons. Thomas hadn't given up on getting inside though.

'Penny for your thoughts?' a familiar voice interrupted.

Thomas turned and saw Merideah standing there. 'They'll cost you a lot more than that.' He grinned.

The short girl didn't smile back. Merideah seldom smiled. Even when Merideah did it was the kind that made a person feel she knew something they didn't. Merideah did know lots of things. Like how to tie a Josephine Knot, whatever that was. That particular knot had been demonstrated on Penders' school tie last week after Merideah eventually got fed up with telling him to do his tie up properly. She'd left Penders to work out how to untie it.

'I was being charitable. It's clear what they are from the fact that your eyes keep wandering over to the tower. It's out of bounds, so you might as well forget it.'

Thomas glanced down at Merideah's jacket. She even wore the prefect badge at the weekends, in her casual clothes. She'd been made prefect two weeks ago, along with Treice Montague.

Merideah pulled the Glass from her pocket. 'Sorry, nothing out of the ordinary.'

Thomas nodded as he took the Glass. Merideah looked a bit disappointed, but it was hard to be sure. Over the last few weekends, Jessica and Penders had also tried sleeping with the Glass in their hand, but it hadn't glowed and there'd been no dreams about a giant serpent or statue-like people. Jessica had reported that she'd dreamt about shopping. Penders had a dream about eating a giant marshmallow.

Thomas placed the Glass back in his pocket. 'Maybe something triggered it, though I can't think what.'

Merideah looked out through the doors. 'Perhaps it's best to put it away before you go to sleep?'

Thomas shrugged. 'I suppose.'

Merideah nodded. Thomas now saw what played upon her face. It was frustration at not being able to explain the experience Thomas had had, and the glowing of the Glass on that evening back in September.

As Thomas watched Merideah leave, he thought about his own feelings. He, too, wanted to know what the glowing meant. If only he could get inside the tower. At least he'd know what was making the Glass glow.

Thomas heard a chair scrape. He turned to see Demelza picking up pieces of cereal and toast from the floor. She looked surprised as her eyes met Thomas's.

'Oh, sorry, thought everyone had gone. Just getting some treats for Tregeagle.'

Thomas smiled and was about to leave when he had an idea. 'Demelza, does Tregeagle ever go anywhere near the tower?'

The girl stood. 'Oh, yes. There's lots of big juicy insects in the walls.'

'Has your rat –' Thomas paused. He couldn't believe he was asking this. 'Has your rat seen a door to the tower?'

Demelza thought for a moment. 'I don't think so. At least I've not seen one in the images he shows me. That's how we communicate, by images in the mind. But there must be a door, because Tregeagle's seen students in there.'

'Students in the tower?' Thomas asked.

'Yes,' replied Demelza. 'Students that disappear and reappear. I'm not sure how exactly. A rat's mind can be hard to work out.'

* * *

Thomas peeked through the round window. He and Penders had been waiting in the boys' dormitories since twenty past nine. Now all was quiet.

Penders yawned. 'So, no Jessica?'

Thomas shook his head. 'She might tell Merideah, by mistake.'

'Ah, understood. I think she swallowed that rulebook since she became a prefect.'

Miss McGritch appeared at the top of the stairs, her long, dark brown dress almost touching the floor. Thomas glanced at Penders. 'Here she is.'

Penders put his face to the glass. After the Housekeeper entered the girls' dormitories, Thomas eased open the door. 'Let's go.'

'Where exactly are we going anyway?' Penders asked, as he followed Thomas down the stairs.

'If students have been in the tower then there must be a door!' Thomas led Penders right at the bottom of the stairs. 'The tower touches the side of the Manor. Maybe the door's there – on the inside.'

'It's a big "if",' Penders said as they crept through Block A and into Block B. 'That girl's not right in the head, if you ask me.'

He'd told Penders about his conversation with Demelza. Penders wasn't convinced. Thomas stopped just before they reached the Headmaster's office. He could hear muffled voices coming from a corridor to their left.

Thomas grabbed Penders by the arm. 'Someone's coming!'

They dove into the Caretaker's office and closed the door. Then they both pressed their ears against the door. Two pairs of feet approached. One pair had a limp.

'Prothero will be returning early tomorrow morning. His arm's broken. Hopefully he'll learn to be more careful with me next time,' came Gallowglas's voice.

'Ah, right you are.' Stanwell's voice sounded no more than a few feet away.

'Quiet, I heard something,' Gallowglas hissed.

They couldn't have heard him or Penders. They'd made no noise. Surely Gallowglas's hearing couldn't be good enough to hear them breathing. Then Thomas heard it: the soft pad of a third pair of feet toward them from the direction of the entrance hall.

'A little late for lessons, Mr Goodfellow,' said Gallowglas, as Thomas heard him and Stanwell step forward.

'Good evenin' to you.' Stanwell's voice followed.

'Ah, hello,' Goodfellow said. 'I left some test papers in my class yesterday. Just drove by to pick them up, so I could get them marked for Monday, you understand.'

'I see,' said Mr Gallowglas.

'Well, I best get them and go. A lot to get through, you know!' Mr Goodfellow said.

Mr Goodfellow's footsteps disappeared off in the direction of the staff room. Gallowglas and Stanwell Clear's voices edged nearer to their hiding place. Penders stopped breathing.

'Well, I best be gettin' the mud off my ol' boots before I check the boys' rooms,' Stanwell said. The handle began to turn.

Thomas and Penders backed away from the door. Both held their breath.

'Wait,' Gallowglas said, and the handle turned back. Thomas and Penders let out a silent breath of relief. 'Make sure Mr Goodfellow leaves the building after he's got his papers. He's been asking questions about the Club and snooping about. He's a risk if you ask me, though no one ever does.'

'The 'igh Cap said we need a science teacher to comply with that natural cubiculum,' Stanwell said.

'National Curriculum,' the other corrected. 'And the High Cap pays far too much attention to such things in my opinion.'

'Right you are. Well, I'll go and see Mr Goodfellow do be doin' no more snoopin' then.'

'I'll check the boys' dorms,' Gallowglas added.

'As you wish, Mr Gallowglas.'

Stanwell lolloped off in the same direction as Mr Goodfellow. Gallowglas paused for a while before the limping sound of his footsteps disappeared down the corridor toward the entrance hall.

'Oh, great,' Thomas said after emerging from the Caretaker's office. He looked down the corridor in despair.

Penders, leaning against the wall in relief, raised an eyebrow. 'What's wrong now?'

Thomas ran a hand through his short hair. 'Gallowglas is checking the dormitories.'

'No problem. We can wait until he comes back down and –'

'Penders,' Thomas interrupted, 'I didn't lock my room. Mr Gallowglas checks all the doors.' Thomas locked his door every night since that first night when he'd heard the door open and close, and Gallowglas's footsteps outside. But he hadn't thought to lock it on his way out this evening.

'You sure?' Penders asked.

'That I didn't lock my door?'

'No, that Mr Gallowglas checks them.'

Thomas began walking up the corridor toward the entrance hall. 'Yes, I know his footsteps. He always checks the doors.'

'He's never checked mine,' Penders muttered as he followed.

Thomas reached the end of the corridor and looked up at the landing. 'You were probably asleep and didn't hear.'

The two boys ran gingerly up the stairs and crept into the dormitory. There was no sign of Mr Gallowglas. The shower block to the left sounded empty, and all Thomas heard from the toilets was the odd gurgle of the water system.

'He must've gone through the common room already,' Thomas said and his hopes sank. There would be no way now to overtake him without being seen. When Mr Gallowglas checked Thomas's door he'd find it open and the room empty.

'Come on,' said Penders. 'Let's follow, we might get a chance to slip past.'

Thomas followed, but he didn't think that chance would come. Moving carefully through the common room, they stopped at the corridor that held the doors to the rooms of the upper-year students. Mr Gallowglas wasn't there.

They tip-toed past the low tables and red, padded chairs until they reached the end of the common room. The door that led to their corridor hung open. Thomas and Penders cautiously poked their heads around the door. Mr Gallowglas was walking slowly up the corridor. He was over half way up and not trying any of the doors as he passed.

'See,' Penders whispered, 'he doesn't check the doors.'

But as he said it Thomas watched in dismay as Gallowglas approached his door and put his hand out to try the handle.

Just then the washroom door opposite Thomas and Penders opened and out walked Treice Montague in a rather garish pair of blue-striped, though very well-pressed, pyjamas. He held a toothbrush.

Treice saw the two boys immediately and, despite Thomas's and Penders' frantic signals, said, 'Hello.'

Thomas pointed up the corridor and Treice glanced around just as Mr Gallowglas turned to see who'd spoken.

'Mr Montague,' Mr Gallowglas shouted. 'You should have long since been in your room. And it's "Hello, sir" when you address me.'

'Erm, yes, sir. Sorry I'm late. I couldn't' – at this point Treice looked at Thomas and Penders again. Penders was trying desperately to convey the message that they wanted to get back to their rooms without Gallowglas seeing them – 'erm – I couldn't seem to turn the tap off. I think it's stuck. I didn't want to leave it running all night, so I thought I'd better find some help.'

'I'll have Mr Stanwell check it tomorrow,' Mr Gallowglas said. Thomas and Penders gave Treice pained looks.

'I – I don't think I'll be able to sleep until I know it's off,' Treice said.

'What? Oh, very well, let me see,' said Gallowglas.

Thomas and Penders quickly hid behind a sofa. They heard Mr Gallowglas walk past and then enter the washroom. Thomas risked a look and saw Treice moving into the washroom behind the teacher, and this time it was him who made the frantic hand and arm signals for them to run.

Thomas and Penders moved as swiftly and silently as they could. Thomas got to his door and they both disappeared inside. Thomas fumbled in his pocket for his key and locked the door.

They both slid down onto the floor and sighed in relief.

'Close,' said Penders. 'We owe Treice one!'

# – CHAPTER ELEVEN –

## *Goodfellow's Flight*

'I wanna prove something,' Penders said suddenly the next morning. Treice Montague had just walked into the assembly hall. It being Sunday, Treice wore his casual clothes. Even so, they seemed very nice, and Thomas thought his trainers were the whitest things he'd ever seen.

Penders put his toast down. 'Treice!'

Treice looked over, smiled, and came and sat opposite them. 'Hi.'

Penders said hello. 'Treice, does Gallowglas check your door when he comes round at night?'

Treice frowned. 'No, I don't think so.'

'Maybe you were asleep,' Thomas added.

Treice picked up a carton of orange juice and poured himself a drink. 'I think I'd have heard if he tried my door. I'm a light sleeper. Takes me ages to get to sleep. An owl on the other side of the field woke me up the other night.'

'There you go then, he doesn't check mine or Treice's or probably anyone else's. Only yours,' said Penders. He then turned his attention to his third piece of toast.

Thomas and Penders had spoken about it before Penders had slipped off back to his room last night. Thomas wanted to believe it was some random check, but it seemed Gallowglas did check his door alone. But why? Was Gallowglas going to injure him like Prothero? Or was Gallowglas after something? Was Goodfellow after something too? Perhaps they were looking for the same thing?

'Thanks for last night,' Penders said to Treice in a lowered voice.

Treice put his glass down. 'Oh, that's OK. Anytime! What were you doing anyway?'

Thomas shifted in his seat and Penders looked at Treice with a mouthful of toast. Apricot jam clung to his bottom lip.

'Something strange is going on, and Gallowglas is involved.' Thomas looked around to make sure no one else was near enough to hear. He quickly related the events of last night, though left out why they were in Block B in the first place.

Treice looked from Thomas to Penders and back to Thomas again. 'Mr Gallowglas injured a student?'

Then William Prothero walked in. His arm had been set in a cast, which he wore in a sling.

Treice bent closer to Thomas and Penders. 'I've not told this to anyone before, but last Thursday I was avoiding some girls – er, I mean I was alone in the boys' changing rooms – and Mr Gallowglas and Miss McGritch came in. They didn't see me because I was behind the lockers. I heard them speaking though. Mr Gallowglas said something about getting rid of Mr Goodfellow, and Miss McGritch agreed.'

'You think Gallowglas is gonna kill the science teacher?' Penders asked incredulously.

'Who's going to kill the science teacher?' came Jessica's voice from behind Treice. Thomas and Penders had been so engrossed that they'd not noticed her and Merideah approach. She looked briefly at them and then smiled at Treice.

Treice looked very embarrassed, and didn't know what to say. Whether his discomfort stemmed from their conversation or because there were two girls standing right behind him, Thomas couldn't tell.

Thomas decided to fill the girls in. 'Treice rescued us last night; we almost got caught by Mr Gallowglas.'

Jessica sat down next to Treice, who shifted uncomfortably. 'I see,' she said. 'Thank you. Thomas and Penders do need looking after sometimes.'

Treice smiled awkwardly. 'Oh, it was nothing really.'

Jessica turned back to Thomas and Penders. 'And what exactly did you do last night?'

Thomas glanced at Merideah, who remained standing. He couldn't read her face. He and Penders quickly filled in the girls on what had happened, what they'd overheard, and what Treice had just told them.

Merideah folded her arms. 'Do you know how much trouble you'd be in if a teacher had caught you?'

'No one did.' Penders sighed. 'Merideah, we've got proof that Grim Gallowglas is hurting students' – he nodded toward Prothero – 'and trying to do away with Goodfellow.'

Merideah rolled her eyes. 'You've not got any proof at all. There's probably a perfectly reasonable explanation for everything you heard – or misheard!'

Penders shrugged. 'And what would that be?'

Merideah checked her Alice band and prefect badge were both straight. 'If you'll excuse me, I have prefect duties.'

'She'll go and blab to the Headmaster about us,' Penders muttered after Merideah had left the hall.

Jessica put a hand on Penders' arm. 'She's leaving so she doesn't have to report us for what we're about to plan.'

'And what would that be?' Thomas asked.

Jessica showed her braces in a grin.

\* \* \*

Thomas, Penders and Treice made their way cautiously out onto the landing, and then swiftly down the stairs to the front door. All the lights had been turned off, but moonlight filtered in from windows high in the walls. It was enough to see, for Thomas at least. Penders and Treice kept on bumping into each other.

'You shouldn't have such long legs!' Penders muttered.

Thomas saw something move.

'Thomas?'

'It's us,' Thomas replied.

Jessica detached herself from the shadows. 'You're late.'

'Sorry – I had to go back and lock my room.'

'I've got a torch with me,' Treice said. 'But it might be wise to turn it on when we're in the corridors.'

'Good thinking!' Jessica said. If Treice reddened, it was too dark to tell.

'Shhh,' Thomas hissed. 'I think I hear footsteps.'

He cocked his head. 'They're coming from outside.' They could all hear them now – footfalls on the cobble path leading to the front door.

'Quick, down here!' Jessica moved into an alcove that served as a place to store coats.

The children disappeared into the gloom of the hanging coats. Thomas peeked out from behind a large duffle coat. The footsteps had stopped. A key slipped into the lock and slowly the door eased open. A furtive figure stepped into the hallway. The moonlight struck his face. It was Mr Goodfellow. He crept past the alcove, and looked about before slinking off around the corner in the direction of Block A.

'Why's he creeping about like that?' Penders whispered.

'Let's follow him,' Jessica said, as she moved out from under the coats.

They followed Mr Goodfellow as he worked his way through Block A and into Block B. Mr Goodfellow had produced a small torch from somewhere, so they kept well back.

The teacher turned just before he got to the Headmaster's office, and made his way down the corridor that Gallowglas and Stanwell had come down the night before. Thomas and the others followed, but slowed as they got near the corner. The light of the torch had stopped, and they could hear the jingling of keys. Then, without warning, Mr Goodfellow came running toward Thomas and the others, but he didn't see them as he fled past. Thomas heard the door open. And he heard feet, lots of feet.

'Run!' Thomas said.

The children ran back the way they'd come. Mr Goodfellow was some way ahead of them. Then Treice slipped and went down. Jessica stopped to help him up. The fluorescent lights flickered into life as the boots approached the end of the corridor.

'Quick, in here!' Penders darted into a classroom.

Jessica and Treice followed on his heels, but Thomas's eye caught something lying on the floor. It was an envelope, and no doubt the cause of Treice's fall. Thomas grabbed it and dove it into the classroom just as the owners of the footsteps stepped into view. Thomas left the door ajar. It was too dark for anyone to see them in there. Thomas peeked out of the classroom from his position on the floor. Mr Gallowglas stared down the corridor, behind him a group of students who looked to be from different years.

Gallowglas spoke to the students, but didn't take his eye off the corridor. 'Return to your rooms. I have some business to attend to.'

Gallowglas walked down the corridor, his face set like stone. Thomas thought he heard the front door close. Gallowglas quickened his pace.

Penders sighed in relief after Gallowglas and the students had passed by. 'We've come so close too many times to finding out what his detentions are like.'

Thomas ignored Penders' remark. 'Maybe it's some sort of evening class?'

'I've no idea,' Jessica began, 'but I saw Duncan Avebury.'

'Who?' Penders asked.

'Melantha's older brother. He's in the fourth year.' She paused. 'I do hope Mr Goodfellow's all right.'

\* \* \*

Mr Hartworth took the science class the next day. Normally quite at home in his technology room, he seemed uncertain in his current environment. He was trying to construct a model of a molecule of water, but one of the hydrogen atoms stubbornly refused to stay attached.

Thomas found himself wondering if Mr Gallowglas really had 'got rid of' the science teacher. Maybe he'd buried the body in the woods outside, or perhaps there'd been an accident with a javelin? No, he would've heard about that. Maybe Mr Goodfellow had been done away with in a more subtle way. After all, Mr Gallowglas did know about all those poison berries.

The hydrogen atom fell off again, and rolled under Reginald Quaint's desk. At that point the bell rang and everyone moved off to their next lesson, leaving the teacher to search for the rebellious atom.

'Where's Mr Goodfellow, sir?' Thomas asked just as Mr Hartworth came out from under Reginald's desk with the atom.

'Oh, Mr Farrell!' Mr Hartworth said, almost dropping the atom. 'I thought everyone had left. I don't know what's happened to Mr Goodfellow, but I've been asked to stand in until further notice. It could be some time, I hear.'

Thomas made his way out. He was surprised to find Jessica, Penders, Treice and even Merideah waiting outside for him. Merideah had obviously been filled in by Jessica, though Thomas was sure she'd deny any knowledge of it if asked.

'Well?' Penders said.

'Well what?' Thomas asked.

'Did he say what happened to Mr Goodfellow?' Jessica asked.

Thomas looked at Merideah who stared back coolly through her spectacles.

'Oh, well, I – I had to tell Merideah,' Jessica defended herself. 'I mean, we're all a team now, right?'

Penders nodded his agreement, but soon stopped when he saw Merideah glowering at him.

'You should've gone to the Headmaster,' Merideah said to Penders.

'And how would we've explained what we were doing out of our rooms in the first place?' Penders countered.

Merideah didn't seem to have an answer for this, and so Thomas answered the question. 'Mr Hartworth doesn't know what's happened to Mr Goodfellow, but he said he's been asked to cover for him until he hears otherwise. He said it might be some time.'

Penders' eyes narrowed. 'I reckon Gallowglas has done him in.'

'Nonsense,' Merideah said. 'What I'm more interested in is why Mr Goodfellow sneaked into the building last night.'

'He was scared though, I reckon. He left the place pretty sharpish.'

'That's right,' Thomas added. 'He even dropped an envelope.'

Merideah pushed her spectacles up her small nose. 'You found an envelope?'

Jessica, Penders and Treice looked at him expectantly. He hadn't told them about it. 'Well, Treice slipped on it, so I guess he found it really.'

Merideah raised an eyebrow. 'I see. So where's this envelope now?'

Thomas opened his science exercise book. 'I've got it here.' He'd stuffed it in his pocket last night and forgotten about it until this morning when he'd put it in his science book so he'd remember to give it back to Mr Goodfellow. He passed it to Merideah.

Penders frowned. 'Are you going to hand it in?'

Merideah shrugged. 'Of course, but I'm going to look at what's inside first.'

Penders shook his head. 'And you're a prefect!'

Merideah examined the envelope. 'Well, Mr Goodfellow won't mind if – as you put it – he's been "done in". After all, he may need our help. Besides, we're not opening it, because it's not sealed.'

She held the envelope up to show that the flap had simply been tucked in, then she pulled out its contents – a few pieces of paper. 'They seem to be photocopies of newspaper articles about missing persons from various places across the British Isles. There's another sheet listing their locations and ages.'

'My dad says people go missing every day,' Penders said.

'Yes,' Merideah confirmed after a few moments scanning the pages, 'but according to this list these particular missing persons had something very interesting in common: they all attended Darkledun Manor!'

# – CHAPTER TWELVE –

## *Through the Stones*

The large, furry coat hanging above Thomas tickled his neck. Jessica, Merideah, Penders and Treice sat near him, all staring up at the landing.

'This floor's hard,' Penders complained. 'So, what we doing again?'

Merideah drew a breath. 'If you hadn't been so interested in your rice pudding, you might have listened to what I said. We have to wait for Miss McGritch to go to the girls' dorms. Then we can grab the main set of keys she leaves in her office.'

'Right, and why do we want those?' Penders asked.

Merideah ignored him. They'd all met at the end of lunch that day. Merideah had taken a quick look down the corridor that Gallowglas and the students had emerged from on the night of Goodfellow's last appearance. She'd found a door, marked 2B, that wasn't shown on their maps. It was locked. Merideah's attitude had changed a lot since she'd seen the contents of Mr Goodfellow's envelope. She now considered it her duty to uncover what was really going on at Darkledun Manor. She'd even committed them all to tell no one, not even the Headmaster. Not until they had some evidence.

Jessica had done a little digging too. Curious about the Club Thomas had told them Gallowglas mentioned, she'd found out from Melantha Avebury that her brother, Duncan, was a member of something called the Family History Club. It met at the weekends and its members often went on trips to parish record offices, cemeteries and churches. It seemed innocent enough, though Thomas didn't think Gallowglas the most likely candidate for leading such a pastime.

'What if McGritch gets back early?' Penders asked.

Jessica snorted. 'Miss McGritch is never late or early, she's always precisely on time. I hear her pass my door at exactly twenty-one minutes past ten every evening.'

Treice moved his luminescent watch up to his face. 'She should appear about now.'

No sooner had he said it than a door swung on its hinges and Miss McGritch's quick but measured footsteps approached from the direction of Block B. He hushed the others, and then tried not to sneeze as his nose came in contact with the furry sleeve of the coat. The corridor lights went off, and the Housekeeper walked into the entrance hall.

They all watched as Miss McGritch ascended the stairs and went to her office. Thomas heard the large bunch of keys hit her desk, and she soon appeared with the smaller bunch of silver keys which serviced the girls' rooms.

Once Miss McGritch had passed through the doors into the dormitories, Merideah stood up and told the rest to stay put. 'Treice, start timing. I'll go get the keys. Better one of us gets caught than all.'

Merideah made her way gingerly yet purposefully up the stairs. Then, without a sound, she slipped quickly into Miss McGritch's office and was soon out and coming down the stairs with the bunch of keys in her hand.

'OK, let's go!' she whispered.

Thomas, Penders, Jessica and Treice emerged from their hiding places in the cloakroom and followed Merideah cautiously toward the dark, deserted corridors of Block B. Once through the first set of doors, Treice switched on his torch to light the way ahead.

'Turn that off! We'll be seen!' Merideah whispered sharply. 'That thing could guide a ship on a foggy night.'

Treice was quick to comply, and the powerful beam of his torch was replaced by a narrower, more discreet one from a small torch strapped to Merideah's wrist. With her combat trousers and determined little face she looked like a soldier, albeit one with spectacles and an Alice band holding back her hair.

They soon reached Stanwell's office. Much to Thomas's relief, no light seeped out from under the Headmaster's door.

Careful to make no noise, they slipped down the corridor to room 2B.

Merideah turned her light onto the bunch of keys in her other hand.

'There must be at least twenty keys on that,' Penders remarked with some alarm. 'Are you sure it's even on there?'

Jessica put her ear against the door. 'Miss McGritch always has these keys on her when she's downstairs.'

'Jessica, try them.' Merideah handed the bunch to Jessica, keeping the torch beam fixed on them.

Jessica tried a small bronze key. It didn't fit. Then she tried another and another. None of them seemed to work.

'Wait a minute,' Thomas said, grabbing Jessica's hand just as she was putting another similar bronze key into the keyhole. 'Most of these keys look the same. Miss McGritch must have a way of telling them apart.'

Jessica pulled the key out of the lock and asked Merideah to bring the light nearer. They all saw a small letter and number scratched into the surface.

'6A,' Thomas said. 'There must be a 2B!'

Jessica flicked through the keys until Merideah's light fell upon a scratching that resembled *2B*.

'There it is!' Jessica said as she inserted it into the lock. She turned the key and pushed the door open.

'Where's the light?' Penders asked.

'Hang on,' Merideah said. 'Let's all get inside first, just in case someone sees.'

After they were all inside, Treice shut the door carefully. The lights came on. Merideah had found the switch.

Penders surveyed the room. 'See? Desks and chairs, yup, definitely just a classroom. Shall we go back now?'

'Wait.' Merideah switched off her torch and began looking around. 'Mr Goodfellow must've been trying to get in here for a reason.'

Thomas studied the room. The blackboard was different; it seemed to be built into the wall, whereas the other classrooms had blackboards mounted on rolls so the teachers could write their way around the whole thing. By the blackboard hung a big wooden clock with a pendulum. On both sides of the room stood wide bookcases, but they didn't just contain books. In small compartments sheets and scrolls had been neatly stored. Thomas walked over to one of the compartments and pulled out a sheet. Someone had written *1891* in the top left-hand corner. He scanned the paper. It seemed to be a list of names, though the handwriting proved very hard to read.

'What are they?' Penders asked.

Jessica appeared at Thomas's elbow and pulled a sheet down from the bookcase. 'Census reports. We had to research our family tree at our old school. I remember these.'

Merideah tapped her chin. 'Seems to be what Duncan said: a family history class. They must do their research here when they're not out on a trip to a graveyard or something.'

'Maybe that explains the mud on the floor,' Treice said, more to himself than anyone else. He stood near the clock, peering down.

Merideah bent down. 'Lots of different sizes of footprint; must be the Club members then. But why here?'

Jessica knelt on the floor. 'Maybe the cleaner missed this spot?'

Penders yawned. 'Thomas, let's check the Glass so we can go.'

Of course, he'd almost forgotten, it was the reason why he'd first come to Block B. He removed the Glass from the bag and found it had a faint glow within it.

'What's that?' Treice said, moving a little closer. 'And what's that light inside it?'

'That's what we want to know,' said Jessica as she quickly got to her feet. As she did so she brushed Treice who was still staring at the Glass. He stepped back, but his feet hit the wall and he grabbed the only thing within reach to catch himself – the clock's pendulum. The chain made a distinct click.

Just as Penders was about to laugh, and Jessica offer an apology, they heard a grating sound.

'Craters!' said Penders, as the blackboard disappeared upwards to reveal an entrance to a dark chamber.

Merideah moved into the entrance and the others cautiously followed. Once they realised where they were, Jessica turned to Thomas.

'This is the tower. You were right, Thomas. The door was in the Manor, but it's a secret door!'

The moon shone unnaturally brightly through the windows high above. Two large stones, each the height of three men, stood about three yards apart in the centre of the chamber, and upon them rested a similar stone so as to form a sort of huge stone doorframe. The rock glittered eerily.

'What on earth *is* that?' Penders asked, his eyes wide.

'I don't know,' said Jessica. 'Looks like a bit of Stonehenge.'

'I've seen stones like this before,' Merideah announced. 'I was with my father, somewhere in southern Ireland. They were cruder than these though. These are magnificent!'

As a group, they moved toward the stones. Jessica, first to reach them, touched one of the upright stones. 'It feels' – she hesitated and frowned as if trying to find the right words – 'it doesn't feel hot or cold – somewhere in between.'

'Would that be "warm"?' asked Penders.

'Thomas!' Jessica said. 'The Glass!'

The Glass glowed very brightly now. They all stared at the small orb. Inside mists swirled about the unmoving serpent.

Merideah looked at the Glass and then back to the centre of the tower. 'It's the stones, Thomas. The Glass must be reacting to how close it is to the stones.'

'Sorry, so what's that again?' Treice asked, indicating toward the Glass.

Thomas didn't take his eyes off the Glass. 'It was my father's. We're not exactly sure what it is.'

'Look!' Penders said, pointing at the stones.

The stones also glowed now. More than that, the stones were making a noise.

Jessica drew back. 'Why are they humming?'

'Perhaps they don't know the words?' Penders offered. No one laughed.

Thomas moved closer to the stones and the humming seemed to increase in intensity. It wasn't loud, in fact it was quite soothing, a bit like a babbling brook on a hot summer's day in a peaceful meadow.

'Be careful, Thomas,' Merideah warned.

But Thomas wasn't concerned. Indeed, he felt very comfortable indeed. He touched the stones. Jessica was right: they weren't hot or cold. But they weren't warm. That wasn't the right word. Living, yes, that was the word. They felt alive. Intrigued, he moved around the pillar, and so through the hole the stones formed.

A flash of golden light surrounded him and he found himself standing inside a cavern made of the same glittering stones, except here their silver shimmer lit the whole chamber. The cavern seemed familiar to Thomas, as if it knew him, and he it. It seemed aware of him, or perhaps aware of the Glass. The cavern wall triggered something in his memories, but it remained just outside his reach, like a word on the tip of his tongue.

Through another entrance Thomas could see a moonlit scene of tall, thin trees. It didn't look at all like the wooded area that surrounded the Manor. These trees had silver barks, unlike those around the school. He looked behind and saw a similar entrance. This one, however, provided a view of the tower where stood a very confused-looking Penders, Treice, Jessica and Merideah.

Thomas waved, but they didn't seem to see him. Then Jessica came forward, concern on her face but mingled with determination. She approached the entrance to the cavern, but then disappeared.

Concerned, Thomas stepped back through and the same golden light briefly enveloped him again.

Penders spoke first. 'Thomas! What happened? Where'd you go?'

'It leads to a cavern, and there's some sort of exit on the other side,' Thomas explained, as the rest came forward.

Jessica looked from the entrance back to Thomas. 'Why'd nothing happen when I walked through?'

Thomas shrugged.

Merideah scanned the stones with her amber eyes. 'Let's try it together.'

The golden light flashed again as Thomas stepped back through the stones, this time with the others.

'Craters!' said Penders, again.

'Cool!' said Treice.

'It's amazing!' said Jessica, as she stared around the cavern in wonder.

Merideah said nothing.

'That,' Thomas began as he pointed toward the far side of the cavern, 'seems to lead somewhere else.'

'Come on,' Penders said. 'Let's see what's on the other side.'

They all passed through accompanied by a golden flash of light.

'How beautiful!' Jessica stood with Thomas, Penders, Merideah and Treice on a grassy patch of ground atop a small hill.

Thomas's senses seemed to sharpen. He could smell lush grass and see the silver trees stretching out around them. The moon rode high and bright, and the sky held a multitude of shimmering stars. Enormous dark mountains loomed up on either side of them. They must have been standing in a deep and very narrow valley. The stillness of the night was deafening.

'Look!' Penders stared back, and Thomas and the others turned with him.

The cave had vanished and, instead, a stone structure just like the one in the tower stared back at them. Perhaps it was the same one somehow in two different places. It was flanked by two identical structures, except they faced away from it. And, like a mirror image, yet another stone gateway sat on the far side of the hill.

'What is this place?' said Penders, but he didn't expect anyone to know the answer.

'Fascinating.' Jessica touched the stones as if to make sure they were real. Penders and Treice did the same, though more cautiously.

Merideah stared up at the stones. 'I wonder what those symbols mean?'

On the stones, a series of letters had been inscribed. Maybe this wasn't the same stone they'd come through. He'd seen no such writing on the one in the tower. Although Thomas couldn't understand their meaning, the symbols did seem familiar.

'They're very old,' Thomas said.

Merideah shook her head. 'They aren't weathered. I'd guess they were quite new.'

'The symbols don't fade with time, those who put them there intended them to last forever,' Thomas said. Merideah turned and looked at Thomas, her eyes narrowed.

'How can you know that?' Penders asked.

They were all staring at him now. They were right, how could he know? But know it he did.

'We should explore,' Thomas said.

'We must be somewhere near the Manor,' Merideah said after a while. She didn't sound too convinced though.

Treice stared out into the sparse forest about them. 'These trees don't look like the ones around the school.'

'They aren't. These are aspens and silver birches. The trees around the Manor are oaks and beeches largely.' Merideah glanced at the trees, but her interest still dwelt upon the inscriptions. She walked over to take a look at the other stones.

'Be careful,' Penders said. 'You don't know where you'll land up if you walk through one of those.'

'I'm always careful,' she replied. 'And I don't think I'll go anywhere without the Glass, anyway.'

Eventually the children began to drift down the hill to explore the area. Thomas hung back, still in wonder at the new sharpness to his senses. It was as if his ears had had water in them all his life, and now they'd suddenly been cleared. He'd always had good eyesight of course, but even that seemed sharper. The number of stars he could see in the night sky surprised Thomas. The whole vault of heaven teemed with pinpricks of yellow, red, blue and many hues in between. It didn't seem like the same sky he'd known all his life, but it must have been.

Treice had turned his powerful torch back on and the group was moving away. Thomas hurried to catch up.

'Where'd you suppose we are?' Penders asked as Thomas fell in beside him.

'I don't know,' said Thomas. 'I think we need to find some kind of landmark.'

'Like that, you mean?' Merideah said from ten paces in front. She shone her torch up ahead.

Penders stopped in his tracks. 'Whoa! That mountain's made of huge stone bricks!'

Jessica scanned the structure. 'It's not a mountain, it's a wall!'

Before them arose a stone wall made of the biggest blocks of stone Thomas had ever seen. He couldn't imagine how heavy they were, or how they had been placed one upon another.

'It must've been built by giants,' Penders said, not content with his first announcement.

'Treice,' Merideah said, as she tried and failed to see up the wall with her own small torch. 'Shine that fog light of yours up the wall.'

Treice swung the beam of his powerful torch up the stonework, but it failed before it reached the top – if it had a top.

'Look there,' Jessica said, pointing. Treice moved the beam back to a section of wall.

'It's a snake,' Treice said.

Thomas froze. A snake? He looked up and sighed. It was just a carving. 'No, it's a serpent.' He held up the Glass. It was glowing only faintly now. The serpent shape on the wall bore a strikingly similar pose to that of the serpent in the Glass.

'What's that?' Merideah spun around and looked into the trees to their left, the narrow beam of her torch strobing the silver barks.

'What?' Jessica asked, somewhat nervously.

'I thought I saw something move,' Merideah said.

Thomas was the first to hear it, a sort of metallic noise as if someone was carrying a lot of pots and pans.

'There!' Penders said, pointing in the darkness.

Not twenty yards from where they stood, a figure had appeared. A figure in bronze armour. Thomas couldn't make out a face behind the metal visor, but upon its head sat a flat helm, and in a gauntleted hand a long spear that now pointed directly at them.

'Run!' said Merideah. 'Back to the hill!'

They ran, but as they neared the hill two more armoured figures blocked their way. More appeared. The pursuers moved in to form a circle around them. They lowered their spears and pointed them at the five children.

Thomas and his friends huddled back to back. As Merideah's and Treice's torches darted about the circle, Thomas saw that each figure had the same red-lettered Roman numeral crafted into the front of its flat helm: the numeral VII. Treice's torch lingered on one of the figures. Thomas swallowed hard. There were no eyes inside the helm.

'This isn't looking good,' Penders whimpered.

'Disengage!' came a stern and yet familiar voice from the top of the hill.

The spears were lifted in one synchronised move, their blunt ends hitting the ground as one as the suits of armour froze to attention. All clinking and clanking ceased. The children looked up and saw Mr Gallowglas, descending the hill. Thomas's heart sank, but he still had the presence of mind to conceal the Glass.

'Stay back!' Merideah shouted at Gallowglas, a look of challenge in her determined amber eyes.

'And just what do you propose to do, Miss Darwood?' Gallowglas lifted his hand and the armoured figures parted to let him through.

Penders balled his hands. 'Are you going to get rid of us the same way you did with Mr Goodfellow?'

'Goodfellow was a snoop. He suspected too much, so we got rid of him,' Gallowglas announced quite casually.

Jessica gasped. 'You and McGritch murdered the science teacher?'

'No one said anything about murder, Miss Westhrop,' came another familiar voice from behind Gallowglas.

Mr Trevelyan appeared and, with him, Stanwell Clear. The latter held a lantern on a pole in one hand. Was the Headmaster part of this too? Thomas couldn't believe it. Thomas had looked to him as someone he might go to when all else failed, someone who would keep him safe from Mr Gallowglas. Thomas moved closer to Jessica. They'd been foolish to trust anyone else. Whatever happened, Thomas wasn't going to let anyone hurt Jessica.

Trevelyan blinked. 'Miss Darwood, would you kindly stop shining that torch in my eyes. Mr Clear's lantern is quite adequate, I think.'

'Sorry, Headmaster,' Merideah said weakly, and pointed the beam back toward the suits of armour who didn't have any eyes.

Trevelyan and Stanwell walked through the opening in the fence of spears and flanked Gallowglas. 'Well, Mr Gallowglas, we seem to have captured our quarry.'

Gallowglas looked at the five of them grimly. Thomas couldn't tell what he was thinking though. He always looked at everyone grimly.

'We know about the missing students too,' Penders said suddenly. 'I suppose you're going to just bump us off as well!'

Thomas felt terrible. He'd started all this. If it wasn't for him, none of them would be here now. 'Please, sir, it was my fault. I wanted to know what was inside the tower and –'

'Yes,' Trevelyan interrupted, 'I guessed as much, though I'm sure Jessica and Merideah played their part too, eh?' A smile played upon the Headmaster's lips, then – to Thomas's surprise – Mr Trevelyan winked at him. 'It's never happened before.'

'What's never happened before?' Merideah asked, keeping the torch firmly on the armoured figures.

'First-year students in the Grange.'

'The Grange?' Jessica said.

'Yes, you are in Darkledun Grange,' the Headmaster explained. 'But that is besides the point. Now, Mr Penderghast, it was I, not Mr Gallowglas, who "got rid of" Mr Goodfellow. His services were no longer required. I believe he already has an offer of a job at another school in England, which is probably best for all concerned. And, you will be glad to know, we've not done away with any students either. 'Blige me, after years of trying to teach them something, we're not going to then "bump them off", as you so eloquently put it. What a colossal waste of time and effort! I'm sure you'd agree.'

Trevelyan paused and cast his eyes over the five children before him. 'Now, Mr Gallowglas, what shall we do with our guests?'

Gallowglas grunted. 'Have them swear to tell no one of this place and never return, or else.'

Thomas gulped, and thought he heard Penders do the same.

Trevelyan brushed at his tie. Thomas couldn't quite tell the colour in the light of the lantern, but it looked as if it might be bright yellow. 'Or else what? We can hardly lock them up. I think their parents might notice if they didn't return for Christmas.'

Gallowglas didn't respond.

'I says we do give 'em a very long detention with Miss Havelock. That oughta do it,' Stanwell chimed in, but he smiled and cocked his head toward the children afterward.

Gallowglas sighed.

Trevelyan looked up at the star-filled sky for a moment before answering. 'No, there'll be no detentions. I think we shall go with an "or else". We shall, I think, give them a tour of the Grange, and answer their questions, "or else" I'm sure their curiosity will never be satisfied, and we shall have to mount a constant vigil on the tower.'

Gallowglas folded his arms, his face unreadable.

'Mr Clear,' Trevelyan began, 'have the carriage ready for Saturday morning, will you?'

Stanwell grinned. 'I will do, sir! Oh, yes, most certainly I will do!'

Trevelyan extended his hand. 'I think we'd better get those keys back to Miss McGritch so she can finish locking up, Miss Westhrop.'

Jessica handed over Miss McGritch's keys. 'We were just borrowing them.' She smiled weakly.

'Of course, of course,' Mr Trevelyan said, as he took the keys and passed them to Gallowglas.

With one final stare at the children, Gallowglas turned around and headed for the hill. He didn't seem very pleased. Thomas watched as he disappeared though the stones, though he saw no flash of light.

'Return to your posts!' Trevelyan shouted, and the suits of armour started to shuffle off. Thomas watched them walk stiffly away into the trees until they were lost in the gloom.

'Mr Trevelyan, what are those?' Jessica asked, as the clank of the flat-helmed figures disappeared into the night.

Trevelyan gave a satisfied smile. 'They, my dear, are the renowned Darkledun Guards. They watch over this place, help keep it safe.'

'But there's no one –'

'No one in them?' Trevelyan interrupted Jessica, a boyish grin on his face. 'Clever, eh? Now, children, there's something I must have your word on. Mr Gallowglas isn't wrong to employ caution, though he may choose to pay it a rather higher sum than I myself would. What I'm about to tell you must never be shared with anyone outside of this place. Do you agree to this?'

The children nodded.

'Right then, now where shall I begin?' Trevelyan said, as he put his hands behind his back.

'Perhaps by telling us what those are?' Thomas said, pointing back at the stones on the hill.

'Ah,' Trevelyan said, turning to look at the standing stones. 'That's as good a place to start as any. Cnocmorandolmen it is called, a rather long name, but a pleasant hill all the same. Those stones are Way Gates. They lead to certain places. The one nearest to us, as you know, leads to the tower at Darkledun Manor.'

'Exactly how far are we from the Manor?' Merideah asked.

Trevelyan frowned. 'Exactly is a very difficult word. All I can say is that we are a lot closer and yet a lot further than any of you could imagine.'

Merideah's brow puckered at the answer, but it was Jessica who responded. 'Are we still in Scotland?'

Trevelyan surveyed the surroundings. 'We are in the realm of Avallach, Miss Westhrop.'

'I've never heard of it,' Merideah said.

'You won't find it on any map you've ever seen. You see, Avallach isn't part of your world, though it once was. It lies hidden and separate, yet in places the two still touch. The Way Gate you just came through is one such place.'

'Why do you say *your* world? Don't you mean *our* world?' Jessica asked.

'No, I'm not from your world, though I have rather enjoyed exploring it these last few years. Indeed, it's given me quite a few ideas, I must say.' Trevelyan nodded to himself. 'But we'll save the rest of this conversation for daylight. We'll meet in Stanwell's office at the Manor at nine o'clock on Saturday morning. Now, I have your word that you'll tell no one what you've seen?'

The children nodded eagerly.

'Good,' Trevelyan said. 'Then I think it's time to return to our beds. I have some marshmallows and a cup of hot chocolate waiting for me, and it's very likely now a cup of lukewarm chocolate.'

'Dinnsenchas!' the Headmaster said, as they approached the Way Gate. The stones shimmered and hummed as they'd done when the children had first come through. Trevelyan ushered the children through the stones in a flash of golden light. After they'd departed, Cnocmorandolmen stood still and silent once more in the moonlight. Yet something new hung in the air. Something that hadn't been there for many years had returned.

# – CHAPTER THIRTEEN –

## *Darkledun Grange*

Thomas sat in the Caretaker's office. He'd arrived with Penders and Treice just before nine o'clock, and found Jessica and Merideah already there. Ten minutes had passed and still there was no sign of Stanwell Clear. Mr Trevelyan had told them to wear 'old clothes', but Merideah and Treice didn't seem to have any. Treice wore his very white pair of trainers that looked like they'd just come out of the box. Merideah wore her khaki combat trousers (with more pockets than Thomas cared to count), and a pair of petite hiking boots. Penders' jeans were definitely old, as at least a couple of holes attested. He wore them whenever he wasn't in his uniform, and Thomas suspected he had no others. Thomas had two pairs of trousers, both second-hand. Today he wore his corduroys and a light blue woollen jumper that Aunt Dorothy had given him in the middle of the summer a couple of years ago. The gift served him well this morning; outside Stanwell's window an early frost clung to the Manor's grounds.

No one had said anything since they'd arrived, except for Penders announcing 'Isn't it exciting?', to which he'd received only silence. They had, of course, spoken a great deal to each other since their strange experience a couple of days ago. Although they were all looking forward to the day, Thomas also sensed some concern in the others. Questions still remained unanswered after all, such as the reason for the disappearance of the students, and the nature of Gallowglas's involvement with Prothero's injury. Still, thought Thomas, if they wanted to do away with him and the others, they could have done so easily that night in the place Trevelyan called the Grange. There was something more to it all for Thomas, of course. This Grange had some connection with the Glass, and that meant that Avallach must have some connection with his father. That thought alone swept aside any real apprehension from his thoughts. In fact, he felt quite excited despite not replying to Penders' question.

Stanwell's thin face appeared around the door. 'Sorry I do be late.' He placed a net against the wall. 'A kind soul threw some leftover crisps in my ol' pond for my little fishes, but forgot to take 'em out of the bags.'

A few minutes later they stood in 2B watching the concealed door slide away to reveal the inside of the tower.

Stanwell stopped at the stones and spoke the same strange word Trevelyan had used the night before last. 'Dinnsenchas!'

The stones hummed slightly as they'd done before.

'Right, come along. You do be following Stanwell!' The Caretaker walked through and the children followed. Thomas passed through the Way Gate last. The golden light flashed around him, and he found himself back in the strangely lit cavern. A sense of familiarity hit him again, but he shrugged it off to keep up with the others.

Cnocmorandolmen sat like a precious stone in a ring of silver and jade. The place looked quite different in the light of day, yet still enchanting. A little frost touched the grass, but already it had begun to melt, making everything sparkle as if it were newly cleaned. Thomas's senses felt the same way – new, clean and sparkling. The smell of the wet ground and trees seeped into his nostrils, the glistening hues of melted frost struck his eyes, and the soft sounds of the grass underfoot caressed his ears.

The wall loomed before them, even more imposing in the light of day. It thrust up higher than anything Thomas had ever seen. The stone wall curved away in both directions. High up the face, the huge stone serpents kept watch over the valley. The similarity to the serpent in the Glass was uncanny. They were even encircled by rings, as if to represent the Glass itself.

Stanwell, however, led them toward the other side of the valley, careful to avoid the other Way Gates. The opposing 'mountain' they'd seen on their night-time visit appeared to be a vast wall of earth. Thomas judged the distance between the two walls to be about two hundred yards, with Cnocmorandolmen set halfway between them.

Not long after they'd entered the sparse wood, it ended abruptly about twenty yards short of the earthen wall. Roots and branches sprouted from the wall as if torn from the ground. It seemed, like the stone wall, to have no end to its height or, for that matter, to its length. Most remarkable of all was the giant wooden door set within it. Its height was that of ten men, and its width that of a house. Branches and vines grew over it with more vigour than did the wisteria over the side wall of the Westhrop's home. The door looked as if it hadn't been opened in a very long time.

Penders stopped and gawped. 'Whoa! It'd take a hundred men to open that!'

'One, I think, but not a thousand men could force it if it didn't want to be opened. Still, that isn't our path, and guests have no need to force doors.'

The children turned toward the sound of the voice. There, in front of a long wooden hall partially hidden by the trees, stood Mr Trevelyan. He wore a plain short-sleeved grey robe, tied about the waist with a rope. It was quite a contrast to his usual attire, though his silver-chained monocle still hung about his neck. He looked very strange, but everyone was far too polite to say anything, though Treice's eyebrows were just about as high up his forehead as they could go without disappearing under his curly fringe.

The children greeted the Headmaster as Mr Clear disappeared into the wooden hall. A few moments later a horse whinnied and a carriage emerged from the building. It reminded Thomas of the sort he'd seen on old Christmas cards, but then another coach, attached by what looked liked black wooden poles, followed the first coach – and then another, and another, and another and another, until a six-coach carriage stopped before them, drawn by a team of six jet-black horses.

In the driver's seat sat Stanwell Clear, who grinned at them from under a three-cornered hat. 'This do be the Darkledun carriage, and she's at your services!'

'Well, we can't be standing here all day,' Trevelyan said, as he moved toward the first coach and opened the door. 'Now, everyone hop in.'

Thomas and the other children made their way into the first coach of the black carriage while Trevelyan climbed up beside Stanwell. Inside, the coach boasted leather seats and fine mahogany panelling.

The carriage lurched forward just as Thomas closed the door behind him. Suddenly a part of the roof of their coach slid open and Trevelyan's delighted face appeared. 'You can get a better view if you stand up!'

'Great, a sunroof!' Penders stood on his seat and stuck his head through the hole.

Treice preferred to remain seated and look out of the window, which was just as well as it was a squeeze for the other four to all fit their heads through the hole. A gentle breeze ruffled Thomas's blond hair as he looked through the trees to his left and saw the sun's rays on the earthen wall high above. Everything appeared crisp and new. He could hear every bird's song and every rustle of a leaf against another.

'What's on the other side of the wall?' Jessica asked, as she stared at the great stones, clearly visible through the thin trees.

Trevelyan leant back. 'The rest of the Grange lies beyond the Inner Wall, young lady. That's where we're going!'

'And what's behind the other wall?' Thomas asked.

'A whole world, Thomas. The world of Avallach.'

'Right, 'ang on!' Stanwell raised his voice. The carriage lurched again and the speed increased threefold. The trees bent inward the further they went on, creating a leafy tunnel. Thomas saw a bronze-armoured Darkledun Guard every now and again, standing motionless in small man-high alcoves set in the Inner Wall. The Guards, who didn't look quite so menacing in daylight, paid the carriage no heed as it hurtled by.

'Wow!' Jessica was gazing directly ahead, filled with the same sort of look she had when she spotted something nice in a shop window.

'What is it?' Penders asked, as he tried to see around Jessica, who was now in his way.

Merideah pushed her glasses up her nose. 'It's another giant door.'

'That's the Inner Gate,' Trevelyan shouted back.

An enormous door, every bit as large as the one near Cnocmorandolmen, now rose before them. A few Guards lined the base of the wall either side of the Gate, their flat helms above their faceless visors displaying the Roman numeral V. The Darkledun carriage slowed as they drew close to the Gate.

'Goibhniu!' Trevelyan bellowed. In response the Gate began to open inwards. On the wall above the door were yet more of the serpent shapes. They were easier to see here because they were lower down. Thomas turned away from their slitted eyes.

'Master Clear, keep us at a canter,' said Trevelyan. 'We don't want to miss anything.'

'Yes, Master Trevelyan, sir!' Stanwell pulled on the reins and the six black horses slowed as they came through the Inner Gate.

Thomas caught his breath. Before them a pale red road of stone led through a landscape of verdant grass and tall, majestic oaks, ashes and hawthorn trees, as beautiful as they were green; early autumn seemed to be lingering here longer than outside the Gate.

'The wall's gone!' Thomas heard Penders shout from behind.

Thomas looked back. Penders was right. The stone road led to a now free-standing Gate flanked by a few trees, fields, and a blue-white sky. There was no sign of the wall. Then the Gate itself winked out, replaced by a seemingly unending landscape.

'Maybe it's done with mirrors,' Merideah said, but Thomas doubted that was true.

To his left Thomas saw a grassy plain that ended in a lake that sparkled cold in the sun's rays. To his right a thick, tall forest grew, and it seemed to Thomas as if a shadow hung over it. The road soon crossed a stone bridge that forded a narrow river, a silver ribbon in the green of the fields. Now, up ahead, large shapes loomed. Buildings. A huge tower, much bigger than the one at the Manor, sat next to an old stone building that reminded Thomas of a castle. They seemed familiar to his eyes, though, of course, they couldn't be.

Trevelyan cast a glance back at the children. 'You now see before you' – he swept his hand out toward the buildings – 'Arghadmon Academy!'

'Seems a bit of a waste to use it as a school,' Penders said, shaking his head, as the road gave way to a dirt track that led into a garden.

Trevelyan smiled. 'Not a school, Mr Penderghast – an Academy!'

The garden was filled with delicate trees, lush hedges, wide bushes, and colourful flowers all of which were in full bloom despite it being the wrong time of year. Thomas could smell the flowers' heavy scents, and their colours appeared even more vivid than Mrs Westhrop's garden gnomes.

The track ran straight through the garden toward the buildings. The carriage stopped near a statue of a warrior through whose head water bubbled to fill a fountain. Next to the fountain a large, yellow square had been outlined on the ground in which the words *LANDING ZONE – KEEP CLEAR AT ALL TIMES!* had been written in yellow paint.

Trevelyan had already climbed down from the carriage by the time Thomas and the others had all piled out. 'You now stand in the Gardens of Arghadmon. A delightful spot for a wander and a ponder, but perhaps another day, eh? Well, follow me!'

Trevelyan led them toward the Academy. Stanwell had jumped down to see to the horses. They'd not gone many paces before Thomas saw a large hedge with a single narrow archway set in its midst. Penders and Merideah, who were closest to it, moved nearer the archway to see what lay inside.

'Do not enter the Restless Maze,' warned Trevelyan, without looking back. 'It cannot be trusted.'

The hedge shuddered, groaned and then rustled all along its edge. The children moved away from it as quickly as they could.

The path ended in a yard fronting a huge building that, now that Thomas saw it, looked more like a cathedral than a castle, except there were no stained-glass windows. Large wooden doors stood between two smooth, dull-grey pillars. A couple of Guards flanked the door, each with the Roman numeral I upon the front of their flat helms.

Trevelyan turned to the Guards. 'Would you be so kind?'

The suits of armour came to life at the Headmaster's words, pushing the great portal inward. When the doors lay open, the Guards froze again.

Trevelyan bent slightly and lowered his voice. 'At my age, I find the doors a trifle heavy – though strictly speaking it's not part of their duty. I trust you won't tell them?' He straightened again. 'Right, follow me.'

Trevelyan led them into perhaps the biggest room Thomas had ever seen. Three long tables, each surrounded by chairs made of the same dark wood, sat upon the reddish floor. Four large fireplaces, two on either side, rested in the pillared walls beneath paintings depicting battles. On the far wall a giant crown wreathed in fire had been embossed into the wood, and to each side of it hung a green drape bearing a golden serpent. Thomas's hand went to the Glass. He told himself it was mere coincidence, serpents and dragons existed on many flags and emblems.

Penders looked around, wide-eyed. 'It's big!'

'Indeed it is. This is the Hall of Arghadmon. This is where the Academy meets for the great feast days.'

'What do people learn here?' Merideah asked.

The Headmaster looked her directly in the eye. 'How to survive, Miss Darwood, but we shall speak of that later.'

'And, more importantly, what do you eat here? Or is that what you meant by surviving?' Penders asked.

Trevelyan chuckled. 'I should've liked an academy of cookery, but alas our times do not allow for such luxuries. But don't worry, Mr Penderghast, the Grange puts on a good spread all the same.'

Thomas grinned and looked around at the paintings. Most looked a little odd, especially Marganus the Misplaced, an ancient king of Glywysing, according to the words at the bottom. The king's crown sat unevenly upon his ginger head, bending one of his ears down. But it was the painting above it that caught Thomas's attention. Its ornate wooden frame surrounded a land of many pools and rivers. In the midst of this landscape sat a walled hill defending a grim-looking fortress. Thomas thought he'd seen the fortress somewhere before, though he didn't know where. Perhaps it was some famous place in his world that he'd seen in a book. As Thomas turned, he thought he caught Trevelyan's eyes flicker down from the painting to him.

'Now, let's explore the Tower, shall we?' The Headmaster led them to the right, down one of the two corridors that led from the Hall.

Unlike the Hall, the corridor had no wooden panels, or even any paintings. It was made entirely of stone except for a gossamer-like substance that covered the windows in place of glass.

Penders stopped and prodded the strange substance. 'Eww, it's sticky!'

Trevelyan stopped and turned. 'Mr Penderghast, it takes the spiders a long time to spin the web glass. Please desist from poking holes in it!'

Jessica scrunched up her face. 'It's made of spiders' webs?'

'Yes, one of my ideas. Do you like it? There was a nasty draft through here before I had them made. And they're so much cheaper to replace than glass, though admittedly a tad less easy to clean – what with all the flies and things. Anyway, keep up!' Trevelyan spun around and continued down the corridor.

The corridor ended in a door.

'Welcome to the Tower,' Trevelyan said as he opened the door.

Jessica suppressed a scream. There in the doorway stood a short man – if man he was – dressed in faded multicoloured robes. His wrinkled face was black as coal. He smiled, showing small white teeth. A look of displeasure swept across Jessica's and Merideah's faces.

'Ah, High Cap. Greetings on this fine morning!'

'Hello, Master Fabula!' Trevelyan replied enthusiastically. 'Children, this is Master Fabula. He's the storyteller here at the Grange.'

'Felicitations!' Master Fabula announced with a florid bow.

'Storyteller?' Treice said. 'My parents said telling stories is bad.'

'Not those sort of stories, Mr Montague,' Trevelyan corrected. 'Master Fabula teaches oral tradition.'

'The history of dentistry?' Penders offered.

'No,' Master Fabula began. 'I relate the stories of our past, so that we don't forget them.'

'Can't they just be written down?' Thomas asked.

Merideah sighed impatiently. 'That's not the point. Relating stories orally is an art in itself quite separate from writing them down.'

'Quite right, Miss…?'

'Miss Merideah Constance Darwood,' she replied. Penders' eyes rolled up to the stone ceiling above.

'Well, it's a pleasure to meet you all, but I must practise the epilogue for a fireside tale this evening, so if you'll excuse me?' Master Fabula said, inclining his head.

Mr Trevelyan nodded. 'Of course.'

After Master Fabula and his rustling multicoloured robes had gone, Mr Trevelyan ushered them through the door.

'I've never seen a man with jet-black skin like that before,' Thomas said, after they'd passed through the door.

'His mother was a Dewg,' Trevelyan said.

'A Dewg?' Thomas asked.

Trevelyan waited until Jessica had closed the door before he replied. 'Yes, one of the races of Avallach, and not a very kindly people it must be said. But Master Fabula was brought up by his father and knows only of the Dewg from his own stories.'

'Why'd he call you "High Cap"?' Treice frowned and glanced at the top of Trevelyan's head.

'We don't use the term Headmaster here, it's High Cap instead.'

Thomas had heard the title before, when he'd overheard Stanwell and Mr Gallowglas talking in the corridor that night. So Mr Trevelyan was the High Cap.

Penders didn't look convinced. 'But you don't wear a cap.'

'No, Mr Penderghast, but we don't call the teachers at the Manor "masters" and yet there I am the Head one.'

'Fair enough, I suppose,' Penders agreed.

They now stood on the gound floor level of the Tower surrounded by a vast kitchen. Stoves lined the walls where stone work surfaces did not, and herbs hung from the ceiling along with pot and pans.

Trevelyan, unlike Penders, ignored the kitchen and made for a spiral staircase that wound its way up through the Tower. The stairs were of marble, and the black banisters were topped with silver. They walked up the stairs and round and round until Thomas felt quite dizzy. Landings led off the stairs, but Trevelyan led them past all these until they reached what Thomas made the fourth floor. Here the staircase ended.

The circular room's central feature was a large map that had been painted on the floor. Several brass statuettes served as map markers, though Thomas didn't recognise any of the names on the map. A few shelves dotted the largely bare walls, but they held only the odd book or two.

Before anyone could ask any questions, Mr Trevelyan led them to a ladder fixed onto runners that ran the length of one of the longer shelves. The Headmaster leapt onto the bottom rung and coasted several shelves down until the ladder stopped beneath a round hole in the ceiling. 'Right, up you all come!'

Thomas was the last to ascend the ladder. He felt as if he'd just come up through a manhole in the street, except that this street was the roof of a tower complete with battlements.

Trevelyan swept his hand through the air. 'From here you can see the entire Grange.'

Thomas looked down to the Gardens of Arghadmon below. His eyes followed the garden path as it became the road they'd travelled down in the carriage. He saw the river, the stone bridge, the dark forest, the lake and grassy plains. On the left of the road spread a patchwork of fields where crops grew. About a mile away, or so he guessed, the road branched off to the right and ran, with an occasional bend, to a small cluster of buildings on the near edge of the lake. Further on the landscape went, in lush grass and blue sky dotted with trees. There seemed no end to it.

'Where did the Gate and the walls go, sir?' Thomas stared out toward where he thought the Gate should have been. 'It feels as if we're inside, but it looks as if we're outside, if you see what I mean?'

Trevelyan leant upon the battlements. 'We're inside a sidhe mound.'

'A sidhe mound?' Jessica asked. 'What's that?'

'You might think of it as a hollow hill, Miss Westhrop,' Trevelyan explained.

'But I can see the sky, the sun, the horizon!' Treice said as he looked around.

'Yes, clever, isn't it? But we're inside a hollow hill nonetheless.'

*Sidhe.* The word echoed in Thomas's mind. Had he heard it before? It seemed familiar. Thomas had an overwhelming feeling that he'd been here before, here on these very battlements. But, of course, that was impossible.

## – CHAPTER FOURTEEN –

# *Arghadmon Academy*

Mr Trevelyan turned to the right after exiting the Hall, leading the children across a wide stretch of grass that gently dipped until they reached a long circular wall that looked to be the foundation of another tower. The wall stood only a couple of feet high and if there had ever been a stone floor it was now entirely covered in dirt and grass. Behind the structure lay a number of wooden buildings.

Inside the walled area was a spectacle to behold. Dozens of armed young people dressed in fawn robes practised sword or staff strokes against wooden dummies or one another. Mr Gallowglas stood in the middle of the activity, barking instructions and reprimands for poor moves.

'Welcome to the heart of the Academy. We call this the Ring!' Trevelyan beamed.

'Combat training?' Penders asked.

'Yes, the cadets are all taught the basics of how to use a sword and staff, though some prefer other weapons.' Trevelyan stepped over the wall and sat down. He was soon joined by the children.

'Hence Prothero's injury?' asked Merideah.

'Indeed. Mr Gallowglas is a fine instructor, but a little hard on them at times.'

Penders watched as Mr Gallowglas swung his staff and knocked a cadet's legs out from under him. 'And I thought press-ups were bad.'

The cadets looked to be older than Thomas and his friends, though some only by a couple of years. But it wasn't their age that caught his attention. Although most seemed quite normal, others most certainly were not. Several of the lean cadets sported ginger hair, spiked up as if gelled, but even these were not the focus of Thomas's eye, for every now and again he caught sight of a cadet with pointed ears!

Mr Trevelyan pulled a large ivory key from his robes. 'Now, if you'll all kindly follow me into my office?'

Penders looked around. 'What office?'

Trevelyan thrust out the key inserted it into something the children couldn't see. Suddenly a door materialised, a plain wooden door with a silver knob.

'This one!' the Headmaster announced as he opened the door. Inside, inexplicably, lay a room.

'Most peculiar,' Thomas heard Merideah mutter to herself as she passed through the door behind him.

Once through the door, Thomas found himself standing in a room filled with books, papers, maps, framed pictures, and numerous objects he couldn't put a name to. A bright-red carpet adorned the floor and upon it sat a large desk and chair that looked to be several hundred years old.

Trevelyan moved over to the desk and sat in the large wooden chair. 'Please pull up a seat, there are a few about if you can find them – or just sit on a pile of books!'

The children eventually all found seats. Thomas ended up sitting on a stack of books, the topmost of which was entitled *An Insight into the Mind of the Clabbersnapper* by Gylburne Tailz. He briefly wondered what a Clabbersnapper might be before his attention wandered to some of the other strange items in the room. A glass case behind Trevelyan's desk contained a number of interesting items, including an hourglass in which the white-yellow sand stubbornly refused to move into the lower half of the vial, and a mirror that showed a reflection of an empty room. However, it was the picture on the wall that his eyes felt drawn to. It depicted a dozen silver-clad knights on silver-grey horses galloping through the clouds, each with a silver lance.

'Would anyone like a drink and biscuits?' Trevelyan asked, to which everyone replied that they would.

Trevelyan picked up a small silver bell from his desk and gave it a tinkle. Suddenly six tall goblets appeared on the desk followed a couple of seconds later by a plate of chocolate biscuits the size of saucers.

'Neat!' Penders' eyes were almost as wide as the biscuits.

Trevelyan smiled as he separated the goblets into pairs. 'Indeed, Mr Penderghast. Now, which drink will you take? We've two blackcurrant-and-apple, two peach-and-grape, and two lemon-and-gooseberry! Choices! Choices!'

Penders grabbed a blackcurrant-and-apple. The others were quick to grab hold of a goblet, leaving Thomas a lemon-and-gooseberry drink along with Mr Trevelyan.

'Ah, a fine choice, Mr Farrell!' Trevelyan said before taking a sip from his goblet.

'But I didn't make a choice,' Thomas protested.

Trevelyan smiled. 'You chose to choose last. You see, there's always a choice!'

Thomas frowned and then took a sip of his own drink. It tasted much nicer than he thought it would.

Merideah put her drink down on the desk. Her face looked serious. 'So the missing students came here?'

'Well, where shall I begin?' Trevelyan tapped his goblet. 'We find some pupils at the Manor more willing to believe than others; usually it's because they've more of the Old Blood in them.'

'The Old Blood?' Jessica asked.

Trevelyan swirled the liquid around in his goblet. 'Yes, there are some in your world who still have the blood of Avallach in their veins. As I told you before, our worlds weren't always separate. Even after they became so, many Way Gates allowed those from one world to cross into the other. People met, got married, had children. Their descendants are what we call the Halfkin, although true Halfkin haven't been known for centuries now.'

Merideah tapped her chin. 'Are you saying that the Family History Club are Halfkin?'

'I think all the Manor students are,' Thomas said, as his mind churned. This must have been why the school was for gifted students. They had the gift of the blood of Avallach.

Everyone looked at him, including Mr Trevelyan who seemed to have a twinkle in his eye. 'Yes, Thomas, though we must except Miss Westhrop, here.' He turned to Jessica. 'Though, of course, we're very honoured to have a representative of your world among us.'

Jessica smiled and showed her braces.

Trevelyan put down his lemon-and-gooseberry drink. 'We try to make sure all the students we take on are strong-blooded Halfkin. Alas, most reject this heritage and pass from the Manor unaware of who they really are. The blood of Men, and that world, is stronger in them.'

Treice seemed a little shocked. 'You mean we're not – I'm not – fully human?'

Trevelyan grinned. 'It makes little difference whether you are or not, if you choose not to believe it. But time will tell. He often does.'

The idea that his people once dwelt in Avallach didn't faze Thomas. Indeed, he felt the idea settling, as if a long-standing question had finally been answered.

Trevelyan continued. 'How students respond to Miss Havelock's lessons gives us a good idea of who might be receptive. Then we set up some extra lessons for them, teach them a little about Avallach from a purely mythical point of view you understand. We know by then which ones to invite into the Club. Of course, you five bypassed all that. I don't think Miss Havelock was very happy about it.'

Penders made a poor attempt to stifle a burp. 'Excuse me!'

The High Cap raised an eyebrow, but then continued. 'Most of the Club members return to Avallach once their education at the Manor is complete. Some never return to your world – those few without family usually. Hence the apparent disappearances.'

Merideah's face softened and she relaxed a little. 'So, does the Academy teach archery?'

The High Cap picked up his goblet. 'Indeed it does, though I must say I'm a terrible shot myself.'

Penders eyed another biscuit. 'Sir, the disappearing walls, this food and drink, the web windows –'

'Web glass,' Trevelyan corrected.

'Yeah, web glass. Sorry. Well, I mean, how does it all work? Is it magic?'

'Magic,' Trevelyan said with a curious light in his eyes as Penders stuffed the biscuit in his mouth. 'Well, that's a very human way of looking at it. Let us for now just say there are certain things that exist here that don't exist in the world of Men, certain things that work one way here and another way in your world. We call it the Old Power.'

Thomas thought there was some truth to that. After all, Mr Trevelyan could make chocolate biscuits appear from nowhere, but Penders could make them disappear almost as quickly, and he didn't even need a magic bell.

'Now, I've some good news for you all, or at least I hope you'll think it good news. I've spoken with my colleagues and we'd like to extend the offer to all five of you, from the Feast of Fires onward, to attend the Academy every week.'

Jessica almost bounced off her seat. 'Oh, that would be wonderful!' The rest of the children agreed enthusiastically.

'When exactly is this Feast of Fires?' Merideah inquired.

Mr Trevelyan raised his eyebrows. 'Ah, yes. I forgot! You call it Hallowe'en in your world.'

'Hallowe'en? That's just a couple of weeks away!' said Penders.

'Yes, indeed,' the High Cap began. 'However, the offer would be restricted to Saturdays, so as not to deprive you of your normal schooling or valuable homework time.'

The children nodded, though Penders looked a bit disappointed.

'Well, from the look on your faces I assume you all accept this offer?' Trevelyan asked.

Everyone, including Penders, said they did.

'That's splendid. However, there are some very strict rules for your safety here. I must ask that you especially not stray outside the grounds of the Academy. Is that clear?'

The children nodded as one.

'Does this mean we get to join the Family History Club? You know, as a sort of cover?' Penders asked.

Trevelyan nodded and then smiled. 'It's a rather good cover, isn't it? No one has ever asked to join the Club, so we can always control who has membership!' The High Cap suddenly looked a little more serious. 'However, it's not entirely a ruse, you know. You saw what was in 2B, I assume? Well, genealogy helps us find those in your world who have the blood of Avallach in them. But, as to your question, yes, Mr Penderghast, you'll be members of the Club. We'll speak of the details at the Feast.'

Trevelyan stood up and cast a wary eye at a grandfather clock. 'Oh dear, I've taken too long. I'm sorry.'

'Sorry for –' Jessica's words were cut off as the hands of the clock swung to one o'clock and an almighty bong sounded so loudly that the glass in the room reverberated and everyone put their hands to their ears.

'I must get that sorted,' Trevelyan said once the after-tremors had died away. 'I normally just pop in here for a few minutes at a time. Anyway, we best get you back to the Manor or you'll miss lunch, and I'm sure you wouldn't like that, would you, Mr Penderghast?'

Penders shook his head. 'Certainly not, Headmaster – I mean High Cap, but we won't be back in time for us to have seconds.'

Trevelyan chuckled. 'Well, 'blige me! We can't have that. We shall have to take a more direct method in our return. Thomas, could you move a little closer.'

Thomas did as he was told.

'Good, you should be clear of any danger now,' the High Cap said, as he stood up. 'Lift to High Cap's Study!'

Suddenly, out of nowhere, a lift landed in the corner of the room behind Thomas. It stood entirely free of the walls, and appeared to have no cables, pulleys or other attachments. The ceiling above it remained quite intact, as did the floor below it – though several unlucky books stuck out from the edges, dented and squashed by the impact. The lift's wooden doors parted silently.

Mr Trevelyan walked into the strange box. 'Well, get in!'

'What *is* this?' Merideah asked, as they all crowded in.

'An idea of mine based on some inspiration from your own world after visiting a department store. I call it the Anywhere Lift. It will take you anywhere within the Academy,' Mr Trevelyan explained as the doors closed. 'Though cadets may only use it with the approval and in the company of an adult.'

Thomas studied the inside of the lift. There were no buttons on the wall, only a sign that read: *PLEASE SPEAK CLEARLY.*

'OK, hold tight everyone. Lift to gardens!'

Suddenly Thomas felt as if they'd been catapulted into the air. After about three seconds the lift came to a sudden stop, causing Penders to hit his head on the wooden wall, and Treice to fall against Merideah; a fall from which he recovered with amazing speed.

Trevelyan's face looked a little flushed. 'My apologies, I haven't been able to track down the reason why it does that yet. To be honest, I don't like to use it too often, and never after a meal.'

The doors opened and the children found themselves back in the Gardens of Arghadmon again. Thomas noticed they were next to the fountain, and that the lift occupied the painted yellow square he'd seen earlier.

The thin-faced Stanwell Clear waited for them in the driver's seat of the Darkledun carriage, apparently unconcerned that a lift had just landed outside, in a garden, and only a few yards away from him. The black mares that pulled the carriage seemed only mildly interested.

'I need to attend to some things here.' Trevelyan stopped as he reached the doors. 'Mr Clear will take you back. Don't forget to keep what you've learned to yourselves! Oh, and remember never to stand in landing zones!'

And with a wave he stepped back into the Anywhere Lift, the doors closed and it shot up into the air.

'Striking!' was all Treice could say. The rest stood there with open mouths.

'Ey!' came Stanwell's familiar voice. 'Do you be standin' there gapin' while your dinner's soon for servin'?'

That broke Penders out of his awe, and he headed toward the carriage followed somewhat more slowly by Thomas and the others.

The Caretaker adjusted his three-cornered hat. 'Two of you can sit up 'ere with ol' Stanwell if you like, but you do be needin' to 'old tight, or else you do be goin' straight under the wheels and that'd be a right shame!'

The two girls went straight into the first coach. Thomas and Penders looked at each other excitedly before climbing up to sit next to Stanwell. Treice ducked into the second coach and thus avoided the girls.

'Hello, Mr Farrell and Mr Plundervast, glad you could join me and the 'orses! Now 'old tight!' Stanwell said.

'It's Penderghast,' Penders corrected.

'Oh, right you be, yes!' Stanwell said, sounding not at all convinced, as he flicked the reins and goaded the six horses forward. It wasn't long before they passed the turning that led to the buildings Thomas had seen from atop the Tower.

'Stanwell?' Thomas asked. 'What are those buildings by the lake?'

Stanwell smiled. 'Ah, that be Darkledun Village. They do be sellin' some fine potatoes in there little ol' market.'

'And the name of the lake?'

'That's Darkledun Lake.'

'Makes sense,' Penders muttered.

'And the river?' Thomas asked as they crossed the stone bridge.

'The Darkledun River?' Penders offered.

'Oh no, Mr Fenderblast, that do be the Darkledithy. Runs all the way from the lake to the north road, and then into – into there.' Stanwell nodded his head toward the forest.

'It's a very big forest!' Thomas said, as the carriage thundered past. The forest, by Thomas's reckoning, covered about a quarter of the entire Grange.

Stanwell lowered his voice. 'Yes, that be Muddlestump Wood.'

'It's beautiful to look at,' Jessica said. Thomas looked back and saw Jessica and Merideah's head sticking through the hole in the top of the first coach.

'Yes, Miss Westhrop,' Stanwell said. 'But I wouldn't be doing any more than lookin'.'

'Why?' Merideah asked.

'Anyone who goes into Muddlestump Wood never comes out again. That's why it's avoided. No one comes near 'ere, except the carriage and the Suits, that is,' explained Stanwell.

'Suits?' Penders asked.

Stanwell nodded. 'Aye, it do be what the cadets call the Darkledun Guards. Though we 'ave lost a few of those tin buckets to Muddlestump o'er the years. They get a bit confused sometimes and wander off the road.'

'And they never came out again?' Penders gulped.

'That's right. They do never come out!'

'Are there wild beasts in it, like wolves and bears?' Jessica asked.

Stanwell frowned. 'I daresay there might be. Some say it's the lair of many strange creatures. I've not been in it, no one's been in it, else they wouldn't be out of it, if you do be seein' what I mean.'

'Well,' Merideah began, 'if that's the case, no one can really know anything about what's in it, then.'

'Hmm, I guess that do be makin' sense. But I'll tell you this much, there were more things in the Grange when I was first 'ere than do now be found; and many reckon those things wandered into Muddlestump Wood. Good job too!'

Suddenly the Inner Gate blurred into focus up ahead, though the wall remained stubbornly unseen. Thomas briefly thought that maybe the wall had some sort of projection on its inner surface that made it look like an unending landscape, but he couldn't see how that was possible. Perhaps it *was* magic. As they drew closer several Guards with the Roman numeral V on their flat helms appeared.

'Goibhniu!' Stanwell called out and the Gate ahead slowly opened.

'Is Goibhniu the name of the gatekeeper?' Thomas asked.

'Oh no, Thomas, there's no one keepin' any gates here,' Stanwell replied, chuckling. 'Goibhniu is – what would you call it – a sort of password you might say.'

'Really?' Merideah said. 'Can I say it next time?'

'Well, the door do only open for those who've been approved, like, and that doesn't include any cadets, I'm afraid. We couldn't 'ave any ol' Fintan, Fingal, or Flaherty openin' the Gate, now could we?'

Penders, Merideah and Jessica exchanged puzzled looks, but Thomas looked back and studied the dark forest before it disappeared behind the huge wall that wasn't there just moments before.

– CHAPTER FIFTEEN –

# *The Feast of Fires*

A pumpkin wearing a grimace glowed menacingly at Thomas from a nearby table. Hallowe'en wasn't a time of year the Westhrops celebrated. Indeed, they celebrated very little unless it involved the receiving or saving of a considerable sum of money. So Thomas had little experience of making pumpkin heads, which was why he'd chosen to help Penders rather than make his own. Their pumpkin's mouth was uneven and one of the eyes lopsided. It certainly wouldn't win the competition. Several teachers were acting as judges, among them Miss Havelock and the Headmaster.

Mr Trevelyan sat at the teachers' table. He hadn't so much as spoken a word to Thomas or the others since that day in the Grange a couple of weeks ago; though, of course, last week had been half term and spent back in Holten Layme. Thomas thought the Headmaster might have forgotten. He'd told them they would start lessons at the Academy after Hallowe'en. And Hallowe'en had come, but still they'd heard nothing.

After the winner had been announced, all were invited to grab their coats and make their way out onto the field. Ten minutes later, Thomas stood watching Penders duck his head into a large plastic cauldron for the fourth time. Some distance away the fire crackled. Penders' appleless face appeared from the cauldron just as Jessica and Merideah reached them.

Jessica ignored Penders as he wiped the water from his eyes. 'We're to be outside 2B in five minutes. Mr Trevelyan says we won't need anything except our coats.'

'What?' Penders looked at his watch. 'We'll miss dinner!'

Merideah gave him a withering look. 'You can stay if you want.'

Jessica spoke before Penders could reply. 'Have you seen Treice? We couldn't find him.'

'I'll look,' offered Thomas.

'I'll be right there. I just wanna get at least one apple if I'm going to miss me dinner.' Penders plunged his head into the water-filled cauldron again.

Merideah shook her head. 'We're going to get cleaned up. We smell of pumpkin. We'll see you there.'

\* \* \*

Penders traipsed behind Thomas, finishing the last few bites of his apple, whilst Jessica and Merideah stuck close behind Stanwell. Treice walked a few paces up ahead, his face pointing skyward. Thomas hoped he didn't trip and fall. He'd eventually found Treice lying on the Manor's field, just far enough outside the fire's glow to avoid being recognised. Jessica and Merideah hadn't been happy at the boys being late. The Club members had already gone through.

The carriage awaited them, its horses eager to pull away. A number of cadets stood gathered by the middle coach, each wearing the fawn uniform.

'Ah, changed already, that do be good,' Stanwell said to the group as he approached the carriage.

Thomas now recognised the faces of the Club members in the light of the carriage's lanterns. Prothero was there, his arm no longer in a cast. But any word of greeting was quickly cut off by Stanwell.

'We do be late, so all in please! You young'ns will 'ave to get changed on the way. Your uniforms do be in the first coach!'

The Club members jumped into the five back coaches, leaving the first coach free.

'Mr Clear!' Merideah sounded shocked. 'We can't all get changed in the same coach!'

Stanwell pulled himself up onto the driver's seat and placed his black tricorn on his head. 'You can use the ol' changin' rooms.'

'Changing rooms?' Jessica repeated.

Stanwell took up the reins. 'Yes, in the Undercarriage. Now on you get, the 'orses be chompin' at the bit. We'll 'ave to make like an 'ound after a coney, we will!'

The carriage started moving as soon as Thomas shut the coach door. Five packages wrapped in brown paper lay on the seats, each labelled with a name.

Jessica picked up the one bearing her name. 'What did he mean by Undercarriage?'

'That, I assume,' Thomas said, pointing to a small hatch in the floor about two by three feet. A ring protruded from one end.

'We're not opening that!' Merideah said, but too late. Penders had grabbed the ring and given it a tug.

The hatch popped up and the children stepped back, expecting to see the ground rushing past beneath them. Instead, however, they saw a flight of wooden steps leading down.

Penders eyed the steps as they shook from side to side. 'Well, I'm not going down there.'

Merideah raised an eyebrow. 'You opened it.'

Suddenly the carriage leapt violently, and the children were thrown to the floor.

'Sorry 'bout that,' came Stanwell's voice from above. 'The Guards don't be movin' fast enough sometimes.'

'He ran over a Guard?' Penders asked as he grabbed the seat and hauled himself back up.

Jessica stood and looked around. 'Where's Treice?'

They all looked down at the steps.

'Oh dear,' said Merideah. 'Treice! Can you hear us? Are you OK?'

There was no reply.

Jessica started down the swaying steps. 'Come on, he might be hurt.'

The rest followed warily. Thomas came last, glad when he reached the bottom. He found himself in a chamber about twice the size of the coach above, illuminated by four lanterns swinging from the ceiling. Beneath one stood a shaken Treice, though whether his state was due to his fall or the attention

Jessica and Merideah were now giving him, Thomas couldn't tell.

Five doors were set in the wooden walls. Penders opened the nearest one. Inside lay a room slightly smaller than the coach above. A tall mirror had been fixed to one of the walls, and a bench with a shelf underneath sat opposite a coat stand that moved a little every time the carriage hit a bump in the road. A single lantern hung from the ceiling.

'How's this possible?' Merideah asked.

Penders shook his head. 'No idea, but there's one each. I'll grab the uniforms!'

Thomas and Penders were the first to appear out of their changing rooms in their new cadet uniforms, although the girls had been the first to disappear.

Penders held up his arms and examined the clothes. 'I like it!'

Thomas cast an eye over his own uniform. It had obviously been made to measure. The fawn tunic hung low over the belt, covering most of the similarly-coloured trousers. Upon his wrists were bracers of black leather, a complement to the boots. Lastly, a long, hooded cloak, also fawn, hung from his shoulders. Thomas couldn't help thinking he looked somewhat strange. A badge was emblazoned on the right breast of his tunic – the ringed serpent; it seemed fated that the symbol would always be with him.

Treice stepped out of his room, his uniform covering his tall, athletic frame. He looked around nervously. 'Are the girls out yet?'

As if by some unseen signal, Jessica and Merideah appeared together, but they remained silent about their new outfits, which only differed in that instead of trousers they wore skirts. After an exchange of glances, they all made their way back up into the coach. Thomas entered last and shut the hatch door firmly.

'No "sunny roofs" tonight,' Stanwell shouted. 'There be no sun anyway, but the lanterns'll do.'

'I hope it's warm in the Hall,' said Jessica, as she pulled her duffle coat closer about her.

Thomas wasn't bothered too much. Girls were always cold. He looked out of the window. They'd passed the Inner Gate some time ago and were now on the road south. Not much could be seen at night, but Thomas's eyes felt drawn to Muddlestump Wood looming in the blackness. It was as if the trees were gathering all the darkness of the world into their canopies. He shivered and pulled his eyes away from the window.

His eyes fixed upon a black box above his seat. Thomas flipped down the cover. A panel opened revealing a dial with various marks around it, currently in the 'off' position. A slide lever, also with settings marked along its length, sat beneath the dial.

'What d'you suppose it does?' Penders said, reaching out.

Merideah pushed his arm aside. 'Don't touch! Read first. Men never read the instructions!'

Penders scowled as they looked at the panel more closely. Above the dial were the words *SEASONAL SETTING*. The various positions around the dial read *SPRING*, *SUMMER*, *AUTUMN*, and *WINTER*.

'Fascinating,' said Merideah as she spun the dial carefully to *WINTER*. Immediately the coach grew colder and ice started to appear on the windows. Jessica looked as if she was going to freeze on the spot. Merideah switched the dial to *SUMMER* at which point a wave of heat swept through the coach. She looked around. 'Where are the heaters?'

'I don't see any,' said Thomas. 'It's just sort of warm all of a sudden.'

Penders, determined to have his go, switched the dial to *AUTUMN* and the heat diminished immediately. The windows were shut, so Thomas was surprised to see a few brown leaves come fluttering from out of nowhere and settle on the floor of the coach.

Jessica pulled at her hair. 'I wonder how it works?'

'And I wonder what this does?' Penders said, as he slid the slider to a position that, too late, Thomas realised read *REALLY WINDY*. Immediately gusts blustered through the coach, scattering Treice's golden locks about his face.

'Push that back,' said Merideah as she pulled Penders out of the way and reached for the slider. As she did so, they accidentally spun the dial and pushed the slider all the way to the left.

When the children arrived in the Gardens of Arghadmon they stepped out of a coach filled with thick fog. It hung at the door as if not daring to pass.

'I see you found the ol' climate control,' Stanwell said, as he jumped down and disappeared into the coach.

He appeared a few moments later. 'Strange, most do be choosin' "summer" on nights like this, not the pea-souper. Darn 'ard to see the controls when it be on that settin'.'

Merideah gave Penders a hard stare as the fog dissipated in the coach. Penders mouthed a 'what?', but she turned away.

'Well, no time for chat. We do be late.' Stanwell closed the coach door and motioned them all to follow him to the entrance of the Hall. The Club members were nowhere to be seen. They must have rushed inside while Thomas and the other children were trying to find the handle to the coach door.

'There's a leaf in your hair,' Penders said to Merideah before he turned and followed Stanwell.

The two Guards stood at the portals as before, their bronze armour reflecting the light of the torch they each held. As Thomas mused upon this very practical use of the Suits, he walked into something, lost his footing, and landed hard upon it.

'Oi! Get off! Get off!' came a gruff voice from below him.

Thomas sprang to his feet. There on the ground sat not a child but a very short adult. He had the most tangled and wiry grey beard Thomas had ever seen.

'I'm sorry,' apologised Thomas. 'I didn't see you there.'

'No one ever sees old Dugan!' the small man protested as he pushed himself up. He barely came past Thomas's waist in height. 'Tries to help and just gets big people fall on top of him. What sort of thanks is that?'

'Well I –'

'The lad said 'e were sorry, Dugan,' Stanwell interrupted Thomas in a loud voice. 'So don't be gettin' your beard in a bother over it!'

137

Dugan scowled. A large bulbous nose stuck out from Dugan's wizened face. Shabby, well-worn clothes of brown leather covered the rest of his scrawny frame.

'What are you?' Penders asked. 'I mean –'

''E do be a dwarf,' Stanwell said. 'And you need to speak up, as 'e do be as deaf as an ol' 'itchin' post!'

'I'm not a dwarf, and I'm not deaf!' Dugan blurted out. 'I am a Dwerugh. How dare you call me a dwarf!'

'It do be the same thing,' Stanwell said.

'It do be not!' Thomas thought the Dwarf – or Dwerugh, or whatever he was – might explode, so red was his face.

'Dugan Buglebeard 'ere,' Stanwell said, turning to the children, 'be the Sleeper in the 'all.'

'Keeper of the Hall!' Dugan corrected indignantly.

Stanwell eyed the little man suspiciously. 'You were kippin'.'

'I was having a little rest, is all. Poor old Dugan is worked so hard!'

Stanwell rolled his eyes. 'Yes, yes. Anyways, these young'ns 'ere do be first-timers, so they'll need a bit of guidin'.'

Dugan shook his head at Stanwell, and then turned to look at Thomas and the others. 'I can see that. Come on then, we'd best get you inside. Everyone's waiting, you know.'

'Waiting?' Jessica asked.

Dugan opened the door just wide enough for a person to slip through. Inside it looked pitch black.

'Right, everyone be quiet and link hands so you don't get lost,' Dugan instructed.

The children did as Dugan said. Penders had the pleasure of holding Dugan's dirty (and very hairy) hand – something he didn't relish by the look on his face. Dugan led them through the darkness. Penders grunted as he hit something hard.

'Pay attention,' Dugan whispered in a voice that carried.

Penders muttered something under his breath about dwarfs as they continued, and Thomas hoped Dugan really was deaf. He didn't want to be led into a wall. Thomas could see the dim light of the night sky in the windows now, and although the rest of the Hall lay still and dark, he'd the distinct feeling that they weren't alone.

'Here you are. Release hands,' Dugan eventually said. Chairs scraped on the floor. A small hand guided his hand to the back of the chair beside him. 'OK,' Dugan said a few seconds later, his voice low. 'Everyone sit down.'

They sat down and silence fell. After several moments he thought he might risk whispering to Penders, but before he could do so a heavy chair scraped on the floor from the other side of the room.

'Welcome, cadets of Arghadmon Academy!' came a cheery voice that Thomas immediately recognised as belonging to the Headmaster. 'Welcome to the Feast of Fires!'

As soon as he finished these words, fires sprang up in the Hall's fireplaces, torches flared alight, and candles flickered into life until the whole room was lit by many flames. An enormous cheer went up. They were surrounded by about two hundred cadets seated in their uniforms around three long, wooden tables.

As the cheers died down Thomas's attention shifted to the Headmaster. He stood between Gallowglas – now dressed in a beige tunic and a black cloak – and a young woman in a brown dress. It took a few moments for Thomas to realise this woman was Miss Havelock. With her hair down and her glasses gone, she looked much younger, if no less stern. About a half dozen other adults sat at the head table near the wall. Some of them Thomas recognised from the Manor, but others he hadn't seen before.

The unmistakeable Master Fabula, dressed in the same colourful mismatched robes as before, sat listening intently to Mr Trevelyan. There were no cadets or adults who looked like him.

Trevelyan cast his eyes toward Thomas. 'Now, I have a special announcement. Tonight we have with us five new cadets, youngest of any to have entered the halls of the Academy from the Otherside. Perhaps I could ask them to stand?'

They stood. Thomas looked around warily. For some reason he felt less nervous here than at the Manor, even though a multitude of strange faces now looked at him.

The High Cap smiled. 'May I introduce Jessica Westhrop, Merideah Constance Darwood, Treice Montague, Marvin Penderghast – or Penders as he prefers to be known – and Thomas Farrell as honorary cadets of Arghadmon Academy? They'll be joining our younger cadets for one lesson every week. I ask you all to make them especially welcome.' Trevelyan's face turned serious. 'Now, may I remind all junior cadets to remain within the confines of the grounds, especially now the nights are drawing in; and also to refrain from throwing stones at the Darkledun Guards. They may not feel it, but Master Bellows has to mend the dents. Any cadet caught in the act will receive extra duties at the forge! Now, to happier matters: Let us eat!'

He clapped his hands and immediately a line of green-liveried servants began filling the tables with all manner of wonderful food. A broad smile spread across Penders' face.

The meal itself, much to Thomas's pleasure, tasted very nice and wasn't at all strange. The main course was potato and cabbage stew, complemented by barmbrack, a sort of bread. Dessert consisted of a bowl of ice cream, a large toffee apple, roasted pumpkin seeds and bonfire toffee. At about the time that the slower eaters were finishing their dessert, and Penders was finishing his third helping, the High Cap stood and raised his arms for silence.

'As those who have attended the Feast of Fires before will know, we like to recount the Tale of Avallach at this point every year, so that we do not forget what should not be forgotten.'

Trevelyan paused as if some sorrow was suddenly upon him, but it was soon gone and his smile back upon his rotund face. 'It is my privilege, therefore, to introduce our teller of tales for this evening's recounting – Master Fabula!'

And with those last words Master Fabula stood and gave an ostentatious bow to a cacophony of clapping and cheering that continued until he stepped up to a small stone dais. The final claps fell silent as Master Fabula raised his wide-sleeved arms and all the candles and torches went out, leaving the room lit only by the four fires.

'Cadets of the Academy' – he shot a look through narrow eyes toward Thomas and the others – 'it is my great honour and distinct pleasure to present to you this evening, at the Feast of Fires, the tale of Avallach's very beginnings. Clear your minds, open your ears. Stare into the flames, and let them invoke the memories I will now stir to life in word…'

Thomas looked into the flames of the fire behind Fabula. Firelight danced upon Fabula's multi-hued robes.

'Avallach,' Master Fabula began with a voice that seemed to fill the whole Hall, 'was a proud Alfarian king' – some of the blond youths in the room nodded in approval – 'and the last to have known the ways of the De Danann before they withdrew from the land to their sidhe. In the latter days of his reign, when many of the Humbalgogs' – here Master Fabula indicated toward the large brown-haired group of cadets seated near Thomas – 'had begun to deny the Old Power, he and his enchanters summoned a great veil of mist and forever divided our world from that of those Humbalgogs who meddled with science and machines. And in later times our world was called Avallach to distinguish it from the Otherside – the World of Men.'

Though too dark to be sure, Thomas thought many of the cadets looked in their direction.

'But,' Master Fabula began again, a sadness now in his voice, 'King Avallach was not the only one to know the ways of the De Danann, the Everliving Ones, for there dwelt a lord among them, by name Cernunnos, strong in the Old Power, and ruthless.' At mention of this name there were a few intakes of breath and mutters across the Hall. 'And he did not withdraw from the land as had the rest of his kind, but rather sought power in Avallach. And he made war with King Avallach and all the Free Peoples. And so began the Great War, and there was a great division among the people. And in that day the Humbalgogs' – Master Fabula pointed at the brown-haired cadets – 'and the tall warriors of the Firdheeg' – he swept a hand toward the red-haired youths in the room – 'and the noble Alfar' – his hand gestured toward the long, golden-haired cadets – 'stood against Cernunnos and those who served him: the Fomorfelk, the Dewgs, the Drough, and all the foul creatures dedicated to his cause. And so that war has continued to this day. And so on this night, every year, we tell the tale and recite the Lay of Avallach in memory of the fallen, and to honour those who still fight the Dread Lord.'

A hush filled the room. Even Penders had forgotten his toffee apple. Master Fabula raised his arms and everyone stood. Then the room went black as all the fires went out. After a few moments, Fabula began to recite the Lay, and as he finished each couplet, a fire burst back into life and the cadets echoed the words back to him:

*A Fire to remember the Last King,*
*Who sundered Avallach and the World of Men;*
*A Fire to ward off the Horned One's Power,*
*To send him back to the Forgotten Tower;*
*A Fire to mourn the Fallen Lord,*
*Arghadmon, slain by the Horned One's sword;*
*A Fire to bring Hope out of the Dark,*
*Two Children bearing the Everliving Ones' Mark*

Master Fabula bowed as the candles and torches suddenly flared alight again. In silence Fabula walked back to his seat. Everyone sat down, but no one clapped or cheered. Thomas could see all the faces clearly now – faces filled with thoughtfulness, reverence and, here and there, a look of sorrow or loss. What had he walked into when he came through the stones? A war? Was it safe here? He touched the Glass. It was glowing, he could sense it. A warmth flooded through his body. His fears fell away like ice melting before the heat of the sun. He was meant to be here. He knew that more than he knew anything, war or no war.

## – CHAPTER SIXTEEN –

# *Thayer Gaul*

'It isn't natural to get up before it's light,' Penders moaned as he stumbled bleary-eyed down the stairs behind Thomas and Treice.

Thomas smiled. He was used to getting up early in the Westhrop household. After all, he'd made the breakfast every morning since he was nine. He wondered how the Westhrops were coping now that he'd gone.

It was quiet in the Manor, the dawn's light growing as the night faded. Up above, a window rattled. It sounded as if it would be a blustery Saturday. They were going to visit a graveyard today. At least, that was what they had to say if anyone asked. The Headmaster had spoken to them briefly after the Feast of Fires, telling them to be outside 2B at half past seven the following Saturday morning for their first class. He hadn't said what the lesson would be. Penders wanted to do some sword fighting. He'd be on about it since they'd seen the combat training in the Ring.

Thomas, Penders and Treice arrived at 2B a few moments later to find Stanwell and the girls waiting. Penders plonked himself down on a desk, rubbed his eyes and cast a tired gaze over the room. 'I wonder if my family tree's in here somewhere?'

Stanwell pulled on the pendulum of the clock. 'Oh yes, Master Plunderfast, it surely be. I seem to recall you be a Cromwellian.'

Penders, who'd long since given up correcting Stanwell over his surname, repeated the Caretaker's last word. 'Cromwellian?'

'Yes, there be these key ancestors we look out for. Cromwell be one of them. 'e was an 'alfkin. 'is mother were a 'umbalgog.

'umbalgogs like order and don't 'old with kings,' replied Stanwell as the blackboard grated up to reveal the entrance to the tower.

Penders had Humbalgog ancestors? The cadets Fabula had pointed out at the Feast of Fires had been Humbalgogs. Thomas wondered where his line led, but he'd probably never know. Without knowing the details about his mother and father it was impossible to trace a family tree.

Twenty minutes later they were standing in the Hall of Arghadmon. The fires were dead now and the place empty.

Stanwell looked agitated. 'Where be that Bogglebeard? Never rely on a dwarf, mark my words!'

Thomas reached beneath his cloak for the bag hanging from his belt. Bringing the Glass had felt right, after all it had led him here in the first place. As for the marbles, maybe the younger cadets might like to play a game or two, or he could teach them the rules if they didn't have marbles in Avallach.

The old Dwerugh appeared from the corridor that led to the Tower. He carried a tray with a half-dozen silver bells.

'It's 'bout time,' Stanwell murmured. 'You been kippin' again?'

Dugan scowled as he placed the tray on a table. 'Extra duties! I'm busy enough as it is, and now I have to prepare breakfast like some old maid!'

Penders perked up at the word breakfast, but looked upon the tray in confusion as Dugan scuttled off back the way he'd come.

'Well, children,' Stanwell began, after Dugan had gone. 'Eat up! Your first lesson do be at eight of the clock. You can't miss it. Remember to be leavin' enough time to get there now. I shall meet you by the fountain in the gardens after your lesson. Do be prompt! Don't dilly or dally!'

When Stanwell had gone, the children approached the tray. Penders picked up one of the bells. 'Well, I guess it works the same way as the one Trevelyan had.'

Penders rang the bell and a plate of toast appeared on the table next to the tray. Picking a piece up, he bit into it. 'Mmm! Strawberry jam! Still warm too.'

Thomas picked up another bell and gave it a tinkle. Five goblets of juice appeared.

Penders looked at his bell. 'I wonder what would happen if we took one of these back to the Manor?'

Jessica examined them. 'I don't think they'd work in our world anyway.'

'Thomas's Glass worked in our world,' Penders said through a mouth full of toast.

Merideah shrugged. 'I'm not sure that glowing's the same thing as producing food out of thin air.'

'I'd rather have a supply of food anytime I wanted, not an extra lamp.' He turned to Thomas. 'Sorry, mate.'

'Nothing surprising there, then.' Merideah drained the remainder of her goblet.

'I wonder what the glowing means?' Jessica asked no one in particular.

Treice looked up from his bowl of cereal. 'Maybe it detects magic?'

Merideah tapped her chin with a finger. 'Well, I'm not sure what was magical about Thomas's dreams.'

Treice stared back at them with blank eyes. Jessica filled Treice in about the Glass glowing.

'You got the Glass?' Penders asked. 'We could see if it glows near these bells.'

Thomas pulled the Glass from his bag and held it close to the bells. It remained quite unaffected. He hadn't expected it to glow. The Glass only seemed to illuminate near the Way Gates or when he slept with it in his hand. When he had those terrifying dreams of the serpent.

Merideah stepped closer to examine the Glass, but she brushed against Treice who stood up abruptly to make way for her. Unfortunately, in doing so, he knocked the orb from Thomas's hand and it rolled down the length of the table. Thomas grabbed for it too late. The Glass fell heavily to the ground and rolled across the floor until it came to stop at the wall. He dared not look at first, thinking he'd see a crack, but it seemed quite unscathed, and, more than that, it was glowing. He picked it up. 'What this time?'

Merideah's face was intent as she and the others approached. 'Move about. See what happens.'

Thomas moved to the right. After ten paces the Glass began to dim. He tried the opposite direction and the same thing happened. He stared up at the southern wall of the Hall with its huge image of a fire-wreathed crown embossed between the two serpent-embroidered drapes. The other children silently gathered behind him. He touched the Glass against the wood-panelled wall and a doorway outlined in silver light shimmered and disappeared, leaving open an entrance to a small chamber.

Merideah called out something about being careful, but Thomas wasn't listening. He stepped through and, one by one, the others followed. Inside they were welcomed by a bare room with a stone podium thrusting out from the middle of the floor. Upon it lay a large and very old-looking parchment. It was quite empty.

'Well, what a silly room.' Penders looked from the podium back to the doorway. 'Why go to all the trouble of hiding it, if all it contains is a blank piece of paper?'

Thomas shrugged. 'Don't ask me.'

'Well at least we know what the Glass does now,' Merideah said.

Penders looked at her. 'We do?'

Merideah pushed back her Alice band. 'Yes, it seems to find hidden doorways: the stones, the entrance to this chamber. They're both doorways of a sort.'

Merideah was right, Thomas was sure of it, but what about his dreams? Did it open some kind of doorway there, too?

Penders headed back out. 'I'm going to finish my breakfast.'

Merideah gave him a withering look before she and the rest of them followed.

As they stepped out of the room the doorway disappeared and the wall returned to normal. Not a second later, Dugan appeared down the corridor.

He stared at them suspiciously, no doubt wondering why they were all walking away from the wall. 'You should've finished by now. You'll be late, and she'll not like it!'

'Ah, right. Well –'

'No more talking!' the Dwerugh interrupted Jessica. 'Poor old Dugan will do the washing up.'

Dugan pulled the plate of biscuits from the table before Penders could reach it, and started shooing them all off in the direction of the Tower. 'Off with you now, to the Map Room. Don't be late!'

The children made their way up the spiral staircase and to the room with the giant map on the floor. The chamber was much as they last saw it, except that it now had two occupants. Miss Havelock, minus her glasses, stood in a long, dark gown, her hair flowing down her shoulders. By her side, dressed in the fawn robes of the Academy, stood a boy, or what looked like a boy. He was large-boned, muscular, and his skin the colour of ash. He looked at the children with eager grey eyes.

Miss Havelock frowned. 'You're late!'

A look of dismay spread across Penders' face. It didn't look like they'd be doing any sword fighting today.

'Normally, when Halfkin are accepted into the Academy, we like to prepare them by explaining a little about the Grange, our history, our cultures, and, of course, the War. As you chose to bypass my lessons, and as I really don't have time for private tutoring, you'll just have to get along as best you can. You're younger than the other cadets from your world, so you'll have time enough to learn. But to help you along, the High Cap has asked that Thayer Gaul' – she indicated the boy to her side – 'be your guide. He knows the Grange well enough to keep you from danger, and will accompany you on your visits. Are there any questions?'

No one answered.

'Well, Thayer will give you a tour of the village and answer the questions you seem too shy to ask,' Miss Havelock continued. 'Now, if you'll excuse me, I need to attend to some other matters.'

Miss Havelock walked over to a shelf and pulled a large book down. Seeing everyone still standing there when she turned back, she raised her eyebrows at Thayer Gaul who nodded nervously and led the children out of the room.

They followed Thayer without a word until they were outside, at which point Jessica could contain herself no longer.

'My name is Jessica Westhrop –'

'Yes, I know your name. I know all your names. I was at the Feast of Fires when the High Cap introduced you,' Thayer interrupted, stopping and looking at them all with eager eyes. 'I am very pleased to be your guide. The High Cap was very kind to give me this honour.'

Jessica smiled as they walked in silence into the gardens.

'Why'd you have grey skin?' Jessica asked, just as they began traipsing up the dirt track that led to the road.

The squat boy looked at her. 'I am one of the Fomorfelk. We all look like this.'

'Fomorfelk? Didn't Fabula mention those at the Feast of Fires?' Jessica continued, as Thayer plodded on into the gardens.

Thayer looked a little pained. 'Yes, it is one of the races of Avallach.'

Though slow of speech, the boy seemed keen to answer questions, even those asked by Jessica.

'So each race has a different skin colour? Like Fabula with his black skin? He's a Dewg, right?'

'He is,' their guide confirmed, 'but the other races have skin like your own, except the Hobhoulards of course.'

Jessica didn't ask about Hobhoulards, but she nodded as the boy spoke. 'I've not seen anyone else here with grey skin.'

'I am the only one of my people within the Grange, just like Master Fabula.'

It was not far to the village. They passed through small fields filled with pigs, chickens or cows as they approached the collection of wooden buildings. Thayer walked slowly, much to Jessica's frustration, and she only stopped herself from breaking into a run by asking what shops existed in the village. Thayer mentioned a tavern, a grocer, and a few other basic stores, none of which seemed to appeal to Jessica, even when Thayer went into detail about what each of them sold.

The village was pretty basic. Wooden cabins of various sizes sat across an area about the size of two football pitches. The village was bordered on the north by the river where boats with nets bobbed. Men, women, and children went about their business, all of them with quite normal skin, though a one or two had pointed ears.

'This is where I live,' Thayer announced as they approached the blacksmith's. 'Father is at the armoury today, but this is where he does his work for the village.'

'Your father?' Merideah asked. 'I thought you said you were the only Fomorfelk here?'

Thayer's expressionless face turned toward them. 'He is not my real father. My parents were both killed. Master Bellows brought me up as his own. I have lived in the Grange most of my life.'

Thomas could not help but relate to the boy. 'Do you remember much about your parents?'

Thayer shook his head and headed toward the river. 'I do not even remember much about life before Master Bellows brought me to the Grange.'

'Can you tell us more about the Academy?' Merideah asked.

Thayer sat down on the bank and the others did the same. 'It is where we train for battle. It is a safe place. That is why you will see some of the sons of Avallach here and not just Halfkin. Chiefly it is Humbalgogs here, they all have brown hair, but a few Alfar and Firdheeg also attend.'

'The Alfar are the ones with the pointed ears, right?' Treice said.

'Yes, and the Firdheeg are the ones with the red hair. They come from the forestlands. They are good with the spear. The Alfar prefer the bow and the horse. Have any of you wondered which race you have in your blood? It must be exciting to be a Halfkin.'

Merideah tapped her finger on her chin. 'Well, Thomas has blond hair and blue eyes, so maybe he's got Alfar blood in him.'

Thayer nodded. 'Maybe. Maybe not. I am not sure it always works like that.'

Thomas bit his lip and looked at Jessica. He hadn't told anyone he wore filtered contact lenses. Still, what with his hair, he probably was of Alfar blood. Maybe his mum or dad had had an Alfar ancestor. He needed to know about his family history. He couldn't say why. He just did. And this time he had a feeling that the Glass would be of no help.

## – CHAPTER SEVENTEEN –

# *The Hall of Tales*

Thomas, Merideah, Jessica, Penders and Treice exited the Darkledun carriage as soon as it came to a stop in the Gardens of Arghadmon that morning. Thayer joined them just as they were finishing breakfast and apologised for being late.

'I had to carry some tools to the forge for my father,' Thayer explained as he led them out of the Hall and toward the Ring where men were setting up weapon racks, no doubt for that day's training.

'Do we get to do some fighting?' Penders asked, his eyes alight.

Thayer looked at him blankly as he led them past the walled area. 'Cadets cannot enter the Ring or practise with weapons without the Chief Instructor's permission.'

'And that would be?' Penders queried. Looking around eagerly.

'Master Gallowglas,' replied Thayer. Penders' face grew dark. 'But we are not going to the Ring. Come, we must hurry or it will start before we arrive.'

Before anyone could ask what the 'it' was, a red-haired cadet brushed past Thayer, knocking his shoulder. Thayer didn't lose his balance. He was a well-set lad, but the other boy didn't stop or say sorry.

Merideah looked on in anger, but the offender had disappeared around a building before she could say anything to him. 'How rude!'

'What was that about?' asked Penders.

'I am Fomorfelk,' said Thayer, as if it explained everything.

'So what?' Merideah chimed back in.

Thayer sighed. 'The Fomorfelk serve the Horned One.'

Penders puckered his brow. 'The Horned One?'

'Cernunnos,' said Merideah. 'Fabula called him the Horned One in the Lay of Avallach.'

Penders' eyes widened. 'You serve that bad guy, Thayer?'

Thayer looked dolefully at Penders. 'No, I was lost overboard a Fomorfelk ship when I was two years old. I have only ever known the ways of the Humbalgogs since then. They are a good people.'

'Unlike others!' Merideah hissed, glaring back to the building the red-haired boy had disappeared around.

Thayer clasped his hands together. 'The Firdheeg have suffered much at the hands of the Fomorfelk. Many cadets here have lost brothers, sisters or a mother or father under a Fomorfelk sword.'

So exactly who is this Cernunnos anyway?' Penders asked as Thayer started to lead them off again.

'He is a powerful enchanter. He is very old, though how old I do not know. It is said that he rides in a chariot that can fly, and is attended by giant black dogs with red eyes that can take an arm off in one bite.'

Jessica squirmed. 'That's nice.'

'No, it is not nice,' began Thayer, who evidently had no grasp of the concept of sarcasm. 'Cernunnos is bad, very bad. He hates the Humbalgogs, the Alfar, the Firdheeg and the Dwerugh. He especially hates the High Cap. He tried to kill him once or twice, I heard.'

'Cernunnos tried to kill Mr Trevelyan?' Penders asked.

'Yes, before the High Cap came here. It is safe here in the sidhe though. Well, relatively safe as long as you know the dangers.'

'Dangers?' Jessica asked.

'Oh, do not worry. The High Cap asked me to keep you away from the bad places.' Thayer stopped by a long wooden hall. Outside stood the members of the Family History Club, all in their cadet uniforms.

A young blonde girl swept toward them before Thomas could ask what dangers might lurk in the Grange. 'Hello, Jessica!'

'Hi, Tara!' Jessica turned to introduce Tara to Thomas and the others. Although in the second year, Jessica had started to become good friends with her. She was short, perhaps a tad taller than Merideah, and looked younger than her age. Thomas saw Duncan Avebury too, and wondered how he kept the Grange secret from his sister Melantha.

The door of the wooden building was made of thick oak and covered in ornate carvings. Small figures, on both horse and foot, populated the central panel. Creatures twisted their way around the borders. Thomas searched in vain for any image of a serpent. Merideah traced her finger over the figures with a look of admiration on her face.

Penders glanced from the door to Thomas. 'Think the lesson's on wood carving?'

'It's storytelling,' said the short sandy-haired Miles Merlock. Thomas liked Miles. He was friendly.

Penders looked at Miles. 'Ah, with Master Fabulous?'

Tara smiled. 'Fabula, though he is fabulous at telling stories.'

'Oh,' said Penders. 'My dad's good at doing that too, especially when he's been fishing –'

'No, it's not quite like that, you'll see – or maybe I should say "hear",' Miles politely interrupted. Tara giggled.

Thomas stole a glance at Treice, who leant against the wall, staying apart from the girls.

The door swung open with a creak. Thomas winced.

Merideah stepped back. 'Those hinges need oiling.'

'Greetings and felicitations!' a familiar voice cried from within the building. 'Enter the Hall of Tales!'

The cadets filed in ahead of Thomas. The hall inside had no windows and no decorations of any kind except for a huge fire place in the middle of the room beneath a large hole in the roof. Master Fabula occupied a wooden chair, every bit as ornate as the door, next to the fire, and around him were strewn beanbags of varying colours – purple, crimson, dark orange, and emerald green. They looked quite out of place in this world and Thomas had a sneaking suspicion that Mr Trevelyan might well have procured them from some hip Scottish furniture store.

Thomas found a beanbag not far from Master Fabula's feet. The tutor's multicoloured robes looked even more tattered and faded now that Thomas saw them up close. Master Fabula sent a puff of pipe smoke into the air to mingle with the firelight before he spoke.

'Greetings and mirth! Welcome once again. I trust you all had a pleasant Feast of Fires?'

Many of the cadets nodded, and some gave a hearty 'Yes, sir!'

'And how are our young cadets?' Fabula smiled at Thomas and his friends, showing too many incisors.

'Now,' Master Fabula began, as he cast his gaze across the cadets, 'last time we spoke of the coming of Arghadmon, Captain of the Free Peoples. This week we shall tell the story of Arghadmon's first victory against the dread lord Cernunnos himself. I speak of the heroic tale of the Battle of Hammerhoe!'

The cadets muttered in excitement, even though some of them, such as Duncan, must have been at least fifteen. Weren't they a bit old to sit at someone's feet and listen to stories? To be honest, Thomas felt a bit too old himself, but he thought it'd be interesting to know more about the person who gave the Academy its name.

Master Fabula looked around at the walls. His eyes glittered like metal orbs. The room fell quiet, as if the cadets were waiting for something spectacular. The fire dimmed, and shadows played eerily upon the walls.

'Before any of your mothers brought you into the world, a great army led by the dread Cernunnos came to the northern borders of the land of the Humbalgogs, intent on murder and ruin. An army composed, it is said, of over ten thousand Hobhoulards strengthened by a thousand Fomorfelk warriors.'

Master Fabula paused and tapped his pipe on the arm of his chair.

'Now Arghadmon dwelt in Alfheim among the Alfar, when news reached him that Cernunnos was on the move, marching his dark army toward the lands of the Humbalgogs. Arghadmon was granted as many warriors as could be spared by the King of Alfheim, but they were few. But horses the

Alfar had many, and so Arghadmon persuaded their king to lend him the use of as many sure mounts as could be found. And so it was that Arghadmon rode north with two thousand steeds but no army save a few score Alfar warriors.'

Master Fabula raised a hand as if he were conducting an orchestra, and suddenly from all around came a great noise of horses' hooves, of neighing and of whinnying. Many of the younger cadets gasped in excitement.

'And in every village and town he passed through, Arghadmon raised the Serpent Banner. Thousands of Humbalgogs flocked to the defence of their homeland under that emblem.'

That must be why the Grange had the symbol of the serpent everywhere, thought Thomas. It must have represented the Free Peoples. But how was the Glass connected with it? And how did his father come to have it?

Master Fabula went on to tell – with various sound effects – how Cernunnos and his army were eventually routed by the army of Arghadmon at Hammerhoe. The tale enthralled Thomas. Thomas touched the Glass and felt himself suddenly in the midst of battle.

A squat, green-skinned warrior dressed in black leather armour jumped down from a rock, narrowly missing Thomas's head. But the strange warrior didn't seem to see him, and ran toward the mass of the battle, a curved sword swinging in its short arms.

Thomas looked around. The grassy field played host to a ferocious battle. Green-skinned warriors screamed and slashed at enemies with their scimitars. Grey-skinned men with larger swords or maces appeared to be on the same side. Brown-haired men who wore little in the way of armour were falling back before the onslaught. Then there was a cheer. Others, taller than them, were pushing to the front line and, at their head, a man with long hair that shone the colour of the moon, and eyes like emeralds.

But before Thomas could see any more, he was somewhere else. On the edge of the battlefield perhaps. The baying of dogs sounded in his ears, and then the beasts burst out from a wooded area up ahead. Behind them emerged a chariot driven by a figure wearing great antlers upon his head.

The dogs stopped not a hundred yards from where Thomas stood clinging to a boulder, as if it could defend him. The huge hounds bayed, but now their attention seemed fixed on something else, something behind Thomas. He turned and swallowed hard. The giant serpent stood, extended to its greatest height, not a stone's throw away. It seemed larger now than Thomas ever remembered.

The chariot charged forward. The serpent shrieked and thrust itself forward at tremendous speed, its wings flapping like great sails. Thomas could feel the rush of air they generated. He was trapped. Still gripping the boulder, he pressed himself against it and awaited his doom.

'And this is the end of the tale,' Master Fabula finished as Thomas opened his eyes and found himself clinging to the beanbag. Everyone clapped as the fire flared up again. Fabula stood, bowed, and sat down again. 'Now, are there any questions?'

Thomas pulled his hand from his marble bag and silently rebuked himself. He looked around. No one appeared to have noticed his daydream – if it was a daydream.

One of the younger girls put her hand up and asked what the horses looked like. Master Fabula told her they were snowy white with mottled manes. Several other questions followed. Then Thayer put his hand up.

'Yes, Master Gaul?'

Thayer put his hand down, but was slow to ask his question. 'Were the Fomorfelk all killed?'

Master Fabula paused before he answered. 'I'm very much afraid they were if my memory serves me well, and it normally does.'

Thayer nodded, but Thomas thought he saw a little sorrow in the boy's normally expressionless face.

No one else raised their hand and Master Fabula, after exhaling one final large puff of smoke, dismissed the class, at which point the carved door swung open of its own free will.

Everyone headed for the door except Thomas. Master Fabula had turned toward the fire.

Thomas coughed. 'Master Fabula?'

'Yes?' The teacher turned around, smiling.

'Why did Arghadmon have a serpent on his banner?'

Master Fabula placed a black hand on the mantelpiece. 'It was the symbol of his lineage.'

There it was again. Lineage. Geneaology. 'Sir, I was wondering if anyone's been able to trace their family history without knowing who their parents were?'

Master Fabula raised an eyebrow. 'Not unless you're Veelan Medrevar.'

Thomas stared blankly at the Dewg.

'Veelan was a Humbalgog enchanter who live about a hundred years ago. He was the last known possessor of the Blood Parchment.'

'The Blood Parchment?'

'It was, as I understand it, a blank piece of parchment but possessed of the power to reveal a person's lineage clear back to the First Fathers of Avallach from a single drop of blood spilled upon it.' Master Fabula laughed. 'Still, the item may never have even existed. You could ask Miss Havelock, she knows more about enchanted artefacts than anyone else at the Academy. But why all these questions about banners and history?'

'Oh,' Thomas said feeling stupid, 'it's just that there's a lot of serpents about. One the drapes, the walls, even on the Academy badge.' He didn't feel the need to tell Fabula about the Glass.

'That is because this Academy was built by Arghadmon. Now, if you'll excuse me, I must prepare my recounting of the Founding of Nieberheim for my next class.' And with that he turned back to the fire and became lost in pipe smoke.

'What were you talking about?' Jessica asked as Thomas left the Hall of Tales, the door closing behind him of its own accord.

'Nothing much. He was just telling me about the founding of the Academy. It was built by Arghadmon.'

'I wonder how he died?' Merideah asked as they made their way back toward the Gardens.

'In a battle, I expect,' said Penders. 'It must be horrible to die like that. No guns or explosions, I guess, just swords and axes. Imagine being hacked down and then chopped into –'

'Yes, Penders,' Jessica interrupted. 'I won't imagine if you don't mind.'

Thomas ran a hand through his hair. Had his father died like that –hacked to pieces on some distant battlefield?

'He was slain by Cernunnos,' Thayer said.

The Fomorfelk must have rejoined them once he'd realised they'd lagged behind after class.

'What are guns?' Thayer asked.

Merideah put her hand to her chin. 'You know what a crossbow is?'

'Yes, I have used one before. A good weapon!'

'Well,' Merideah continued, 'it's a bit like a small crossbow that can fire lots of bolts very fast.'

A spark of wonder briefly crossed Thayer's face. It wasn't the most accurate of descriptions, but probably the best in a world that apparently hadn't yet discovered gunpowder. Or perhaps, thought Thomas, such things wouldn't work here, or weren't wanted. Maybe this Old Power was greater than the science of his world?

Thomas watched Thayer disappear into the distance as the carriage sped north toward the Inner Gate, but he didn't really see him. His mind was caught up with thoughts of the hidden room they'd found in the Hall, and what Master Fabula had said about the Blood Parchment.

# – CHAPTER EIGHTEEN –

## *The Blood Parchment*

During the following week the weather grew colder, and by Saturday a frost covered the ground. It still lay unmelted by the time Thomas and the others arrived in the Gardens of Arghadmon. Thayer Gaul stood waiting by the fountain. He didn't seem the least bit concerned about the chill air. They wore fur cloaks, but Thayer wore none.

'I hope you've not been here since we left?' Penders joked as he jumped from the carriage.

'Oh, no.' Thayer looked at Penders quite seriously.

Penders stopped smiling as they stepped out of the carriage and gathered around. 'So, Thayer. Where are we today?'

'It is a free Saturday. After breakfast you can do anything you want before the carriage returns, as long as you do not wander outside the Academy.'

Thomas whipped out the Glass as soon as they were in the Hall. 'I think we can trust Thayer, don't you?'

The others nodded as Thayer looked from face to face.

Jessica put a hand on the boy's shoulder. 'We're not leaving the Academy.'

Thayer nodded slowly. He looked back at the Glass as Thomas stepped up to the far wall between the drapes, and the concern in his face turned to wonder as the orb began to glow. 'What is that?'

Treice bent his head down to Thayer's ear. 'Thomas's dad gave it to him. It has some interesting abilities.'

Thomas touched the Glass against the wooden panels and, as before, the outline of a door appeared, winking out after a few moments to reveal the hidden chamber.

The children piled in, followed by a more cautious Thayer. The stone podium stood alone in the room. At its top sat the old parchment.

'What are we doing here?' Thayer glanced about the room nervously.

Thomas looked up at the blank parchment. 'Testing a theory.' Thomas put a chair beneath the podium. He'd told the others about the Blood Parchment during the week. At first he thought he might try it alone, but he didn't know how he'd get away from the others. Besides, they had a right to know their own lineages, too. Fabula had said it went back to the First Fathers. Thomas was sure that was longer ago than even Oliver Cromwell. So he'd told them all about it and they agreed to see if the parchment they'd found was the fabled Blood Parchment.

Penders shot a look back into the Hall. 'What now? Dugan will be back soon.'

'Now we find out a bit more about who we are!' Merideah pulled something from her robes. It was her prefect badge.

Penders rolled his eyes to the ceiling. 'Oh please, you can't wear that! It isn't going to impress Dugan or anyone.'

Merideah ignored him and stood on the chair. 'I'll go first.' She opened the badge and pricked a finger with the pin so that a small drop of blood appeared. After pressing her finger to the parchment, she stepped back so that the others could see. Nothing happened for a few seconds, but then a thin red line began to appear, stretching up the parchment and expanding into a great tree of names. Then, finally, a name a little larger than the rest appeared atop the page: *Svart*.

'What does it mean?' Penders asked.

'It's a family tree. My father and grandfather are here.' Merideah pointed to the bottom of the parchment. 'I don't know who Svart is though. Thayer, have you heard the names before?'

Thayer frowned. 'I do not think so, but I am not the best person to ask. My skill is with more practical things. You could ask Miss Havelock.'

The tree faded so that the parchment lay blank again. Merideah jumped down and wiped the pin with a handkerchief. 'Who's next? Thayer? We know your race, so maybe we could use you as a sort of control experiment?'

Thayer didn't seem to know what Merideah was talking about, but he volunteered all the same. Removing a small knife from his robes he cut a gash in his palm.

Thayer got up on the chair and let a few drops of blood fall onto the old paper. Thayer's ancestry gradually filled the parchment and ended at the top with the name *Tethra*.

Thayer clambered down and Merideah offered him her handkerchief. He stared at it blankly.

'It wasn't that emotional,' Penders said.

Merideah shook her head at Penders. 'It's for his hand, silly!'

Penders grinned.

Thayer held up his hand. It had already stopped bleeding. 'Tethra was the first king and father of the Fomorfelk.'

'I thought as much,' Merideah said. 'So that's how we tell what race we come from.'

Penders went next and the Parchment showed the name of Humbal atop his tree. There wasn't much doubt that Penders had Humbalgog blood in him, and so Humbal must've been the father of that people.

Treice went back to someone called Lios. As Treice had blue eyes and blond hair, it was likely Lios was the father of the Alfar.

Thomas and Jessica stood either side of the chair as Treice stepped down. Treice removed himself to the doorway. 'I'll keep a look out for Dugan.'

Jessica watched as the small pinprick of blood faded into the Blood Parchment. She waited, but nothing happened. A disappointed look on her face, she stepped down.

Thomas stared at the blank parchment once he'd climbed up onto the chair. Pricking his thumb, he took a deep breath and pushed it down onto the base of the parchment. He waited, but the canvas remained quite blank. Thomas felt a sudden emptiness.

'I wonder why nothing happened for us?' Jessica said. Thomas didn't know. It made no sense.

Merideah slipped her badge back into her cadet robes. 'I've got an idea.'

\* \* \*

'I don't see why we can't use the Anywhere Lift,' Penders complained, as he puffed his way up the stairs.

'The Headmaster said we can't use it unless we're with an adult,' Merideah reminded him.

'Yeah, but no one would know if we used it, would they?' Penders grinned at Merideah. 'I remember seeing a landing zone on the roof.'

'It only responds to the voice of the adults here at the Academy. Cadets cannot call it.' Thayer's words weren't laboured. Perhaps he was used to the climb.

Penders sighed. 'Not much use it going anywhere if you can't use it. What we need's an Anywhere and Anyone Lift!'

'Or perhaps some exercise?' said Jessica with a hint of sarcasm. Penders didn't reply but focused on climbing the winding stairs instead.

'Why are we going to that room again, anyway?' Penders complained. 'I'm using up all my energy and I didn't get much breakfast before Dugan came and cleared it all up!'

'Perhaps someone noticed the book Havelock took down from the shelf when we were last there?' Merideah asked as they approached the door.

No one answered. Merideah reached for the door knob.

'What if Havelock's in there?' Thomas said.

Merideah shrugged. 'We're allowed to go anywhere in the Academy, aren't we?'

Thayer nodded, though he didn't seem convinced.

Miss Havelock wasn't in the room. Merideah got Treice to hand down the large book from the shelf. Thomas read the title of the book: *An A-Z of Major Events, Characters, Places and Artefacts in the History of Avallach*. It was some kind of encyclopaedia. The children were soon kneeling around the large book as it lay open on the floor.

'Ah, here's B,' Merideah said as she flicked through the heavy pages. 'Ballads – Ballybogs – Bellibones – Yes, here it is: Blood Parchment!' She scanned the entry and then tapped her chin in thought. Treice, Penders and Thayer stared at her.

'Ah, right, yes,' she began as she prepared to read. 'The origins of the Blood Parchment are lost in history, but some say it was created by the Humbalgog enchanters before the Bounding was created in order to provide a means to distinguish between the Humbalgogs and Humans who then both inhabited Avallach. The Parchment would reveal a Humbalgog lineage when it came into contact with the blood of the same, but remain blank when the blood of a Human was exposed to it. It is also said to have been able to determine the bloodline of other races then extant in Avallach. The Blood Parchment fell out of use after the Bounding came into existence, and was subsequently lost to history. Some believe it never existed and was a mere fabrication to impress the enemies of the Humbalgogs.'

'Well, I guess we're one hundred percent human, Thomas,' Jessica said, nudging him. Thomas smiled, but confusion swept through his mind. He felt familiar with the world of Avallach and its people, and a foreigner in his own world of Holten Layme. He couldn't be fully human.

'What's this Bounding?' Jessica asked Thayer.

'It is the border between your world and ours,' Thayer explained.

Merideah's nose twitched excitedly. 'The "veil of mist" Master Fabula mentioned at the Feast of Fires?'

Thayer nodded.

Merideah turned the large pages until she was about half way through the leather-bound tome. 'Lios was the forefather of the Alfar.' She continued to the letter S. 'And Svart was the ancestral father of the Drough.'

'Who are they?' asked Treice.

'I'm not sure if they still exist,' began Thayer, 'but they were related to the Alfar. They were the most trusted servants of the Horned One it is said. Very evil and very powerful.'

Penders smiled. 'That explains a lot about Merideah.'

Merideah fixed her smouldering amber eyes on Penders, but before she could say anything Jessica shouted excitedly.

'Thomas!' Jessica stared at the page now open. There before them lay a drawing of the Glass. Thomas reached down to his marble bag and pulled the Glass free.

'That looks a lot like it, Thomas,' Penders eventually said.

'Yes,' Thomas said, still somewhat dumbfounded. 'But what's it doing in here?'

'Perhaps there's more than one of them?' Penders suggested.

'Read it, Thomas,' Jessica said, as she pointed to the small paragraph below the drawing.

Thomas's eyes found the short entry on the page beneath the illustration. *Gloine Nathair* was the title of the entry, and, immediately following, it read *The Serpent Glass or Serpent in the Glass.*

Thomas looked at Jessica who'd clearly already read it. How could he have known what it was called?

'Out loud,' said Treice, who could only see the writing upside down from where he knelt.

Thomas placed a finger on the text and began to read. 'The Gloine Nathair is a unique object' – so much for Penders' idea – 'of which little is known. It is mentioned in the *Chronicles of Avallach* (Volume I, page 127) as being used by King Avallach's enchanters in reference to the creation of the Bounding. According to Professor Maltheus Nynth (1701-1788) the "small glowing orb" used by Rufus Marmanstane, last of the great enchanters, and mentioned in a later volume of the Chronicles, is this very same art fact – '

'Artefact,' Merideah corrected.

'Artefact,' Thomas said. 'If so, the Gloine Nathair also held the power not only to pass, but also to heal Way Gates. Later Alfar enchanters were unable to use the Gloine Nathair and its power was considered spent. It was subsequently stored away in the vault of the Alfar kings and, as far as anyone knows, remains there to this day.'

There the text ended. Thomas sat back and pondered what he'd just read. 'But how'd my father get it?'

'I don't know, but it explains why we were able to come through the Way Gate that first night, and why Stanwell and the others have to use a password.'

Merideah was right, but Thomas couldn't believe his father was a thief. But how did his father come to possess the Glass? Was someone else looking for it? Was he in danger? He thought about Gallowglas checking his room every night. And why did the book say the Glass had lost its power? He'd used it to enter the Way Gate. He'd seen it glow and felt the life in it. It was far from spent. No, the Glass was very much alive.

## – CHAPTER NINETEEN –

# *The Way Gates*

The Christmas holiday passed all too slowly for Thomas. Even Jessica seemed more interested in returning to Darkledun than staying in Birch Tree Close. Christmas wasn't much to look forward to in the Westhrop household. A single piece of tinsel hung near the front door; a solitary token of the Yule season to any visitors. Not that there were many of those.

Mr Westhrop had wasted no time in renting out Jessica's room. Jessica only had her room until the end of the holiday, when the lodger returned from visiting his parents. Jessica found bicycle parts in her bedroom, and several of her stuffed toys had been shoved under her bed along with some of her adventure novels.

Nothing else had really changed at the Westhrop home. There were no Christmas presents on Christmas day, except one from Aunt Dorothy of course. This year she'd bought Thomas a gigantic blow-up beach ball with the buy-one-get-one-free label still attached.

Other than putting up the single strand of tinsel, Mrs Westhrop seemed to have entirely forgotten it was Christmas. Mr Westhrop knew full well it was Christmas and was doing his best to ignore it, despite a firework display on Christmas Eve not too many doors away. 'Don't they know how much they cost!' Mr Westhrop had complained after the first dozen fireworks scattered their green sparks over his garden. 'Perhaps one or two on Bonfire Night. Yes, that's quite enough for any normal person!' Mr Westhrop had one year calculated the cost of each second of 'pleasure' of a firework's life once lit. Thomas seemed to remember that sparklers were the most cost-effective.

Despite all this, Thomas enjoyed Christmas. The world appeared a little more magical at that time of year. But Thomas couldn't help such thoughts drawing his mind back to the Grange. That was magical too.

The Saturdays at the Academy had been going well. Thayer had introduced them to his father, Master Bellows, and they'd even had dinner in their cabin. Fabula's stories seemed to grow more wonderful everytime they visited the Hall of Tales. In the last week of term there'd been a story involving a waterfall, and the Hall of Tales had produced the most impressive sound of water falling over rocks. Master Fabula's lessons had sparked memories in him. He'd been careful not to touch the Glass during the stories, so he knew the images he saw were entirely his own. But where they came from, he didn't know – an overactive imagination, perhaps?

The revelation that neither of his parents had the blood of Avallach perplexed him. He'd thought long into the night about what that could mean. Maybe his father had been a friend to someone in Avallach. Maybe that was how he came to possess the Glass. Trevelyan knew, Thomas was sure, but this mysterious representative of his father's estate had forbidden the Headmaster from telling him more. Thomas wondered how he could find out who the representative was, but no answer had yet come into his head.

Jessica, despite her initial disappointment, had grown to quite cherish being the only full-blooded human at the Grange, save Thomas. But this brought up other questions: if the purpose of the Manor was to look for Halfkin, then why had he been invited? What possible reason did the school have for accepting his father's wishes in the first place? And why did his father want him there anyway? These questions had occupied Thomas's mind as he'd travelled back to the Manor for the start of the new term.

As Thomas walked through the Way Gate onto Cnocmorandolmen the crisp winter air surrounded him. Yet it wasn't as cold as the world he'd just left behind. It was always warmer here, and more untouched in some way. And then there was the heightened sense of smell, of hearing, of vision. He'd mentioned the sensation at the end of last term, only to be met with blank stares from his friends. But Thomas couldn't believe it was just his imagination.

Miles Merlock and Tara Reeves stepped into the edge of his vision, followed by Jessica, Merideah, Penders, Treice and the remainder of the Family History Club. The members had been waiting outside 2B alongside Jessica and Merideah when Thomas, Penders and Treice arrived that morning. He'd no idea why. Perhaps Stanwell had been too busy to take them through last night, or maybe they had a new schedule for the new term.

While he waited for Stanwell to emerge, Thomas wandered over to the Northern Way Gate. It bore the same familiar symbols. Sometimes their meaning seemed only a sliver away, but then it would slip beyond his reach again.

Thomas reached out and touched the grey stone. This one felt cold and still, as if dead. The other two Way Gates felt warm and tingled his palm.

'Thomas!' Jessica warned.

Stanwell had just come through the Way Gate with the last of the Club members. Thomas ducked around one of the stones and made his way back to the rear of the group. Stanwell didn't like cadets going near the other Way Gates.

When they reached the carriage, Tara and Miles joined them in the first coach.

Jessica spoke to Tara as soon as they were seated. 'How come you're with us today, anyway?'

'The Way Gate wasn't working last night,' Tara said.

'Wasn't working?' Penders turned toward her. 'You mean they don't work all the time?'

'It happens every now and again, though this is the first time – as far as I know – that it's taken so many hours to recover,' Miles explained.

Merideah put a finger to her chin. 'Interesting.'

Thomas decided to take advantage of the momentary silence. 'What about the other Way Gates?'

'Worse, from what I hear,' Miles said.

'Do you know where they lead?' Thomas asked as the carriage hit a bump in the road. Stanwell cried out something about tree roots.

'If I remember correctly, the East Way Gate leads to the land of the Humbalgogs, Humbalhame, and the West Gate to Alfheim, the land of the Alfar.'

Thomas leant forward on his seat. 'What about the northern one? Where does that go?'

Miles shook his head and looked at Tara, but she just shrugged.

'It's cold,' Thomas said.

Penders stopped chewing his gum. 'I can turn the climate control up if you like?'

'We don't want to be plunged into a cloud of fog again,' Merideah said.

'That wasn't my fault,' Penders defended himself. 'If you hadn't –'

'I meant the Northern Way Gate,' Thomas interrupted before the exchange became a heated one. 'It seems "dead".'

Tara shook her head. 'Maybe it's not used anymore. I've never heard anyone speak about it.'

'We could ask Miss Havelock,' Treice suggested. He sat opposite Jessica, staring out of the window. Being with two girls was bad enough, but now Treice had to endure three.

Thomas leant back into his seat again. 'Well, we could, but I think I'll try Thayer first – he's more…'

'Approachable?' Penders grinned.

Thayer waited as always at the fountain. His dull eyes lit up when he saw all the Halfkin were with Thomas. He seemed to enjoy the company of the Club members more than the cadets from his own world. The Club members all rushed off to prepare for their morning of combat training in the Ring as Penders looked on jealously.

'Did you enjoy the holidays?' Thomas asked Thayer after they'd greeted one another.

'No holidays in Avallach,' Thayer said in his usual morose tone.

Thomas immediately felt bad for asking the question. War, of course, had no holidays. He decided to quickly change the subject. 'Do you know anything about the Northern Way Gate on Cnocmorandolmen?'

'I have only been to the Hill of Stones once, when I first arrived. I was very young.' Thayer stared blankly at Thomas. 'The only cadets, besides the Halfkin, who go to that Hill now are those going to serve in the army. Gallowglas escorts them in and out. Maybe you could ask him?'

Penders rolled his eyes. 'Not much chance he'd tell us.'

Laughter filled their ears as they entered the Hall. Not merry laughter – cruel laughter. Dugan Buglebeard stood precariously on a stool furiously scrubbing the wall with a hard-bristled brush. Soapy water dripped down his arms to the floor beneath, where it formed a small pool of bubbles and water. On the wall Thomas could make out words through the foam: *Stubby – scrub this off if you can reach!*

'Hello, sir!' said Thayer to the Dwerugh. 'What are you doing up there?'

Thayer had obviously not seen the writing. 'Up there' wasn't that high. Even on the stool, Dugan was little taller than Treice. Dugan paused and looked at Thayer as if he'd just noticed he was there.

'Well,' he huffed, 'it's good to see that some students still respect their elders! I've been here since the Academy opened, and those Firdheeg have always been the same!'

Thayer blinked. 'You have been up there since the Academy opened?'

Dugan eyed the Formorfelk, but then decided to shake his head instead.

Thomas had an idea. 'Mr Buglebeard?'

Dugan looked him up and down. 'Ah, Thomas Farrell, if I'm not mistaken. I'm afraid I'm too high today to be tripped over so –'

'Er, I don't want to trip over you. I wanted to ask you a question,' Thomas interrupted.

'You do?' Dugan swayed slightly on the stool. 'Spit it out then, I haven't got all day!'

'I wondered, seeing as you've been at the Academy so long, if you knew anything about the Way Gate that seems, well, sort of dead?'

The Dwerugh frowned and his brow became even more creased. 'Maybe I do and maybe I don't.'

Merideah folded her arms and gave Dugan a look every bit as stubborn as his own. 'Well, if you do then can you tell us because we have research to do?'

Thomas preferred asking questions than sneaking about to look in books, but he was glad to have her support.

Dugan shot a look of displeasure in her direction before he turned back to Thomas. 'And why would you want to know?'

Merideah sighed. 'Oh, come on,' she said to Thomas. 'It's not important. Jessica and me want read a book Tara has on the fauna and flora of Avallach. She said we could –'

'NOT IMPORTANT?' For a moment Thomas thought Dugan might launch himself off the stool at Merideah, but at the last moment he controlled himself. 'Why it leads to the Dwerughnook, one of the most beautiful lands in Avallach! You won't find crags as splendid anywhere else! Ah, and the rocky earth and great boulders! Flora and fauna indeed! The Dwerughnook has some of the finest lichens, and brooks teeming with the finest fish – and you should see the size of the hares, oh and the pot-belly boars. You have not lived until you have tasted the meat of one of those beauties!'

'The Dwerughnook?' Thomas asked.

Thayer turned his expressionless face toward Thomas. 'It is where the Dwerugh come from.'

Dugan didn't seem to be listening. 'That was before it faded. Poor old Dugan was shut out! He wanted to go home, but couldn't. He had to stay in the Grange with no mountains, no boulders, no crags – and disrespectful cadets!'

He sat down on the stool. His feet didn't reach the floor but dangled there several inches above the soapy pool beneath.

'It was nine winters ago,' Dugan continued in what for him was a very gentle voice. 'Reports came in of the Horned One leading an army against Nieberheim, the chief city of the Dwerugh. All the Dwerugh from the Grange left to defend their ancestral home, but I got delayed and couldn't leave until a few days later. When Trevelyan took me to Cnocmorandolmen we found the Way Gate had faded. It had done it before, of course, but had always opened again. This time it didn't. I got cut off. Stuck here in this hollow hill that doesn't even look like a hill, or a mountain –'

'There were other Dwerugh here once?' Thomas asked.

'Yes, yes of course! We were the largest group here after the Humbalgogs, "the Hammer of the Free Peoples" they called us when we marched in their ranks.' Dugan's face glowed with pride.

Penders shoved his hands in his pockets. 'Couldn't Trevelyan do something about the Gate? I mean, being a powerful enchanter and all.'

Dugan gave a short gravelly laugh. 'No, Mr Penderghast, it's beyond even his power. The Dwerugh may have built them, but it is the De Danann whose power flows through them and makes them work. Once a Way Gate has faded it has gone forever.'

Thomas frowned. Master Fabula had mentioned that race at the Feast of Fires. De Danann. The name stirred a memory, an old memory, but where could he have possibly heard it before? 'The Dwerugh built the Way Gates?'

'Are you deaf as well as blind?' Dugan scowled, but then seemed to recover suddenly from his bad temper. 'It was Dwerugh masons of Nieberheim who carved out the stones from the mountains, but that was many generations ago.'

'And the writing on the  top of the Way Gates?' Thomas pressed.

'De Danann glyphs. I doubt there's anyone alive today who could read them, save perhaps Cernunnos!'

Thomas nodded. 'But there must be another way to get to your land?'

'Yes, there's another way, but it'd mean leaving the Grange through the Outer Gate.'

'Would that be a long journey?' Jessica asked.

'Long? Yes, or very short. The Horned One controls the lands about the sidhe. Has done for many years. It's infested with Hobhoulards and other fouler things.' Dugan smiled, revealing a mouth of broken and missing teeth. 'Poor old Dugan wouldn't stand a chance. He's not the young warrior he used to be a couple of centuries ago.'

'A couple of CENTURIES ago?' Merideah looked shocked. 'How old are you?'

Dugan stood up on the stool again. 'Four hundred and eighty-seven! Ah, poor old Dugan would love to see his homeland again, that he would. And talk and drink with his old fellow warriors in the mead halls! Yes, that he would…'

The Dwerugh continued to talk to himself as he started scrubbing the wall again. He seemed to have forgotten the children were there. Thomas and the others decided to leave him to his thoughts.

\* \* \*

Thomas lay in his bed that night staring at the Glass on the bedside cabinet, thinking about Cnocmorandolmen, the De Danann, and even poor old Dugan. But it was the image of the Northern Way Gate that prevailed in his consciousness. Something felt wrong. Incomplete. Dugan had said it had 'faded', and nothing could be done about it. But there was more to it than that, he was sure of it.

Thomas looked up at the blue sky. A tall figure carried him away from a stone building, from comfort, from home. The scene changed to one of sunlight and trees followed by a blinding light that left him and the man standing before what looked like a giant fireplace filled with glowing coals, except it wasn't a fireplace – it was the wall of a cavern. It pulsed like a living heart, and that beat echoed from three other caverns. Then Thomas felt fear in the one who bore him – no, not fear, concern; a concern for Thomas's safety. There came another blinding light, and a flash of stone pillars with words written upon them high above. Thomas felt a chill breeze as images of a dark forest passed before his eyes. Then came darkness and silence.

Thomas sat bolt upright. He now knew what he had to do.

## – CHAPTER TWENTY –

## *Cnocmorandolmen*

The winter passed with only a few days of snow in early February, which made Master Fabula's fire-warmed Hall of Tales all the more inviting. March and April grew steadily warmer and wetter, and the Easter holiday came and went at the Westhrops' without so much as a chocolate egg (although Aunt Dorothy would no doubt send one to the family in May after taking advantage of the buy-three-for-the-price-of-one offers). The Westhrops' lodger had gone, the only trace of his stay being a rusty bicycle chain left dangling from the hook on Jessica's door. Mr Westhrop had spent most of the holidays complaining about the thirty pounds the *Holten Layme Weekly Herald* had charged to place a new ad for lodgers. But holidays far from the Manor, and even Master Fabula's tale-filled firesides, hadn't dislodged Thomas's thoughts about the Northern Way Gate. Yet he still hadn't told anyone what he'd decided to do.

'How are you going to get to Cnocmorandolmen without anyone noticing?' Jessica suddenly asked one April morning as the two of them left registration.

Thomas stared at her. 'What are you talking about, Jess?'

'Come on, Thomas, I know the way you think. You're going to' – she looked around to make sure no one was listening or within earshot – 'try and heal the Northern Way Gate with the Glass, aren't you?'

Thomas frowned. It was useless trying to keep anything from Jessica. 'What makes you say that?'

'You were very quiet over the holiday, and you've been in a daze ever since – not to mention that you keep staring at the Way Gates a lot. So you're thinking about something. So I thought back to last term, and then I thought about what it said in that book – about the Glass being able to heal Way Gates. You want to prove that your Glass is the one in the book!'

Thomas sighed. 'Do you remember that dream I keep having?'

Jessica stopped. 'The one where someone's carrying you?'

Thomas nodded. He'd told Jessica about the recurring dream years ago. 'The glowing fireplace I saw, it wasn't a fireplace. It was the inside of a Way Gate. I had the dream again and this time I felt the Way Gates – all four of them – beating together like a heart. They're meant to work together, Jess. It must be why the other Gates are becoming less reliable. If the Glass can open the faded Way Gate then it might lead me closer to knowing who my parents were.'

Jessica thought for a moment. 'But you could give it to Trevelyan. If he can't do it, no one can.'

Thomas bit his lip. He didn't know how to put this, but he tried. 'If my father stole the Glass, or even if he didn't, maybe someone's looking for it? Maybe the Alfar or maybe someone who would give it to Cernunnos. Then everyone in the Grange would be in danger! I don't know who to trust. I think it's what I felt in my dream – someone pursuing my father so they could get the Glass.'

Jessica nodded slowly. 'OK, I understand. So, do you know how to heal it?'

Thomas shook his head. It was one of the things that had stopped him from acting, that and the fact that he just didn't know how to get to the northern Way Gate alone. Stanwell was with them all the time, and McGritch now kept both her bunches of keys with her at all times.

Jessica looked at Thomas for a few seconds as if trying to make a decision in her own mind. 'So, how *are* you going to get to Cnocmorandolmen without anyone noticing?'

Thomas shoved his hands in his pockets. 'I don't know.'

'I thought you wouldn't,' said Jessica with a wry smile. 'That's why I've thought up a plan...'

* * *

The jacket looked out of place on Thayer as the children made their way from the Hall of Arghadmon the following Saturday. Finding clothing large enough hadn't been easy. In the end they'd 'borrowed' a bomber jacket from the Manor's cloakroom because it was the only one both wide enough and short enough for the Fomorfelk. Thomas hoped it wouldn't be missed by the owner. They'd have it back by Saturday evening latest, if all went to plan.

'Remember, keep to the bushes and follow us to the carriage,' Jessica said as they stepped out into the small courtyard between the Academy and the Gardens of Arghadmon.

Thayer nodded seriously. Thomas knew why he'd agreed to the plan. Thayer knew what it was like to be separated from his own people. He wanted to help Dugan. But, more than that, he felt part of their little group now. A friend.

Jessica bent and whispered in Thayer's ear. 'Slip into the end coach when I give the signal.'

'Yes,' Thayer said as he pulled the bomber jacket closer about him and looked about furtively. Thomas hoped this all went OK. If he got anyone into trouble, especially Thayer, he wouldn't forgive himself. Of course, Jessica had roped everyone into the scheme.

Thayer hung back behind a short hedge while Thomas and the others approached the Darkledun carriage.

'There you be!' Stanwell wore a large grin beneath his three-cornered hat. 'Well, jump in and we'll be off.'

Thomas moved to the front of the carriage. 'Er, Stanwell?'

'Yes, Thomas?'

'Could you show me how to drive the carriage?' Thomas said.

'Well, I'm not sure Trevelyan would want you drivin' around,' he said, frowning. Thomas gave him the most disappointed look he could muster. 'But I s'pose ol' Stanwell could show you the basics and you can learn if you watch carefully. Watch mind, nothin' more unless I do be sayin' so.'

'Great!' Thomas said, as he climbed up next to Stanwell and the rest of them stepped into the end coach.

'So how do you hold the reins then?' Thomas asked.

'Ah, well it do be a subtle skill, but you need to be firm too…'

Thomas stole a quick glance behind while Stanwell instructed him on the use of the reins. He saw Jessica make the signal and then a khaki bomber jacket with two legs sticking out of the bottom made a mad dash to the carriage, tripped over the wooden step beneath the door and went flying into the coach. There was a small scream followed by a bump.

Stanwell looked around just as the coach door closed.

'In the end coach today, eh?' he asked.

'Yes, Jessica likes the view out of the rear window,' Thomas replied, a forced smile on his face.

Stanwell nodded. 'Yes, I do be 'earin'. Sounds like she's excited about it already!'

As the carriage pulled out of the gardens, Thomas gave a sigh of relief. The next stage of the plan was going to be far more tricky than the first.

'Y'know,' Stanwell said, as Cnocmorandolmen came into sight through the trees, 'the carriage do seem 'eavier today.'

Thomas gulped. He hoped Stanwell wouldn't question him. Thomas couldn't lie. He'd go red and lose his voice.

'I do be thinkin' some of your friends 'ave put on a little weight. Probably that Plundervast. Always do be eatin' when I see 'im!'

'Ah, yes! Yes, that's probably it,' said Thomas, with a nervous laugh.

'Right, 'ere we are,' Stanwell said, as he brought the carriage to a stop. 'You get changed quickly now!'

Thomas climbed down and moved to the back coach. Jessica was rubbing her knee. He took a quick peek in the end coach. It looked empty.

'Is he out?' Thomas asked, keeping his voice low.

'Yes, he's behind the bush on the other side.' Merideah flicked her head toward a bush.

'Great!' said Thomas. 'We should have plenty of time.'

After Thomas had changed back into his casual clothes, Stanwell took the carriage back to the long, wooden building he called the coach house. Once he'd pulled out of sight, the children called Thayer out from the bush, and they all made their way to Cnocmorandolmen. Thomas pulled out the Glass. Its glow was visible even in broad daylight.

Thayer still seemed fascinated by the Glass, even though it wasn't the first time he'd seen it.

'Stanwell!' Merideah hissed.

Thomas spun around and saw Stanwell making his way though the trees. Why was he back so soon?

Thomas shoved the Glass into Thayer's hand. 'Quick, go through and hide!'

Thayer dashed through the Way Gate but, to Thomas's surprise, the boy came out the other side. It hadn't worked. Just as Stanwell came up the hill Thayer ducked behind the stones.

'You weren't long!' Merideah said, as Stanwell reached them.

Stanwell smiled. 'No, I met ol' Chinwag, and 'e offered to unharness the 'orses later; 'e likes to be doing a night shift every now and again, so I's let 'im.' Thomas had no idea who Chinwag was, but he'd picked a bad day to help Stanwell out.

'Dinnsenchas!' the Caretaker called out, as he walked past Treice and Penders, whose eyes flickered to the stone behind which Thayer hid.

Stanwell ushered the children through and, a little reluctantly, they stepped into the golden flash of light. Thomas wondered what they could do, but Stanwell urged them on.

'Come now, I do be 'avin' to be back in two hours and only 'ave a little time to clean out my pond and get a little bellytimber!' Stanwell said.

Wondering briefly what on earth bellytimber was, Thomas followed the others back into 2B.

After closing the door, Stanwell led the children down the corridor, at which point he left them and went to his office. Thomas and the others kept walking until they reached a turning in the corridor.

Jessica pulled on her hair. 'Why couldn't Thayer get through? He had the Glass.'

Thomas shrugged. 'I don't know.' The door to 2B could be unlatched from inside without a key. It had been Thayer's part to hide in the tower and then open the door. The plan seemed to have fallen apart.

'Maybe the stones briefly stopped working again?' Penders suggested. The Way Gate had failed again some weeks ago, but it had not been brief and the entire Club had been unable to go to the Grange that weekend.

Jessica silenced them all with a raised arm. Stanwell had emerged from his room. They all pressed themselves against the wall.

'My, those were ugly!' Jessica said once the Caretaker had lolloped past them in a pair of green waders.

'Let's go,' Thomas said. He felt terrible. If Thayer had been caught on Cnocmorandolmen, how would he get back to the Grange?

Thomas put his ear against the door to 2B as the others crowded behind. He couldn't hear a thing. He tried the handle, but the door didn't budge. Stanwell had locked it.

'We'll have to go,' Merideah said, casting furtive glances up the corridor. 'Thayer can hide in the carriage and get back to the Grange when Stanwell returns.'

Then suddenly the room to 2B opened and in the doorway stood the Fomorfelk. He hadn't switched the lights on.

Thomas smiled. 'Thayer! You got through!'

'Yes, I slipped in behind Stanwell and hid behind the stones again while he opened that gate in the wall. I am sorry I took so long. It was dark and it took me a while to find this latch.'

'The lights are here.' Jessica flicked the switch after they all slipped into the classroom.

Thayer looked up in awe. 'These long, flat lamps on the ceiling, what gives them their light? I thought the Old Power did not exist in your world?'

'It's electricity,' Merideah said.

Thayer gave her a blank look.

Merideah thought for a moment. 'It's a sort of energy, the same that makes lightning.'

Thayer's eyes widened. 'Your world can trap the power of lightning and use it?'

'Sort of,' Merideah replied as they all stepped through the doorway to the tower.

Thayer closed the concealed gate by means of a lever sticking out from the tower's wall. He looked back, still in wonder, as the stone grated back down and shut out the artificial light. It had never crossed Thomas's mind that someone from Avallach might find his world as fascinating as he found Avallach.

Merideah moved toward the Way Gate. 'Right, let's get on with it then.'

'Wait, I want to try something,' Thomas said. 'Thayer, where's the Glass?'

'Oh, I forgot. Here it is,' he said as he pulled the orb from one of the pockets of the bomber jacket.

Thomas didn't take it from him. 'Try walking through the Way Gate again.'

Thayer shrugged and walked up to the Gate, walked through and stayed quite visible as he came out the other side.

Penders frowned. 'Did it stop working again? How will we get through? Maybe the Glass doesn't work anymore?'

'Maybe,' said Merideah. 'Penders, why don't you try?'

'What? OK, but I don't see how it'll make any difference,' he said as he took the Glass from Thayer and walked through the stones. Nothing happened. Merideah tried too, and Treice and Jessica.

'Dinnsenchas!' Penders said in exasperation, but nothing happened.

'That only works for Trevelyan and a few others,' Thayer said. 'Not for cadets.'

'Did you see?' Merideah said.

'What?' Penders asked. 'I saw nothing. It's not working. We're going to have to find somewhere for Thayer to hide until the Club members come back Sunday evening.'

'No, no. Let me make it more obvious,' Merideah began. 'Thomas, go over to the Way Gate, but don't go through.'

'Well, he can't, can he? The stupid thing –'

'Be quiet!' Merideah interrupted. 'Just observe things for once, Marvin Penderghast!'

'Marvin?' Thayer repeated.

Penders bit his lip, but the red face showed his mood.

'Look at the Glass, not the Gate,' Merideah said.

They all looked. The Glass was glowing.

'It wasn't glowing until I put it in Thomas's hand,' Merideah said. 'Thomas, go through the Way Gate.'

He stepped through the Way Gate. There was the usual flash of gold light, and Thomas found himself in the glowing cavern. He turned around and saw the others on the other side all staring in surprise. He walked back out into the tower.

'It only works for you!' Jessica said what everyone else was thinking. Thomas had worked that much out. Perhaps because it was his father's Glass? But the book in the library said it belonged to the Alfar kings.

'We'd better go through if we're still going to do this,' said Jessica. 'Thomas?'

'Yes,' Thomas said, clearing his thoughts. 'Let's go.'

Once through the stones, Thomas and the others swiftly made their way to the Northern Way Gate. There seemed to be a difference in the order of the symbols on the other Way Gate, but perhaps he was imagining it. Thomas took a deep breath. He held the Glass up and nothing happened.

'Try entering it,' Penders suggested.

'That might be dangerous,' Merideah warned.

'I don't know what else to do,' Thomas said, so he touched the Glass against the stones as he had touched it against the wooden panelling in the Hall. As soon as he did so a blue film flared out across the entrance and the Glass began to glow very brightly. The energy began to crackle. Thomas backed away.

'Quick, to the trees!' Merideah shouted as the blue light pulsated, warped and became even more unstable.

The children moved back down the hill to the edge of the trees as the blue energy crackled and winked out with a loud crack.

'Is it healed?' Thayer asked Thomas as they both poked their heads out from behind the same tree.

Thomas shook his head. 'I don't know.'

Penders had his hand to his chest. There was a pained expression upon his face.

'You all right?' Jessica said.

'Stabbing pain in my chest – really hurts,' Penders, whose face was now red, breathed out with difficulty.

'Indigestion probably,' Merideah suggested.

'Lack of food more likely, I've not eaten since breakfast!'

Merideah opened her mouth, but before she responded a terrible noise ripped through the air. To Thomas it seemed like a wolf's cry, except deeper, louder and a lot scarier. It came from the Way Gate.

'What was that?' Treice asked nervously from behind a tree several yards further back into the copse.

The children stared, wide-eyed, at what now emerged from the Northern Way Gate. Covered in green fur, it possessed a solitary malicious-looking eye above which thrust a thick horn. It was so big that it barely fitted through the Way Gate.

Penders didn't turn his head as he spoke to Treice. 'Does that answer your question?'

Treice didn't answer. The creature had spotted the six children at the edge of the trees, and was looking at them with its very cruel single eye.

'I don't think it's happy,' Jessica managed to whimper.

The creature roared and the children ran. It came thundering after them as they headed for the thicker part of the copse. Glancing back, Thomas saw the beast uproot a tree that lay in its path, snapping it like a branch. The children worked their way deeper into the trees but the foliage wasn't dense enough to hide. Then the coach house came into view. Along the side ran glassless windows. Thomas ran toward them, clambering up and through the nearest window. A bale of straw broke his fall. He found himself in a small cubicle. As he stood up Thayer came blundering through the window behind him.

'Eek!' A thin creature no taller than his waist, clothed in white furs and carrying a small pitchfork, was staring at him and Thayer in shock. It scurried off at breakneck speed, dropping the pitchfork.

'What was that?' Thomas asked.

'Just a hodge-pocker,' Thayer said as he stood up and looked about. 'They help keep things tidy.' Thayer opened the bolt on the door.

Thomas and Thayer slipped into the middle of the building where stood the Darkledun carriage. The others appeared from the stalls at the same time that something heavy slammed against the wall of the building, shattering the planks.

'The carriage!' Thomas shouted. 'Before it breaks through!'

Treice, Penders and the girls dived into the first coach.

'Get the doors!' Thomas shouted to Thayer as he jumped up to the driver's seat. He hoped his brief lesson with Stanwell would pay off.

Thayer ran to the main doors, unbolted them and pushed them wide open. Once Thayer had pulled himself up onto the driver's seat, Thomas flicked the reins. The horses were restless. They could hear the creature trying to break through the side of the building. But they weren't moving.

'Move!' said Thayer.

Nothing changed.

'Rarrrrrr!' The creature had broken through. The horses bolted forward, almost knocking Thomas over the back of the seat. The carriage thundered up the track. The creature ran after them. It was moving fast.

The horses were running out of sheer fright, following the only path they knew. And it didn't look like they were going to pay any heed to anything Thomas did with the reins.

'Did we lose it?' Penders popped up out of the sunroof and cast his eyes about wildly.

Thomas looked back. The creature jumped as it ran, its powerful legs propelling it closer.

Penders gripped hold of the coach. 'It's ugly.'

'It'll be uglier if it gets any closer!' Merideah said, as she poked her head through the hole. 'Can't you go faster?'

Thomas shook his head. 'The horses just bolted – and they're still bolting! We've got no control over them.'

Merideah shook her head as the carriage hurtled past two Darkledun Guards who, had they faces, would've had shocked expressions upon them. Thomas glanced back as the Guards noticed the creature and attempted to stop it with their spears. The creature swatted one into the trees and trampled the other with its hooves. Still, they'd slowed it down, and now Thomas thought they might have a chance of reaching the Inner Gate.

The Gate! How were they going to get through the Gate? They were already nearing the huge wooden portals.

Merideah bounced as they hit a bump. 'I don't remember seeing anything like it in Tara's book on the flora and fauna of Avallach. I wonder what sort of creature it is?'

'An angry one if you ask me.' Penders made room as Jessica and Treice emerged either side of him.

Ahead a dozen Darkledun Guards gathered near the Inner Gate.

'Slow us down, Thomas!' Jessica shouted. 'The Guards will deal with it!'

'I can't slow us down!' said Thomas, as the wooden portal loomed before them.

'Goibhniu!' shouted Merideah. Nothing happened. It was quite pointless of course. Stanwell had said the password for the Gate wouldn't work for cadets. Nevertheless this didn't stop them all from trying, all except Thomas who was desperately trying to rein in the horses before they hit the Inner Gate and splintered the carriage into a thousand pieces, leaving them all to the mercy of the beast.

The Guards were stirring now. They'd seen the creature and were raising their spears in response.

'Open the gates!' Merideah shouted to the Guards, but they didn't seem to understand.

The horses continued. Why weren't they stopping? Surely they could see the Gate now? Perhaps they were so used to it opening that they didn't even consider that it might not. There was no time left, unless the door opened now they were going to crash into it.

'GOIBHNIU!' Thomas shouted in a voice that didn't sound quite his own.

The Inner Gate swung open. The carriage rushed through, almost clipping the sides of the great portals.

They all looked at him, but he shook his head. 'The Guards must've opened it.' But he knew inside that the Gates had opened because he'd told them to. Stanwell's words came back into his thoughts. *We couldn't 'ave any ol' Fintan, Fingal, or Flaherty openin' the Gate, now could we?*

Thomas still held one of the reins. 'Thayer, pull your rein as hard as you can, after three! One – two – three!'

They yanked on the reins with all their strength, but only managed to cause the carriage to veer off onto the grass where the ride became decidedly more bumpy.

'Ouch!' said Penders as he hit his head on the roof of the coach. 'That was my head!'

'Never mind your head,' shouted Jessica. 'Look behind!'

The creature had left the Darkledun Guards in its wake. What was more, the carriage now moved slower on the grass. The creature was gaining on them! Thomas knew their only chance was to get back on the road. But Thomas couldn't get the horses to obey. They moved further from the road and nearer to Muddlestump Wood.

Suddenly there was a thud and the whole carriage seemed to strain. Jessica screamed and he looked back. The creature had leapt onto the end coach, smashing the roof to pieces.

The horses became even more wild, sending the carriage one way and then the other. The creature tore its way up to the next coach. Fortunately the beast crashed through the roof where it proceeded to tear up everything in an effort to get free.

Thomas abandoned the rein and turned around just as the creature leapt onto the coach next to Jessica and the others. Jessica screamed again and disappeared back down into the coach along with Treice, Merideah, and Penders. The carriage bumped again and the creature swayed, but it soon recovered. Leaping, it landed on the first coach and smashed the roof in with its huge hoofs.

Thomas watched in horror as the creature flattened the coach containing his friends. 'NOOO!'

But his scream was cut off as the coaches behind the creature broke off, causing the remaining coach to jolt violently. Something below Thomas snapped and the team of horses raced free of the carriage. He turned around wide-eyed as they all hurtled into the trees, the branches whipping viciously at his face. Then, a second later, what was left of the carriage hit a grassy mound and they were all catapulted into the gloom of Muddlestump Wood.

– CHAPTER TWENTY-ONE –

## *Muddlestump Wood*

Thomas landed in a bush that, thankfully, proved remarkably springy. Thayer, however, wasn't so fortunate and came down heavily next to the splintered trunk of a fallen oak.

'Thayer!' Thomas scrambled out of the bush toward the boy just as the other started to move. 'Are you all right?'

Thayer sat up. 'Oh, yes, thank you. Fomorfelk are almost as tough as the Dwerugh –' He broke off, staring at Thomas. 'What happened to your eyes?'

Thomas put his hands to his eyes. 'What do you mean?'

'They have turned bright green.'

Thomas blinked hard. His contact lenses! They must have come out when he'd hit the bush. 'Oh, it's nothing. I wear contact lenses.'

Thayer stared blankly at him. He obviously didn't know what contact lenses were or why Thomas wore them. Thomas looked around. 'We must've been thrown further than I thought. I can't even see the coach.'

'I think we came over that ridge,' Thayer said, pointing.

After dusting themselves off, they climbed over the ridge and found themselves amid thick trees.

Thomas looked around, confused. 'Where's the coach?'

The two boys skirted the ridge, but neither found the broken coach or their friends.

Thayer shook his head. 'I am glad we lost that creature.'

'Yes, me too, but we seem to have lost everybody else too, including ourselves.' He had to find the coach. If they were still alive, Jessica and the others might be trapped in the wreckage. He looked around again. Surely they hadn't been thrown very far into the trees when they crashed?

A scream suddenly filled the forest. A scream of terror. And yet it filled Thomas with hope. Jessica, at least, was still alive!

'That's Jess!' Thomas took off in the direction of the sound. Thayer's heavy footsteps followed close behind.

Thomas ducked under low branches. When he looked up he saw a strange sight. Treice lay unmoving beneath a tree, and Jessica, Penders and Merideah were staring wide-eyed at an enormous creature. But it wasn't the one that had chased them into the wood. This creature stood covered in brown hair from which poked twigs and leaves. Its teeth and claws – which it was baring menacingly – looked razor sharp, and its eyes were wild with fury. It looked as if it wanted to eat one of them. Jessica and the others didn't run. Perhaps they were too scared, or perhaps they were protecting Treice. If he was alive.

What had he done? It was his idea to try to heal the Northern Way Gate. They'd almost been ripped apart by a giant green creature with a horn on its head, wrecked the Darkledun carriage, and been involved in a rather unpleasant crash. Now Treice might be dead and his friends were in imminent danger of being eaten by some wild, hairy monster. Well, Thomas thought, enough was enough!

Thomas darted between his friends and the dangerous-looking beast. 'Keep back! Leave them alone!'

The creature seemed utterly shocked on seeing Thomas. Its eyes bulged and its growling stopped. Then, to everyone's surprise, it began to sway and then shrink, as if it were a balloon deflating.

It shrank and shrank until it stood no more than two feet in height. 'Og Tiarna!' The whisper seemed filled with wonder. The creature began snivelling about on the ground as if it had just been well and truly told off.

Penders, Jessica and Merideah all looked at Thomas, who shook his head.

'What happened to your eyes?' Merideah said.

Thomas opened his mouth to explain, but then changed his mind and turned back to the creature. 'What are you?'

'Og Tiarna use that tongue? Strange yes, very strange,' the creature said, still in awe. 'But Ghillie Dhu go along with Og Tiarna. Yes, he does.'

'Your name is Ghillie Dhu?' Merideah said.

'Ghillie not speak to Bumbleclogs.'

'Bumbleclogs?' Penders looked at Merideah.

'I think he means Humbalgogs,' whispered Jessica.

'Well, really!' Merideah said, giving Ghillie Dhu a hard stare. 'You were ready to eat us a moment ago. You could at least apologise! And I'm not a Humbalgog.'

'Eat YOU?' Ghillie exclaimed. 'Ghillie not eat horrible Bumbleclogs. Yuck! Ghillie prefer nice mouse.'

'You scared us!' Jessica said.

'Running into Ghillie's patch you were. Try to scare me with your strange clothes and screeching noises.'

'We were screaming because there was a monster chasing us,' Merideah explained.

'A monster?' He pulled a white stick from the undergrowth. It had a hook on one end, like a stunted shepherd's crook. He held it tightly as if someone might try to steal it.

Merideah zipped up her coat. 'Yes, it was as big as you before you – er – deflated. It had green fur and a large horn on its head.'

'Fachan,' Ghillie said.

'Pardon?' said Thomas.

'A Fachan it was, yes, Og Tiarna. Nasty creatures. Like to rip things apart, and no taste: Eat Bumbleclogs! Not like us Gruagachs at all. No, Gruagachs sensible and not eat people.'

Penders pulled a twig from his hair and then looked at the dozens in Ghillie Dhu's fur. 'What's a Gruagach?'

Ghillie eyed him. 'I am a Gruagach.'

Penders looked at Thomas, as if hoping he might get some sense from the creature.

'Ghillie?' Thomas asked.

'Yes, Og Tiarna? I am here to serve,' Ghillie said, his voice fluctuating between rasps and whispers.

'What happened to our friend?' Thomas said, nodding toward Treice. Jessica, clearly having forgotten all about Treice, gasped and ran over to where he lay.

'See tree?' Ghillie said, pointing at the tree below which Treice lay.

'Yes,' Thomas repied.

'Friend didn't.'

Merideah gave the Gruagach a final wary look before joining Jessica by Treice's side.

'He's coming around,' Jessica announced.

'My head hurts,' Treice said, as Penders, Thayer and Thomas rushed over to join the girls. 'Thomas, is that you? What happened to your eyes?' He turned and found himself staring into the wrinkled, furry face of Ghillie Dhu who'd ambled over to his side to see what all the fuss was about.

'Ugh!' Treice scrambled backwards. 'What's that?'

Ghillie looked offended.

'Er, this is Ghillie Dhu, Treice. He's a Gruagach,' Thomas explained.

'Oh,' Treice said, as if it was the most natural thing in the world. There were girls around after all, and he couldn't let them see he was scared. 'What happened to the thing that was chasing us?'

'It's gone,' Thomas said.

Treice let out a sigh of relief and then stood up.

Ghillie backed off a little more. 'Clumsy One is tall.'

'Well,' said Merideah, 'we'd better leave before this Fachan finds us.'

'He not find you,' Ghillie said.

'How can you know that?' Merideah asked.

Ghillie looked around and held his hands up. 'Muddlestump Wood! Even the cunning get lost here. Fachan not known for having much brains. I say he lost for good.'

Thomas looked at his friends. 'I thought we'd lost you – I thought you'd been crushed in the coach.'

Jessica smiled. 'We hid in the Undercarriage. It's all a heap of timber now, but it cushioned us against the crash, I think. When we crawled out from under the wreckage, the creature had gone. We thought it'd gone after you, that's why we were running to find you when – when we came across this!' She pointed at the Gruagach who eyed her suspiciously.

'Well, we should try to find our way out,' Penders said, rubbing his stomach. 'I'd like to be home for tea.'

Ghillie shook his head. 'Hungry One not make it back for tea. Hungry One never have tea again.'

'What do you mean?' Jessica said.

Ghillie twisted his head as he looked at her braces. 'Chatty One in Muddlestump Wood. You not find way out.'

'That is why it is forbidden,' Thayer said glumly and everyone looked at him. 'It is said that once a person steps into Muddlestump Wood he never steps out again. It was one of the "bad places" I was supposed to help you avoid.'

Ghillie's eyes narrowed and he stared at Thayer. 'Now I see, yes I thought so! You are Grey Skin child. You lead Og Tiarna into Muddlestump to trap him here! Ghillie sort you out!'

Ghillie raised his crook staff and started to inflate again so that he was quickly twice the height he had been just moments before.

'Wait, wait!' Thomas said, interposing himself between Ghillie and Thayer. 'He was brought up by Humbalgogs, and he's my friend. He didn't lead us here, we were chased here by the Fachan.'

Ghillie swayed again, then deflated to what Thomas supposed was his normal size. 'Well,' he said, 'Og Tiarna's friend is my friend, but a great misfortune, yes, to be a Grey Skin and also brought up by Bumbleclogs!'

Thayer didn't seem offended by the remark. Merideah, meanwhile, had removed her watch, turned it over and flipped it open. Thomas peered into her hand and saw a compass.

'Right,' she said, pointing. 'That way's east. If we follow it we'll come to the edge of the forest.'

Ghillie was very interested in the compass and jumped every now and again to catch glimpses of it as he followed alongside. Thomas wondered why he didn't just inflate himself instead.

Merideah stopped after about thirty feet and shook her head. 'The compass is now showing us to be walking west, but we've walked in a straight line!' She tried again and again, but the compass kept on swinging around as if it had a will of its own. Finally, she closed it. 'There must be magnetic interference. It's useless.'

'Great, so we're stuck here with no food and a small hairy creature with an attitude problem,' Penders moaned.

The Gruagach's small, beady eyes flashed at Penders. 'I could find mouse for Hungry One. Ghillie always willing to help Og Tiarna's friends!'

Penders grimaced. 'No thanks.'

'If there's a way in then there's a way out!' Merideah said. 'We couldn't have come more than fifty paces into the wood. We just need to test out each direction for the same distance from this central point.'

Merideah pulled a chunk of chalk from one of the many pockets in her trousers. 'The trees are too dense to get our bearings by climbing them, unless we find a really high one.'

Ghillie looked up at a nearby tree through narrowed eyes. 'They not let you climb them anyway. And they not dense – no, they cunning and mean!'

Merideah ignored the Gruagach. 'So, we'll have to try another method.'

'It won't work.' Ghillie sat down and watched the children. 'Nothing will work.'

Thomas got the impression that Ghillie Dhu lived a very dull existence. He seemed glad of the entertainment. But it was no light matter for Thomas and his friends. Thomas had a horrible feeling Merideah's idea wasn't going to work. Muddlestump Wood had decided they were going to stay. Permanently.

After marking a cross on a tree with her chalk, Merideah instructed everyone to explore fifty paces in the direction from which they'd come. Thomas insisted they all stay together. There was no sense in getting separated; Thomas wasn't as convinced as Ghillie about never seeing the Fachan again, besides who knew what other dangerous creatures dwelt in Muddlestump Wood? So everyone followed after Merideah through the wood, even Ghillie who shuffled along behind, his face fixed with an expression of curiosity.

'This is impossible!' Merideah exclaimed about an hour later, just after coming across the fifth tree marked with a white cross. 'The trees keep on moving!'

'Trees not move,' said Ghillie. 'Younglings move and get confused.'

'Can you do any better?' Merideah snapped.

'Ooooh!' Ghillie whooped. 'No, Ghillie not do any better than Bossy One. Ghillie only a lowly Gruagach.'

Merideah gave Ghillie a hard stare, but the Gruagach screwed his face up at her, and she turned away in disgust.

Penders sat down on the forest floor and leant back against the tree with Merideah's cross on it. His stomach rumbled. 'I'm having a rest. I think we should conserve our energy until we can eat.'

'You're always thinking about your stomach,' Merideah said, as she sat down against another tree. She pulled something from one of her many pockets and tossed it into Penders' lap.

'What's this?' Penders said as he picked it up.

'A Cornish pasty. I always keep some on me in case of emergencies.' She rooted though her pockets and threw one to each of the others.

Penders unwrapped the pasty with a smile. 'Merideah, you know a way to a man's heart.'

Merideah gave Penders a withering look, tore open her pasty, and took a bite. The others thanked her for the unexpected food.

'Father taught me to always be prepared. Anyway, Thomas, you never told us about your eyes?'

'Oh, my contacts fell out. They're filtered,' Thomas explained.

'Obviously,' Merideah said. 'I find glasses more comfortable.'

'Oh, there's nothing wrong with my sight. It's just that they used to freak out Mrs Westhrop, so Mr Westhrop made me wear the contacts all the time – except at night of course.'

'How unusual.' Merideah took another bite of her pasty.

Ghillie didn't have a pasty. He ambled over to Thomas. 'What's Cornish posty?'

'Pasty,' Thomas corrected, as he broke off a piece and put it into Ghillie's hands, careful to avoid the sharp claws.

Ghillie sniffed the pasty with his thick, rubbery nose and then cautiously put it in his mouth and began to chew. He stopped suddenly, swallowed, and – eyes alight – his lips curled upwards in what Thomas thought must be a smile. 'Mmmmm!'

Thayer, like Ghillie, had also never had a pasty before, and so naturally took his time eating it. This was unfortunate for the Fomorfelk because it meant Ghillie went and sat next to him, staring up at him with puppy eyes. Thayer's soft nature soon got the better of him and he passed the remainder of his pasty to the Gruagach. Ghillie gobbled it down in seconds.

'They say a young cadet wandered into here a few years ago on a dare,' Thayer said.

'What happened to him?' Jessica asked.

Thayer shrugged. 'He was never seen again.'

Everyone looked at Thayer, but he was staring blankly out into the wood. Thomas felt his marbles digging into his thigh, so he pulled the bag from his pocket.

'What's in the bag?' whispered Ghillie in his husky voice. 'Is it more patsies?'

'Just marbles,' Thomas said, deciding not to tell him about the Serpent in the Glass. 'And it's pasties, not patsies.'

'Marbles?' Ghillie said, ignoring the correction. 'What's marbles?'

Thomas slipped his hand into the bag and pulled out a large marble with a golden band in its glassy depths.

'Ooohhh! Pretty. Yes, Og Tiarna. Pretty.'

Thomas gave him the marble and the Gruagach shuffled off to examine the strange little glass ball.

'Why does he keep on calling you that?' Penders looked at Ghillie, who was now testing the marble's hardness by biting it.

'Calling me what?' Thomas said.

Penders frowned at the creature. 'You know, "Og Tiarna". Probably some made up word.'

Thomas looked up. 'No, it's not. It means Young Lord.'

Penders frowned. 'How'd you know that?'

That was a good question. How could he know? The words weren't English. Yet he knew perfectly well what they meant.

Thomas slowly shook his head. 'I don't know. I just do somehow.'

Jessica cocked her head to one side. 'Don't you find that strange, Thomas?'

'This whole place is strange.' Thomas sighed. 'Maybe I heard it in the Grange or saw it in Havelock's book?'

The others went back to casting glances about the forest, all except for Merideah who seemed lost in thought, though she glanced at Thomas every now and again. Ghillie eventually came back to sit beside Thomas, the marble he'd been given now rolling about in his dark, wrinkled hands.

Thomas smiled. Despite the wild look and crude behaviour of the Gruagach, Thomas found himself glad that Ghillie was with them. 'You can keep it if you want.'

'Keep pretty ball? Og Tiarna is very generous, yes. But Ghillie Dhu has no pockets.' He reluctantly put the marble back into Thomas's hand. 'Ghillie not want to lose pretty ball. Ghillie give it back to Og Tiarna.'

Thomas nodded and opened up the bag to put the marble back in. But, as he did so, Ghillie saw the Serpent in the Glass and his eyes went wide.

'Og Tiarna has fun with us, yes, walking around Muddlestump when he has way out?'

His words got everyone's attention.

Thomas froze. 'What do you mean?'

The Gruagach pointed to the bag. 'Og Tiarna has the Serpent Glass!'

Thomas looked at the others who were all now looking at him. 'It was a gift from my father,' Thomas said, somewhat cautiously.

'Ghillie not doubt that. Why Og Tiarna not use it? Summon the Power?'

Merideah stood. 'Ghillie, how do you know about the Serpent in the Glass?'

Ghillie Dhu stared at her, but then he seemed to remember something, probably the pasty. 'Ghillie served the Ard Tiarnai. Ghillie saw them use it.'

'Who are the Ard Tiarnai?' Merideah asked, looking first to Ghillie and then to Thomas.

'High Lords,' Thomas answered, eliciting raised eyebrows from Penders and the two girls.

'Ard Tiarnai were strong in the Old Power, not like silly Bumbleclogs,' Ghillie explained. 'They were kind to Ghillie Dhu, but then went away and never came back.' Ghillie whispered these words, but then he looked up at Thomas and his eyes lit up again. 'But now Og Tiarna is here.'

Thomas reddened and was suddenly glad of the forest's gloom. Ghillie had obviously decided to attach himself to Thomas and there wasn't a lot Thomas could do about it. 'Ghillie, do you know how to use the Glass to find our way out of Muddlestump?'

Ghillie cackled what must have been a laugh. 'Og Tiarna plays with Ghillie! Gruagach cannot use Serpent Glass.'

Thomas didn't know anything of the sort, and he certainly wasn't laughing. They'd been in Muddlestump Wood for hours now and the gloom was growing heavier. He wanted to get out.

'Maybe if we move around, the Glass might glow when we get near something – like it did with the Way Gate?' Penders suggested.

Thomas nodded. 'Sounds as good an idea as any.'

Thomas got up and started to walk around. Ghillie followed behind, scratching in the undergrowth every now and again to root out small rodents, which he caught and swallowed whole.

'It's disgusting,' Merideah whispered to Penders the third time the Gruagach did it.

'Yeah,' Penders replied. 'But at least he's not eating the pasties.'

Merideah eyed him. 'How did you know I had more?'

Penders grinned. 'I didn't, until you just said that.'

Merideah shook her head and turned her attention back to Thomas.

'This isn't working.' Thomas dropped down against an old gnarled tree. The Glass hadn't so much as glimmered, and Thomas wondered if they were doomed to be trapped here forever like that poor cadet Thayer had mentioned.

'How can it be so difficult to find the edge of this wood?' Penders slipped down beside Thomas and yawned widely.

'Let's rest,' said Thomas.

'Not long,' said Merideah as she and the others sat. 'It's getting darker, and we won't have enough light to see where we're going.'

Penders sighed. 'As if that makes any difference!'

'It will if you fall over a tree root and break your leg,' Merideah said.

Penders leant back against the old tree. 'I'm going to have forty winks.'

'Make it twenty,' said Merideah, but Penders ignored her and shut his eyes. One by one they all closed their eyes, even Jessica.

Thomas found his own eyes growing heavy, and he yawned as he watched Ghillie next to him slowly fade and disappear so that all that remained was his white crook staff that had been lying across his legs. It now hung suspended several inches above the ground. He must be dreaming.

*'Blind,' said the voice.*

*'Sorry?' Thomas stood up. Everyone looked asleep. Perhaps someone had spoken in their sleep.*

*'Thomas?' came the voice again.*

*Was it a woman's voice? It was hard to tell, it was so quiet. More like a wind than a voice.*

*'Yes?' Thomas answered, anyway.*

*'The Wood. It deceives. Trust not your eyes. The blind are not blind.'*

*'Who are you?' Thomas asked.*

'It's Jessica!' The voice sounded in his ear as he opened his eyes to find the girl shaking him. 'Are you all right? The Glass was glowing again.'

The others gathered around, including the inquisitive Ghillie Dhu. Thomas looked down at the Glass in his hand. It wasn't glowing now, but he knew it had been. He stood up. 'I think I might know how to get out of here.'

Ten minutes later, and watched by a very intrigued Ghillie Dhu, each of the children had a sock tied around their head.

Thomas looked around. 'Now, if only we had some rope. I guess we'll just have to hold hands and keep in line as best we can.'

He'd explained what needed to be done, and after some seriously questioning looks from Merideah, they'd all agreed.

After all, there was nothing to lose. A few bruises more wouldn't hurt if they could escape this wood.

'Og Tiarna use this?' Ghillie held what looked like a frayed brown rope in one hand.

'That'd be perfect, Ghillie. Where'd you get it?' Thomas took the rope from the Gruagach.

Ghillie gave a rictus smile. 'It's danglevine. Ghillie see it hanging from tree. Lots of danglevine deeper in wood.'

The single strand of danglevine proved long enough for each of them to wrap around their wrist so that they were all joined together.

'Og Tiarna?' Ghillie said, as they finished forming a line with Thomas at the front.

'Yes, Ghillie?' Thomas asked.

'Ghillie have no socks.'

Thomas realised he'd not even thought about the Gruagach. Muddlestump was his home. Why would he want to leave? 'You want to come with us?'

Ghillie nodded. 'Like the old times. Ghillie fed up with Muddlestump.'

Thomas wasn't quite sure what he meant by 'the old times', but he had pity on him. Thomas removed his trainer, took off his remaining sock, and tied it around Ghillie's head.

'Thank you, Og Tiarna,' Ghillie said in awe, looking up toward the sock as if he'd just been crowned.

Thomas replaced his trainer. 'OK, everyone. Blindfolds down, and no peeking or it won't work. You'll just have to trust me. And don't let go of the rope.'

Ghillie picked up the trailing danglevine behind Thayer and wrapped it around his arm. He then pulled the sock down over his beady eyes.

Thomas pulled down his own blindfold once everyone else had done the same. With the Glass held before him, he started to lead the others through the darkening wood. He tried to keep straight, but every few feet he could feel the Glass give a gentle tug. He followed it without question. After five minutes he could no longer feel the brush of leaves and small branches, and he suddenly realised that his plan had a weakness. How would he know if they'd reached the edge of the wood or just a clearing? Should he risk a peek? No. Thomas knew he was still in Muddlestump Wood. The Glass still tugged at him every ten paces or so, and he could still feel the gloom about him. Besides, he had the feeling that if he took the blindfold off too soon they'd get lost again. He wasn't going to chance it. For some reason he knew he could trust the voice he heard, the voice he now knew had come from the Glass.

Suddenly the ground beneath his feet became soft and even. It was grass. He took a few more steps forward and a breeze confirmed to him that they were no longer in Muddlestump Wood. They'd escaped.

Thomas pulled the sock from his head and stared out at the dimming light of day as it shone its final embers over the expanse of grass. He didn't need to tell the others. They were already taking off their blindfolds.

Treice sighed. 'I never thought we'd see the sun again for a moment there.'

'Or eat another meal,' Penders added.

Merideah turned away from Penders, shaking her head, but then she stopped and pointed. 'Look!'

Several hundred yards away, but approaching fast, marched Gallowglas, his limp accentuated by his speed. Several of the flat-helmed Darkledun Guards followed him stiffly. Thomas stuffed the Glass back into his bag of marbles.

'We're in for it now!' Penders sighed as he kicked off a trainer. 'Trapped between Gallowglas and Muddlestump Wood. What a terrible fate!'

Jessica looked back at the trees. 'Well, you can go back in that forest if you like, but I'd rather have a detention.'

Penders pulled his sock back on. 'If we only get a detention for ruining the coach house, smashing up the Darkledun carriage and crushing half a dozen Darkledun Guards, then I'd say Gallowglas is a pretty generous guy. And I wouldn't say he was a pretty generous guy.'

Jessica shrugged. 'That wasn't our fault.'

No, Thomas thought as he slipped his sock onto his foot, it was *his* fault. But he wasn't going to run from it. Let Grim Gallowglas do his worst, Thomas had only wanted to do what he thought was right. When Mr Gallowglas reached them he didn't look very happy, and it wasn't just because one of the Guards had walked into the back of him before it knew he'd stopped.

'Are you mad?' Gallowglas boomed at the children.

Thomas suddenly remembered he had no contact lenses in. However, Gallowglas made no comment about Thomas's eyes, but cast his cold gaze across all their faces instead.

'What foolishness have you been up to?' Gallowglas glanced at the wood behind them, his eyes narrowing.

'We were chased, Mr Gallowglas,' Thomas said timidly.

Gallowglas didn't reply, so Jessica stepped forward nervously. 'There was this monster –'

'Yes, yes. The Guards have communicated their' – he turned and glanced at the Suits either side of him – 'failure.'

A couple of the Suits, with the numeral V on their helms, lowered their heads in shame. One held a broken spear and the other had a large dent and scratch marks in its breastplate.

'It wasn't our fault,' Merideah plucked up the courage to say.

'Not your fault?' Gallowglas said. 'Was it also not your fault that you sneaked back into the Grange without Stanwell and without permission? Or were you also chased from the Manor? Well?'

No one answered. Penders gulped. Perhaps Muddlestump Wood would have been the better option after all. Mr Gallowglas's attention suddenly switched to something behind Thomas. 'What is that?' Gallowglas said, as he walked past Thomas.

Thomas froze. He'd forgotten all about Ghillie Dhu. He turned around expecting to see Ghillie inflating himself into a giant and preparing to do battle with the teacher, but Thomas couldn't see Ghillie anywhere.

Gallowglas stooped and snatched something up. It was Ghillie's white hooked staff.

'Well?' Gallowglas asked, holding up the staff.

'I think, Mr Gallowglas, that these children have been through a great deal this afternoon,' came Trevelyan's voice from behind the Suits.

Thomas and the children turned to see the Suits parting as they let the High Cap through.

'Is everyone all right?' Trevelyan said, looking around. 'All present and correct?' He too looked at Thomas's eyes, but only for a brief moment. Perhaps, thought Thomas, he was too polite to say anything. 'Good.' The High Cap rubbed his hands together. 'Now, how about a late picnic? You must all be famished!'

Trevelyan sat down, but before he reached the grass a red-and-white checked cloth appeared beneath him. From his robes he pulled out the delicate silver bell and gave it a tinkle. A hamper appeared in the middle of the cloth and promptly opened itself. Hidden shelves shot out, each revealing a white porcelain plate filled with tomatoes, chicken drumsticks, cheese, pork pies, beetroot and large crusts of buttered wholemeal bread. The children eagerly sat down and eyed the food. Thomas felt as hungry and thirsty as any of them (except perhaps for Penders).

'Will you join us?' the High Cap asked Mr Gallowglas.

Gallowglas gritted his teeth. 'No, High Cap, I must attend to the Guards.'

'They can go back to their posts,' Trevelyan said. 'The creature will not, I am glad to say, be as fortunate as our friends here in escaping Muddlestump.'

Gallowglas nodded. 'As you wish, High Cap.' He thrust the crook staff into the ground next to the cloth, turned, and limped off, giving directions to the Suits as he went.

'We're sorry about the carriage,' Thomas said. 'And about the Guards. Can they be – erm – mended?'

'Yes, unlike yourselves had that creature got hold of you. Now,' Trevelyan picked up a piece of bread with sliced tomatoes upon it, 'why don't you tell me what happened?'

Thomas nodded and, after a brief glance at his companions, knew that he'd been chosen to do the explaining. 'It was my idea.'

Thomas told Trevelyan about wanting to heal the Way Gate after discovering it had faded, and in so doing had to tell him about the Glass, though Trevelyan seemed unsurprised. 'I guess I wanted to do something for Dugan, for everyone. My father gave me the Glass for a reason. I just wanted to help.'

Trevelyan looked at him with his boyish blue eyes. 'Indeed, I'm sure you did. And your motives are admirable. But, please, go on.'

Thomas blushed. 'And then this creature stepped out of the Way Gate. It was huge, covered in green fur with a large horn on its head. It chased us into the stables and we jumped on the carriage. It would've got us if it weren't for the Guards slowing it down.'

'That's right,' said Penders. 'And if we'd not crashed in Muddlestump Wood the Fachan would've got us for sure.'

'Interesting,' said Trevelyan, who now stared at the crook staff that Gallowglas had stuck in the ground.

Thomas wondered if he should tell him about Ghillie Dhu. He saw no reason to. The Gruagach had run back into the wood again anyway, taking with it any chance of Thomas learning more from the strange creature.

Trevelyan swallowed his food. 'You seem to display a good knowledge of the fauna of Avallach, Mr Penderghast. I doubt there are many at the Grange who could've identified such a rare creature.'

Penders didn't have a chance to respond because the High Cap went right on talking. 'You do realise that you're all very fortunate?'

Penders stuffed a stick of salted celery in his mouth. Thomas went to pick up his chicken drumstick from his plate, but discovered it had gone. Perhaps he'd eaten it already? No, that was silly – he couldn't have eaten the bones as well. Maybe Penders took it by mistake.

'Oh yes,' Merideah said. 'We do. That creature would've made short work of us if it'd caught us.'

'Perhaps, but I was referring to your little sojourn in Muddlestump Wood. There are creatures in there every bit as fierce as the Fachan, and many more dangerous.' Trevelyan again looked at the crook staff.

'You are the first, I believe, to have ever left Muddlestump's leafy arbours since the De Danann abandoned it many centuries ago,' the High Cap said. 'I suspect this Serpent in the Glass was instrumental in your escape, yes?'

Thomas nodded. 'It seemed to speak to me. It's hard to explain.'

'Then don't.' Trevelyan stood. 'I think you and I need to examine the Northern Way Gate.' The High Cap turned and whistled very sharply. Thomas heard it first. The beat of hooves. Then, from around the forest's edge came a large dun horse. Once it had reached them Trevelyan climbed up with surprisingly little effort for his age and somewhat portly figure.

'I'll be back soon. I suggest you use the time to finish the picnic, you may need your strength, Thomas Farrell,' he shouted, as he put his feet in the stirrups and took the reins. 'Oh, and Thomas,' he turned in the saddle and pointed toward the wood, 'your sock appears to be lying next to a piece of danglevine at the edge of the wood.'

# – CHAPTER TWENTY-TWO –

## *The Serpent in the Glass*

Thomas stared at the danglevine lying abandoned at the edge of the wood. Ghillie Dhu must have taken off the blindfold as he fled back into the trees. Maybe Gallowglas and the Guards had frightened him back into Muddlestump, there to live out his days eating rodents and wondering what it'd be like to have another Cornish pasty. Thomas couldn't pretend he wasn't disappointed. The Gruagach might have told him more about the sidhe and the Glass. Now, he'd never see the creature again. He'd never know.

'Hello, Og Tiarna!'

Thomas almost jumped into the wood at the sound of the voice. He turned around, and before him stood Ghillie Dhu with a half-eaten chicken drumstick in one hand. 'Where'd you come from?'

'Ghillie's been here all the time,' the Gruagach said.

Thomas glanced at the danglevine. 'I thought you'd run back into the wood.'

A deep furrow grew in the Gruagach's wrinkled brow. 'No, Ghillie not go back into Muddlestump. No Og Tiarna in wood. No chicken dumbsticks.'

So Penders wasn't to blame for the disappearing food after all. 'It's chicken *drumsticks*, but how come I never saw you?'

The others had left the picnic now, and gathered around to listen.

'Ghillie not want to be seen, Og Tiarna.'

Thomas frowned. 'What do you mean?'

'Ghillie close his eyes and no one see him.'

'Oh, come on!' Merideah said. 'That's silly. You can't believe people won't see you just because you close your eyes!'

Ghillie flashed a disapproving look at Merideah, and then firmly shut his eyes. Much to everyone's surprise he vanished. Ghillie reappeared again next to Merideah and she gave a start.

'How very disconcerting,' she said, as she stepped away from the creature.

'Craters!' said Penders. 'How'd you learn that trick?'

'Not learn it, Hungry One. All Gruagachs can do it. And it not trick either.' He wrinkled his nose as if insulted.

Thomas watched as Ghillie swallowed the remainder of the drumstick, bones included. 'You mean there are more of you in the wood?'

Ghillie blinked, but didn't disappear. 'Not in Muddlestump, Ghillie never met any there. But he remembers others like him before the Ard Tiarnai left.'

The Gruagach looked lost in thought, but it didn't last long. 'Ah!' Ghillie exclaimed. 'My staff!' He sauntered over to the place where Gallowglas had stuck it in the ground. 'Mean One best not take Ghillie's staff again. No! Ghillie will show him!' He eyed the picnic food that Penders hadn't yet eaten.

Not long after Ghillie had devoured his third drumstick, Thomas heard the sound of hooves in the distance. He looked southward. A group of riders were approaching, Trevelyan at their head.

'Aarrgh! Old One back.' Ghillie thrust his staff into Thomas's hand, shut his eyes, and winked out of sight. Thomas could still feel him though, clinging to his leg.

Behind Trevelyan rode Gallowglas, on a grey steed, and a dozen young warriors with crossbows strapped to their saddles.

'Thomas,' Trevelyan said as they approached. 'Jump up behind me!'

'What are we going to do?' Thomas asked as the High Cap's dun horse came to a stop beside him.

'To finish what was started.' Trevelyan reached out his hand to Thomas.

Thomas nodded.. As he shoved the crook staff in his belt, he felt Ghillie scramble up onto his back. The Gruagach was surprisingly light. Thomas took Trevelyan's hand and managed to clamber up onto the saddle behind him. As soon as he was seated he felt the Gruagach slip into place behind him, his furry arms tightening around Thomas's midriff. The horse whinnied and Thomas bit his lip as one of Ghillie's claws pressed into his side.

'What about us?' Penders said.

'It may be dangerous,' Gallowglas said.

Merideah looked from Gallowglas to Trevelyan. 'The Fachan was dangerous, Muddlestump Wood was dangerous. But we dealt with it.'

Trevelyan chuckled. 'We best let them come then, Master Gallowglas, or else we shall not hear the end of it!'

Gallowglas sighed before instructing five of his men to bear them on their mounts.

The High Cap urged his horse off at a gallop. After a minute, Thomas's fear of falling off subsided, and he enjoyed the rush as the powerful mare ran toward the Inner Gate. They rode swiftly down the dirt track once out of the Gate, and passed several of the Darkledun Guards who were all stiffly making their way in the same direction. When they arrived at Cnocmorandolmen Gallowglas was already there. The riders bearing Thomas's friends came up behind. A number of Suits were gathering around the hill, and more were making their way toward it from the dirt track.

'We should wait for the rest of the Guards,' Gallowglas said to Trevelyan as the High Cap climbed down from his mare.

'I fear we cannot delay much longer. We'll wait for the Fourth Company.' Trevelyan helped Thomas down as he spoke.

Gallowglas started issuing orders to the crossbowmen and Guards, but Thomas wasn't listening.

'Was I wrong to try and heal the Way Gate?' Thomas asked. 'When Dugan said it had faded I –'

'No, you weren't wrong,' Mr Trevelyan interrupted. 'You were only doing what had to be done, sooner or later, if we are to have any chance of winning this war.'

'I don't understand,' Thomas said as Trevelyan led him to the standing stones.

'The Eastern Way Gate' – Trevelyan held his left hand out – 'leads to my land, the land of the Humbalgogs. It only opens when it rains.'

'I'm sorry.' Thomas wasn't sure it was the right thing to say.

'We tried pouring water on it, but that never worked.' Trevelyan looked at the sky. 'Still, it rains every so often, even in a sidhe. The Western Way Gate is less accommodating, though more predictable. It opens only on the night of the full moon. It leads to the lands of the Alfar, as I'm sure you already know.'

Thomas nodded.

'The Gate to your world is pretty reliable, though it's been getting worse of late.' Trevelyan moved to the Northern Way Gate. It looked quite normal again. The blue field of energy had gone. It stood still and silent. 'You already know about this one.' Trevelyan put his hand upon the smooth surface of the stone. 'It faded some years ago, and in so doing cut us off from the Dwerugh. There was only ever one Gate leading to the Dwerughnook.' Trevelyan placed his other hand on the stone. His expression had turned from its normal cheerfulness to one of sorrow. 'The Way Gates unite the Free Peoples. Their fading has hit us hard.'

Thomas moved closer to the stones. 'How'd the power of the De Danann fail? I thought they were strong in this Old Power?'

'All things fail in time in this world, and your world too, Thomas Farrell,' Trevelyan said. 'There is a power even greater than that of the De Danann, and that is Time.'

'So where'd the Fachan come from if the Way Gate doesn't work?'

Trevelyan frowned. 'Those creatures seek out caves or ruined stone buildings in which to dwell. It is said they can survive for years without food. When the Gate finally faded, it's possible that the Fachan entered and then became trapped. But it's strange…' Trevelyan broke off and seemed lost in his thoughts.

Thomas looked at the High Cap, waiting for him to finish his sentence.

'Strange because they're rare, but also strange because they are creatures quite immune to the Old Power, unless it is very strong. No one knows why. It's just the nature of the beast, so to speak.'

Thomas looked at the stones again. 'So what happened when I tried to use the Glass? What was the blue light?'

'I think the Glass fed enough power into the Gate to cause it to eject anything within it. I really would be guessing, but I suppose the Fachan may have been preserved within the stones and when you used the Glass you probably woke it up, and it discovered it was in need of a meal!' Trevelyan looked back over his shoulder. Thomas did likewise. More of the Darkledun Guards were making their way through the forest toward them now.

'Why all the Suits?' Thomas said.

'We have no way of knowing what might be on the other side of this Gate, and if my understanding of things is correct Cernunnos will detect our presence the moment the Way Gate begins to be healed.'

'We're going to heal the Way Gate?' Thomas could feel his heart beating at the words the High Cap had just spoken.

'*You* are. You have the Serpent in the Glass, and it's what you want, isn't it?'

Thomas hesitated. 'Yes, I suppose, but it'd be better if I gave the Glass to you, seeing as you're good with this Old Power.'

The High Cap sighed. 'Ah, Thomas, don't you know yet? Only you alone in this Grange can use the Glass.'

The words surprised Thomas, not because he hadn't suspected the truth, but rather because it had just been confirmed to him. It explained why the Glass hadn't allowed his friends to pass the Way Gates when they held it, and perhaps it also explained why it had given them no dreams. The Glass was meant for him and him alone. His father couldn't have been a thief after all, otherwise how could he, his son, rightfully own the Glass? It belonged to his father, and now it was his – whatever danger that might bring, whatever it required him to do.

Gallowglas approached but ignored Thomas. 'We should take up positions.'

'Quite right.' The High Cap turned to Thomas. 'Are you ready?'

Thomas gave a nod and removed the Glass from his bag. Gallowglas's eyes flickered over the orb, but Thomas saw no surprise in them. Had Trevelyan and Gallowglas known all along that he'd had the Glass? The Serpent in the Glass glowed as Thomas held it up. But what did he need to do? Then the Glass pulled at him, and Thomas knew what he needed to do. He touched the Glass against the stones, and the Way Gate began to hum. A subdued hum.

The High Cap put a hand against the stones and gave a satisfied nod. 'Gallowglas!'

'Guards, enter!' Gallowglas barked.

Thomas watched as the Suits marched, four wide, into the Way Gate. Once they were inside, Gallowglas entered with his crossbowmen.

'Fifth Company, guard the far wall!' Gallowglas shouted as Thomas and Trevelyan entered. Twelve Suits moved toward the far side of the cavern, sank the base of their spears into the ground, and stood still like statues.

The cavern was dimmer than the one in the Manor Way Gate, as if weak or tired. As Thomas looked around he saw Jessica, Penders and the others enter. They stood right at the back behind Gallowglas and his men.

'Now, children,' Trevelyan said before any of them could speak, 'Master Gallowglas will stay in front of you. Should anything go wrong he'll take you back through the Manor Way Gate immediately – do you understand?'

They all nodded solemnly. Thomas wondered what might go wrong. As he really had no idea how to heal a Way Gate, he wondered if anything would go right at all. Where was Ghillie?

'Are you all right, Mr Penderghast?' Trevelyan asked.

Thomas looked at Penders. He looked a little ill and was rubbing his chest.

'Yeah, I'm fine,' Penders said through gritted teeth. 'Just a little indigestion. Too much beetroot maybe. Sure it'll be over soon. Never lasts long.' He looked at Thomas. 'Good luck!'

Thomas felt encouraged by the words, but as Trevelyan led him forward he looked ahead and his heart sank. Where the far exit should've been, Thomas saw a vast blackness. The dim light didn't penetrate it. It was like a great shadow.

Another company of the Darkledun Guards had lined themselves up against this far exit. Thomas thought that Grim Gallowglas must've felt at home in the cavern's gloom. Thomas certainly didn't.

Trevelyan pulled out a copper coin. He mumbled something, but Thomas couldn't make it out. 'Watch!' he said, as he flung the coin at the blackness ahead. The coin stopped and fell to the floor. Was the darkness so thick it had substance to it? The darkness writhed about, as if seeking to escape and wreak havoc.

'Some sort of barrier. I fear Cernunnos has had a hand in this,' Mr Trevelyan began, 'but there's not much we can do about it. Thomas, it is time to use the Glass.'

Thomas took a breath and held up the glowing Glass.

'Keep the Guards between you and the barrier at all times,' the High Cap warned. 'If Cernunnos detects what's going on, he may attempt to counter it.'

Thomas closed his eyes. What on earth was he doing? How could he stand against Cernunnos if he showed up? He was just an eleven-year-old boy! But his father had entrusted him with the Glass. He needed to believe in himself. Pushing the scary thoughts aside, he concentrated upon the Glass, but the Glass seemed quite unchanged. He tried to think about the barrier. Still the Glass looked no different. What was he doing wrong? Then he had a thought. The Glass had glowed strongly when he'd been asleep, or on the edge of it at least. Maybe he should try to sleep? Thomas relaxed and tried to forget about where he was. Shutting his eyes, he tried to calm his thoughts and slow his rapidly beating heart.

Slowly a feeling of warmth tingled from his hand, down his arm, and so on through his whole body. He opened his eyes again and saw the silvery glow of the orb stretching out toward the wall. On it went until it pushed into it. The wall crackled and writhed, but didn't yield. Those around him shifted nervously. Only the statue-like Darkledun Guards remained unaffected. Even so, all he'd done was make the Glass ready for use; he'd no idea how to actually make it heal the Gate. He closed his eyes yet again and, to his surprise, saw the light in his mind. It streaked out like a silver path before him. He pushed it forward, into the blackness. He opened his eyes. The blackness had become a sea of blue storms. Thomas felt the resistance, felt the cold darkness from which the barrier was composed. He focused again, this time with his eyes open, and the stormy ocean became a whirlpool.

Then Thomas felt something claw at his legs, and he almost dropped the Glass.

'Ghillie get front-view seat!' Ghillie Dhu whispered into Thomas's ear after he'd climbed up to his shoulders. 'So what Og Tiarna doing?'

'I'm trying to heal the Way Gate,' Thomas whispered back. No one seemed to have heard his voice above the whooshing and crackling. 'But I don't know how to do it!'

'To see, you must look beyond what you see,' Ghillie advised.

'What do you mean?' Thomas whispered back.

'See through illusion. Ghillie knows it's there. He can see the land though his eyes are closed. Must look harder! Must not get distracted,' the Gruagach explained.

Must not get distracted? That was hard when a sharp-clawed Gruagach that could grow to eight times its normal size was sitting on his shoulders. Thomas looked again. The darkness beneath still seemed solid. Then, just for a moment, he thought he glimpsed some stony hills.

Maybe if he could pretend he wasn't here, but beyond the cavern's mouth – like he did in a lesson when he felt embarrassed and wanted to escape? Yes, that was it. He needed to look beyond what wasn't there, so he could see what was there. Thomas imagined himself behind the writhing ocean. Suddenly he could see hills, rocks, mountains and bits of cloudless sky. It was working! The whirlpool began to grow smaller and with it the barrier thinned and the landscape beyond became clearer. Thomas felt the opposing force yield, dim and dissipate. But just as the whirlpool flickered out,

Thomas felt a new power rushing to fill the void. A raw power, not of illusion but of death.

A chariot flew through the sky drawn by two horses dark as midnight. And its charioteer filled Thomas with dread, for in the flying chariot stood a dark, caped figure with what looked like antlers upon his head. It was the chariot from his dream in the Hall of Tales!

'Cernunnos!' Gallowglas called in warning.

Thomas faltered and the glow of the orb fell, but Trevelyan grabbed his arm.

'The Glass, Thomas! Do not lower it! The wall is down and the way exposed. You must –'

A foul power threw the High Cap back. The force knocked Thomas down as well. Around him a hundred glass balls scattered; his bag of marbles had spilt all over the floor of the cavern. He sat up and suddenly realised that Ghillie Dhu wasn't on his shoulders anymore, but he didn't have time to look for him or even to call his name because two huge dogs the size of ponies had appeared at the cavern's mouth. As black as night they were, their ears red-tipped as if they'd been dipped in blood. Gaping maws dripped foam.

'Ratchet Hounds!' Gallowglas shouted.

The Suits lifted their spears. The Hounds bayed. It was the most chilling sound he'd ever heard. It sapped him of both hope and courage. He forced himself back to the cavern wall, but couldn't get up. Suddenly there was a clash of metal as the Hounds tore into the Darkledun Guards with terrible force. The Suits were no match for the Hounds, and it was only their number that kept the Hounds from breaking through. Then a third Hound Thomas hadn't seen before bounded through a gap that had opened in the line. But it didn't get far, for a volley of crossbow bolts struck it and it fell away yelping.

Thomas glanced back at the men reloading their crossbows as Gallowglas sent all the remaining Suits forward. Behind them Penders and the others looked horrified. Jessica was shouting his name. Gallowglas leant over Trevelyan. The High Cap wasn't moving.

Thomas felt a hand on his shoulder and tensed. The Gruagach had opened his eyes and was no longer invisible, but he stood in the shadows of the cavern. Not that anyone would have noticed him.

'The Gate, it is open. Must close the Gate. Horned One cannot defy power of the Ard Tiarnai once it is closed,' Ghillie explained.

'But I don't know how to close the Gate,' Thomas said as a fourth and then a fifth Hound rammed into the Guards. One of them leapt clear over the embattled Guards and a second volley of crossbow bolts hammered into the beast. It fell wounded, but before the men could reload the fifth Hound broke through the thinning line of Guards. It had the greave of a Guard in its mouth which it tossed away as it landed.

Then it turned its massive head toward Thomas and Ghillie Dhu. It snarled and looked at them with soulless eyes. It seemed to Thomas that though these creatures could be harmed, they weren't entirely natural. Many of the Guards had fallen, mauled and broken, and too few remained to turn and challenge the one that now faced Thomas. Thomas pushed himself up against the wall and waited for that which he couldn't stop. But it didn't come.

He heard Gallowglas shout something, but he couldn't tell what. A battle cry of some sort perhaps. A couple of crossbow bolts were loosed, but they did little more than anger the Hound, though they did take its attention from Thomas. The beast howled and hurtled toward the crossbowmen with the grim-faced Gallowglas at their head. It was going to reach them before they could reload! But then the fell creature lost its footing and slipped, hitting the ground hard. By the time it recovered, a dozen bolts had been loosed into its black hide. It thrashed once and then went limp.

A marble rolled over toward Ghillie who picked it up and looked at it in wonder. 'You never tell Ghillie "marbles" so powerful!'

But the danger wasn't over. Two more Hounds were quickly overpowering the remaining Guards. Gallowglas hung back with his men now, perhaps hoping the Guards would destroy at least one of the fell creatures to give them a fighting chance. Both the Hounds were bleeding, but made short work of the Darkledun Guards.

Thomas stood and looked toward the mouth of the cavern. Cernunnos now approached. He was tall, and wrapped in a yellowish-brown cloak that reminded Thomas of dying leaves. Around his neck he wore a thick golden torque, and upon his head he wore a helm crested with an enormous pair of antlers. His face, like his garb, reminded Thomas of dead leaves, shrivelled and brown. His right hand rested on the hilt of a longsword, but his left hand was entirely missing.

Two of the Suits challenged him. Thomas felt sick as he sensed the foul power again. The Suits were lifted off the ground and crushed like tin cans. One of their flat helms rolled towards Thomas and came to rest by Ghillie Dhu who promptly picked it up, climbed swiftly (and somewhat painfully) onto Thomas's shoulders, and placed the helm on Thomas's head.

'Suggest you use Glass now!' Ghillie said as he shut his eyes and disappeared.

'But how?'

'Ard Tiarnai give Serpent Glass to you and not tell you how to use it! But Ghillie thinks he remembers Ard Tiarnai say it must be felt.'

Thomas concentrated. It took a few seconds to feel the warmth as before, but even then it was but a trickle so thick was his fear.

'Og Tiarna needs to be a bit quicker,' Ghillie suggested unhelpfully. Thomas thought he heard Gallowglas telling Jessica and the other children to run.

Cernunnos's eyes had fixed upon him. They were pitch black, spheres of darkest night; no white touched them and no mercy. Yet, for a moment, Thomas thought he saw surprise in their cold depths.

Cernunnos headed straight for Thomas, mangling another Guard that dared to oppose him, not even sparing the flat helm this time. Thomas gripped the Glass as tight as he could and allowed the warmth to creep into him. The silver glow began to encircle him, to reach out, out toward the cavern's entrance. Suddenly the glow spread out across the mouth of the cavern and Thomas felt its power seeping into the great stones that edged the cavern to form the Way Gate on the other side. An opaque film of silver-white formed across the entire entrance. Thomas was vaguely aware that two remaining Hounds were growling and hurling themselves against the barrier the Glass had created in an effort to finish off what was left of the Darkledun Guards. The film stretched and crackled but it didn't yield and the Hounds soon ceased their attack.

Cernunnos stepped forward now into the Glass's light and Thomas felt a sudden crack, as if a whip had narrowly missed him. Cernunnos had stopped on the outer edge of the silver-white sheet, surrounded in what Thomas could only describe as a dark light. It touched and strove with the silvery glow, testing at first and then exploiting. Thomas could feel it making its way toward him. He knew instinctively that he mustn't allow it to reach him.

*Put down the Glass, boy!* Cernunnos hissed in his mind. The words were like shards of ice.

Ghillie was shaking him and shouting something in his ear, but he could no longer hear the outside world. His only awareness now was of himself, the Glass, and the dark figure before him.

*You cannot win. Surrender, surrender while there is still something to surrender,* the voice breathed inside his head again.

The power of the Glass drew back toward him as if in protection, or perhaps in flight. The opaque film that covered the entrance to the cavern thinned and wavered. Thomas's heart pounded and fear gripped him. He felt a coldness brush against him through the warmth, and he shivered. Perhaps Cernunnos was right. He was just a boy. He knew nothing of the Old Power. Trevelyan had been strong, the strongest perhaps, and Cernunnos had just tossed him away like a child. Perhaps he was dead. Thomas might soon be joining him. He wanted to run. Maybe he could make it to the Manor Way Gate? Cernunnos wouldn't be able to follow him through the De Danann stones. He could leave this world behind forever, and the dark terror that now stood before him.

Then Thomas felt another flow of power. It brought his mind back to the outside world as if he'd been shaken from a daydream. What had he been thinking? Running away and letting others die just so he could save himself?

'Call on them! Call on the Ard Tiarnai!' Ghillie Dhu's voice came strong and clear before it was cut off by the darkness.

The air around Thomas swirled and grew colder. *You are weak, boy,* the chill voice sounded in Thomas's mind. *And victory is mine!*

Thomas's arm shook and his mind raced. He couldn't do it, he thought. This was beyond him. But he couldn't give up. The men in the cavern would be killed. They'd defended him. Put their lives at risk. And then there was Jess and his friends.

*Help me,* Thomas pled silently. *Don't let anyone die because of my failure.*

As though in answer to his call, the Glass flashed and grew bright again. The warmth returned, and then he became aware of a shadow at the other entrance to the cavern. Thomas looked about frantically for help, but everyone seemed frozen to the spot just like in his dreams.

There, sliding now past Penders and the other children, came the giant serpent of his nightmares. Its claws scraped against the cavern floor as it drew closer to Thomas, mouth working as if in anticipation of its prey. There was nowhere to run. He was trapped between the serpent and Cernunnos, just like in the dream in the Hall of Tales. Perhaps it was a vision of the future. A vision of his death.

Thomas turned toward the serpent. Anger mixed with his fear, anger at his inability to avoid this fate. The serpent had stopped now, towering above him on its hind legs. It looked down at him, no doubt sizing up its victim before it struck.

Thomas gripped the Glass tightly. He wasn't going to run anymore. If he was going to die, he would do so with his friends. He'd never had so many friends. He wondered what his second year at the Academy might have been like had he lived long enough to see it.

*Thomas Farrell, the Gloine Nathair is yours to wield.*

And the scales, fangs, claws, and wings all fell away to reveal a woman, robed in white. Her countenance seemed like lightning to Thomas, and her eyes were no less green than the serpent's. Most noticeable of all, however, was the fiery crown that hung suspended above her long golden hair.

Thomas gazed up at her in wonder. 'Who are you?'

215

The woman stared back at him, her green eyes warm like the smile that now spread across her face.

*What do you see?* Her arms lifted, but her lips didn't move.

'A beautiful woman dressed in white,' Thomas replied. 'With a fire above her head like a crown. Where is the serpent? I don't understand.'

*The serpent was of your own making. Your fear. You have faced your fear and it has fled. Now you see what really is, and what ever was. Now trust in yourself, bind the Gate!*

Suddenly he was keenly aware of Cernunnos again, and the foul power seeking to surround him, and the voices shouting orders or crying in fear. But the presence of the woman filled Thomas with a strength and sense of hope, a feeling that his fate wasn't sealed after all. He had a choice. As these feelings took hold the darkness fell back, retreating before the glow of the Glass toward the cavern's mouth.

Cernunnos stepped back at the unexpected resistance. The foul presence wavered. The silvery light began seeping into the stone again, shutting out all that had no right to pass its stone-hewn pillars. Then Thomas's heart leapt as he felt what he'd felt in his dream: all four Way Gates thrummed together, the beat of one power shared between the four. Before him the cavern walls glowed like gold-amber coals, like the fire in his dream. The Way Gates were healed. Then suddenly the glow of the Glass dimmed and withdrew to immediately surround Thomas. Cernunnos attempted to push through the entrance, but something stopped him and he howled in dismay. The tall, dark figure lowered its hand and stared at Thomas. The cold, dark eyes filled with malice, and yet Thomas knew the Horned One could do him no harm now.

*One day you will step outside your prison,* Cernunnos hissed, *and you will not be safe from me then, boy. One day!* And with that Cernunnos turned and slunk away, his remaining Ratchet Hounds following after him. Thomas watched as the chariot took to the air and departed. The world went still again.

Ghillie Dhu let out a short, high-pitched sound and jumped down from Thomas's shoulders to the floor.

'My Lady!' Ghillie bowed so low Thomas thought his nose would touch the ground.

The others had frozen again. Trevelyan lay on the floor, his eyes closed. Gallowglas leant upon his sword and stared at the fallen High Cap, his eyes unreadable. Jessica, Merideah, Thayer, Treice and Penders wore expressions of concern and wonder on their faces. The crossbowmen stood bunched around Gallowglas, eyes fixed on the cavern's entrance.

'Greetings, Ghillie Dhu!' The white-clad woman spoke now with her mouth, and it sounded like the voice of an angel.

Thomas looked at the small creature. 'Ghillie, you know who this is?'

The Gruagach raised his bushy eyebrows. 'Of course, Ghillie know Lady of the Ard Tiarnai when he see one!'

'Who are the High Lords?' Thomas looked at the fire-crowned woman gazing down at him.

The woman smiled. 'De Danann would be a term more familiar to your ears.'

So the Ard Tiarnai were the De Danann! The builders of the sidhe and the Way Gates. The woman seemed to emanate power, the Old Power. Thomas could sense it all around her. He'd always felt it now that he thought about it, ever since he'd had his first dream of the serpent. But now he recognised it for what it was. Not fear. Power.

Thomas looked back at his statue-like friends. 'Have you stopped time?'

The woman seemed amused, and the fire above her head shifted slightly as she moved. 'No, it is not within the power of even the De Danann to do that. Let us say that the perception of time has altered for us.' She looked down to the small Gruagach upon the floor. 'Ghillie Dhu?'

'Yes, My Lady?' Ghillie answered.

'I charge you to teach Thomas. Teach him of the Old Power that is his.'

Ghillie nodded his head eagerly. 'Ghillie will, My Lady.'

She turned back to Thomas. 'Maithfreond will tell you of your father, tell him Brigid asks that the fallen speak. He will know what to do.'

Thomas frowned. 'Maithfreond?'

But Brigid had begun to grow brighter and fade into that brightness. Thomas became slowly aware of his surroundings again. And suddenly his friends were around him.

'Thomas!' Jessica shouted excitedly. 'You did it!'

The others were all praising him, but Ghillie had disappeared before anyone had seen him.

'Those were some dogs!' Penders exclaimed. 'I thought we were goners for sure when that one broke through. If it wasn't for your marbles –'

'We'd all be dead,' Thomas finished and everyone looked at him. 'I think I might need a new bag, Jess.'

'Next birthday!' Jessica grinned, and then gave him a hug.

'Thomas,' a deep voice called. It was Gallowglas. 'Over here.'

Thomas's friends moved aside as Thomas walked over to Gallowglas. The teacher bent over Trevelyan, supporting his head. Thomas knelt down so that his eyes were level with Trevelyan's. The High Cap's face looked pale, his eyes dim, but he managed a weak smile before he spoke.

'You did well, lad.'

Thomas smiled. 'Thank you, sir. How are you feeling?'

But Trevelyan closed his eyes and made no reply.

# – CHAPTER TWENTY-THREE –

## *The Tomb of Arghadmon*

The Headmaster's two-week-long sick leave wasn't something the students of Darkledun Manor thought too much about. After all, everyone got struck down by something now and again. Of course, only Thomas, Jessica, Merideah, Treice and Penders knew exactly what had struck him down – a seven-foot-tall, one-handed dark enchanter wearing a pair of enormous antlers. Gallowglas had sworn Thomas and his friends to secrecy.

The Club had been attending their normal lessons, but Thomas and the others hadn't been allowed to set foot in Avallach since Gallowglas had sent them back to the Manor. Jessica had asked Miss Havelock about their visits to the Academy. She'd been told that it was best to stay away until 'things have been decided' – whatever that meant. Thomas was as frustrated as Jessica. And he'd even more reason to be. What had happened to him that final day in Avallach wouldn't be easily forgotten. Part of his reason for being there had been revealed to him, and now he'd been shut out.

Thomas continued down the unlit passageway, passing the corridor leading to 2B, and making for the early morning light that spilled through the open door ahead. He'd come by full of hope every morning for the last fortnight, but that hope had failed as the days had passed. Maybe Trevelyan was dying. Maybe he'd been permanently hurt and was now confined to a wheelchair, if they had wheelchairs in Avallach. Miss Havelock had only told Thomas that the Headmaster was still weak. That was a week ago. Stanwell knew nothing more, and Gallowglas remained as silent as a stone.

Thomas reached the Headmaster's office and peered through the half-open door. The desk remained unoccupied, as it had every time he'd come. Thomas turned to go, but then he heard humming. Thomas didn't recognize the tune, but he recognised the hummer. Thomas poked his head through the door. There, bearing a plate of biscuits and two glasses of milk on a tray, stood Mr Trevelyan. His countenance and eyes were back to their normal brightness, both vying for supremacy over the bright clothes he wore.

'Well, 'blige me, don't stand there with wide eyes all day,' Mr Trevelyan said, as he placed the tray on his desk. 'I've brought some chocolate-chip biscuits and milk to fill that open mouth of yours!'

Almost without thinking, Thomas ran and threw his arms around the waist of the old man. 'I knew you'd be OK. I knew!'

Mr Trevelyan gently pulled Thomas from his lime waistcoat and looked him in the eye.

'I'm sorry for' – Thomas began, tears rolling down his cheeks and finding it hard to get the words out of his mouth – 'for all the trouble I've caused.'

Trevelyan smiled. 'Thomas, what you did needs no apology, indeed it needs some praise. We've already sent scouts out to see if we can make contact with the Dwerugh – and I think there's one person in the Grange who will be especially happy to know that he can visit his kith and kin again!'

'Dugan?' Thomas said.

'Yes, and to be honest I think many others at the Grange will be happy for him to visit the Dwerughnook too.' Trevelyan winked.

Thomas smiled, but the happy thought was immediately replaced by a darker one. 'What about Cernunnos? Won't he be waiting?'

Trevelyan straightened his tie. 'After what happened at the Way Gate, he'll think twice before attacking without an army behind him.'

Thomas wiped his eyes and felt his contact lenses press against his pupils. By Gallowglas's order, Thomas had put in his spare ones as soon as he got back to the Manor. 'What would've happened if I failed?'

'The Outer Circle of the Grange would have fallen to Cernunnos, and those who survived would've been trapped behind the Inner Gate for the rest of their lives while all about them the Free Peoples of Avallach would have succumbed to the Horned One's malice.'

Thomas swallowed hard.

Trevelyan took his seat behind his desk. 'Was there another question?'

'Yes.' Thomas sat down opposite the Headmaster. 'You knew I had the Glass all along?'

Trevelyan nodded. 'Yes, the representative of your father's estate informed me that it had been left to you.'

Thomas bit his lip. 'I saw one of the De Danann, in the Way Gate. She said her name was Brigid.'

Trevelyan picked up a biscuit, and indicated for Thomas to do the same. 'Yes, I thought she'd come to you eventually.'

Thomas picked up a glass of milk. 'She spoke about someone called Maithfreond. Do you know who that is?'

'It's a terrible mouthful, isn't it? I don't know what my parents were thinking. It's why I prefer "Trevelyan".'

'You're Maithfreond?' Thomas suddenly remembered the invitation letter he'd received last year – it was signed 'M. Trevelyan'.

The Headmaster nodded and smiled.

'She said that the "fallen must speak". She said you'd know what to do.'

Trevelyan didn't answer for a while. 'Yes, I suppose that would be best now, considering all that's happened.'

'You know her then? You've seen her?' Thomas bit into a biscuit.

'Once, yes. But let's speak of this elsewhere.' He pulled some keys from his jacket and led Thomas quietly to 2B. It wasn't until they were on Cnocmorandolmen that he spoke to Thomas again.

'This sidhe, the walls of which you see before you, once belonged to the De Danann – to Brigid to be exact. She surrendered the Grange to our stewardship nine years ago.

Without this this haven I think it safe to say our cause would have suffered greatly, perhaps even have been lost by now.'

Thomas looked from the walls back to the Headmaster. 'But what's this got to do with me?'

'Well, to answer that you must allow me to follow the final instructions that Brigid gave to me nine years ago.' Trevelyan moved down the hill and beckoned Thomas to follow.

They were soon inside the coach house. The Darkledun carriage had all but been repaired, as had the building itself. Several of the small white-furred hodge-pockers worked on the final touches to the coaches. On seeing the High Cap they became excited, but Trevelyan calmed them down and they got back to work. Trevelyan led Thomas to a dun horse. It looked like the one they'd ridden two weeks ago. The High Cap saddled the horse and Thomas was soon seated behind him. Trevelyan rode slowly, but they were soon inside the Inner Gate and trotting down the road that led to the Academy.

Thomas looked at Muddlestump Wood as they passed it by and he wondered what had happened to Ghillie Dhu. He'd not seen – or felt – him since leaving the Northern Way Gate. Perhaps the experience had scared the Gruagach? Perhaps this time he really had gone back to Muddlestump? But what of his promise to Brigid to teach Thomas about the Old Power? Thomas couldn't believe he'd disobey her.

It wasn't long before they arrived at the Hall of Arghadmon. Trevelyan led Thomas to the fireplace at the far western end of the room. 'Here's the entrance.'

Thomas glanced at the fireplace. 'The entrance to what?'

'To the place of the fallen. You'll need to use the Glass of course.'

Thomas pulled the Glass from his pocket. He'd yet to find a new bag for his marbles, so they lay at the Manor in his small chest-of-drawers. 'You're not coming with me?'

The Headmaster shook his head. 'No, Thomas. I'll wait here for you.'

The Glass glowed as Thomas stepped into the ashes. Suddenly the fireplace flared into life, and for a moment Thomas thought he might be burned alive, but the flames disappeared as soon as they had come, and, with them, Trevelyan and the Hall of Arghadmon.

Thomas found himself looking across a marble floor and up smooth pale grey walls. He stepped out of the fireplace into a chamber about half as wide as it was long. Both ends sported windows of stained glass. The window to his left bore the image of a silver-scaled serpent with a fire above it in the shape of a crown. In the other window stood a tall, silver-haired man clad in armour of the darkest blue and bearing a sword. His green-stained eyes flashed as the sun cast its early-morning beams through the window. Fabula's description had been vivid enough for Thomas to recognise the image before him as Arghadmon, but the storyteller had never mentioned his green eyes. Then the image of the green-eyed warrior came back into his mind – the one he'd seen in the dream in the Hall of Tales – and he realised that it was Arghadmon he had seen on that dreamworld battlefield.

A large stone block dominated the floor of the chamber. Almost as tall as Thomas, it measured twice his length, and its top had been carved into the likeness of a man in sleep. Thomas instantly recognised the armour and sword from the stained-glass window. This was the tomb of Arghadmon. Thomas put his hand out to touch the stone. It was cold. There were words inscribed upon the side facing him. He couldn't read them at first, but then the Glass in his hand shone a little brighter and its glow touched the strange glyphs and their meaning suddenly became clear:

*Here Lies Fearghal, Son of Brigid, Returned At Last to the Hollow Hills*

Thomas stepped back, removing his hand from the stone. This was his father's tomb! The knowledge sank into him like a chainless anchor. How could Fearghal and Arghadmon be the same person? Thomas refused to believe it, but the silver-blond hair and green eyes in the window bore testimony to the truth of it. As Brigid's son he would be De Danann, but how could that be? The De Danann supposedly withdrew to their sidhe hundreds of years ago and had no more to do with

Avallach. He didn't understand. Yet he knew it was true. It was why he knew their language. It was why some things here in Avallach seemed so familiar.

His eyes rested upon the stone carving. The image of his father. The face was strong, yet kind, and above it sat two serpent heads, the bodies of which ran down the length of the tomb until the tails wrapped about a carving of an open book just beneath the feet. He traced the carvings. More symbols adorned the great sword clasped between the two stone hands. He reached out to touch the blade, but the edge, undulled by time, cut his finger. He winced and put his finger in his mouth. How could it be so sharp? He followed the line of the great sword as he moved down the tomb until his eyes caught hold of the open book. Blank stone pages stared back at him. Why would there be no words for such a great leader and warrior? Maybe the tomb hadn't been finished before being hidden away? Thomas ran his hand over their smooth surface as if to confirm that they really were blank, but in so doing his finger left a trail of blood upon the stone-carved page. He wiped the stone, but the blood remained. He wiped it again, this time with his sleeve, but the stain on the book didn't go away.

Thomas stared at the page. He felt like he'd just desecrated his father's tomb. Then he watched as the blood began to form into lines and then into writing, just like the Blood Parchment. Fearghal's name appeared on the page, then Brigid's above it, and then above that others until it reached the top of the page where the name *Danu* winked into sight. Unlike the Blood Parchment, the writing glowed brightly as the tree completed, then, as if in response, a voice, deep, gentle, and familiar, filled the room.

'Thomas, son.'

Thomas looked around. The voice came from the walls, just like in Master Fabula's Hall of Tales.

'You now know the truth of who you are. I am sorry it had to be this way. I am sorry your mother and I could not be there for you.'

It was his father's voice – he remembered it now from when he was a child. 'Father?'

'What you now hear are my last words to you, spoken before my death. Listen carefully, for you shall not hear my voice again in this world.'

Thomas looked to the image of Arghadmon in the stained-glass window. The eyes were looking at him.

'There is something I would have you know. I sent you to the Otherside for your protection. I have asked faithful Erendrake to look out for you, and Brigid, your grandmother, will do what she can. You may trust them both, but you must learn to trust yourself too, and that may prove the harder task. The Gloine Nathair, should you desire it, will guide and aid you until you are its master. Only those of De Danann blood may wield it. Let it be your guide, day and night, and it will teach you things that I am no longer able to do. Farewell, Thomas. Son.'

The voice faded and Thomas saw the blood on the page do the same. Then words rose up through the page, words not of blood but of stone:

*Here Lies Fearghal, Son of Brigid, Husband of Eleanor, Father of Thomas, Returned At Last to the Hollow Hills*

'No! Wait!' Thomas cried, sensing the presence leave. 'Father?' His voice cracked.

But there was no reply, not even when he fell to the floor and wept...

Thomas wasn't sure how much time had passed when he eventually stumbled out of the fireplace and back into the Hall of Arghadmon where Trevelyan still waited, hands clasped behind his back.

Thomas turned and made his way silently toward the back wall. Lifting the Glass, he pressed it against the panelling and the chamber opened to their view.

A look of pleasant surprise filled Trevelyan's countenance. 'Well, bless my soul! It's amazing what one can find behind a wall! If I'm not very much mistaken, that's the Blood Parchment.'

Thomas nodded.

The Headmaster looked at Thomas thoughtfully. 'Ah, I see. You are wondering why nothing happened when you placed a drop of your blood upon it?'

Thomas nodded again, still unable to form his thoughts into words.

'The Blood Parchment was created long after the De Danann departed. The blood of that people, and indeed of Men, cannot be detected by it. It was made to discern the mortal races of Avallach alone.'

Thomas still had more questions. 'Why did my father have two names?'

'Ah,' Trevelyan began, 'that's easily explained. Arghadmon's a title the people gave him because of his long, silver-blond hair. I don't think many knew his real name.'

Thomas watched as the chamber of the Blood Parchment disappeared. Then his eyes wandered up to the fire-wreathed crown on the wall. It made sense now. 'My father said someone called Erendrake would look out for me.' Thomas looked at the Glass still in his hand. 'He's the person in charge of my father's estate, isn't he?'

The High Cap didn't answer, but turned and looked at the painting across the room on the far wall, the painting of the fortress on a hill. 'As you must now realise, your father's estate includes the Fortress of Arghadmon.'

Thomas hadn't realised at all, but now he knew why the place was so familiar to him. He'd spent the first two years of his life here. 'Do you think I could stay and look around for a while? It's just that it means more to me now, if you understand.'

Trevelyan smiled and walked toward the doors. 'I do understand, Thomas. I'll be at the fountain in a couple of hours.'

After the High Cap had gone, Thomas looked at the paintings on the wall and wondered what significance they'd held for his father. One was of the Battle of Hammerhoe. The battlefield even looked like the landscape in his dream. Marganus the Misplaced now stared back at him with a knowing look in his eyes.

The Grange, this strange yet familiar place, was his inheritance. It was why the Inner Gate had obeyed his voice. Thomas wanted to try something. 'Lift to Hall!'

The Anywhere Lift thudded down out of nowhere and the doors slid open. Thomas walked in. 'Lift to Battlements!'

The Lift lurched, landed, and opened its doors. Thomas found himself on the roof of the Tower. He passed quietly over to the edge of the Tower and looked out over the battlements, wondering how many times his father had done the same. He felt that familiar feeling again, but this time he knew what it was. He'd come home.

And as he gazed out across the Grange a small furry figure, no taller than his waist, appeared beside him from out of nowhere. A figure with a white crook staff in his hand, and a flat helm upon his head.

THE END.

# Thank you for reading!

## DID YOU ENJOY THIS BOOK?

You can post feedback, and find out about this author's other books, on his blog at writers-and-publishers.com, or facebook.com/dmandrewsauthor, or follow him on twitter @AuthorDMAndrews

CPSIA information can be obtained at www.ICGtesting.com
Printed in the USA
LVOW10s1525130515

438364LV00001B/82/P

9 781781 767733